SUPERSYMMETRY

Also by David Walton

Superposition

SUPERSYMMETRY
DAVID WALTON

an imprint of **Prometheus Books**
Amherst, NY

Published 2015 by Pyr®, an imprint of Prometheus Books

Cover design by Grace M. Conti-Zilsberger
Cover Image © Media Bakery

This is a work of fiction. Characters, organizations, products, locales, and events portrayed in this novel either are products of the author's imagination or are used fictitiously.

Inquiries should be addressed to
Pyr
59 John Glenn Drive
Amherst, New York 14228
VOICE: 716–691–0133
FAX: 716–691–0137
WWW.PYRSF.COM

19 18 17 16 15   5 4 3 2 1

Library of Congress Cataloging-in-Publication Data

Walton, David, 1975-
    Supersymmetry / by David Walton.
        pages ; cm
    ISBN 978-1-63388-098-6 (pbk.) — ISBN 978-1-63388-099-3 (e-book)
    1. Physicists—Fiction. 2. Quantum theory—Fiction. I. Title.

PS3623.A454S87 2015
813'.6—dc23
                                                                    2015011713

Printed in the United States of America

To Karen
My theory of everything

PROLOGUE

Jacob Kelley spent the last minutes of his life at a baseball game. He hadn't been to Citizens Bank Park in years, not since his children were young, and he reveled in the vivid hue of the brightly lit Kentucky bluegrass, the low roar of the crowd, the squeak of hinged seats, and the smell of popcorn and beer. The stadium was aging now, no longer the sparkling novelty it had been in his youth.

In the eighth inning, the Phillies took the lead with a three-run homer. With the best closer in the league warming up in the bullpen, the rest of the game wasn't much more than a formality. Jacob considered leaving early to beat the traffic, but it wasn't often he came out to a game. He wandered off to find a pretzel and a beer instead.

It was strange to be alone. Baseball was a much different experience without kids along, chattering and begging for treats and poking all the chads out of their all-star ballots. But the kids were all grown up now. He had tried to convince the twins to come with him, but Sandra was on patrol and Alex was working hard on an upcoming demo. Claire lived on the West Coast now, with her own family, and Sean was in the Marines on overseas assignment. It was sad when a family started breaking up, each child finding a different place in the world, but he supposed it was inevitable.

He had to admit he was enjoying himself, even without them. The game was close, and it was a good crowd—41,528, according to the big screen. He could leave behind his worries about Alex and Sandra; there was nothing in the world but the crack of the bat and the soft collision of ball and glove. Baseball was a clean sport, precise and mathematical. Jacob was a physicist, or had been before he switched to teaching, and the analytical nature of the game appealed to him. It was sports boiled down to pure numbers.

Jacob took a bite of his pretzel and sighed. He was going to have to tell them. He should have told them already, but it had never seemed like the right time, and somehow, one or the other of them always had an excuse that kept them from coming to the house together. He wanted to tell both of them at once, since it affected them both. He would have to call and insist that they come together. Maybe next weekend they would be free.

On the way back to his seat, Jacob stopped short. He knew something was wrong before his mind could even process what it was. The space over his seat was contorting, changing shape, refracting light like a huge drop of water. He had seen it before, but it wasn't supposed to happen again. Not here. Not now.

He dropped his pretzel and cup, heedless of the beer splashing on the concourse, and backed away, unable to tear his eyes away from the distorted space over his seat. The wrongness grew, bending the metal and plastic around it like light through a lens. Other people started to notice. Fans pointed and shouted, and those sitting nearby scrambled to get away.

It expanded rapidly in a sphere, silently warping everything in its path. A woman who was slow to get away screamed as her leg was caught, and then she herself was enveloped. People started to panic then, everyone pushing and shouting and shoving to get to the stairs. Jacob turned to run as well, though he knew it would do no good.

The distortion grew larger. Everything nearby seemed to be stretching and curving away. Without warning, the growing sphere sucked back into nothing. *This is it*, Jacob thought. *I'll never see my children again.* There was a bright flare of light, and then the whole stadium tore itself apart around him.

CHAPTER 1

I t would be the disaster of their generation, like the fall of the Twin Towers or Kennedy's assassination. Sandra Kelley was one of the early responders, one of the first to see the stadium lying crushed, torn apart as if by an angry giant. She was less than two years out of police academy, a junior officer still doing patrol on the night shift. She had seen victims of traffic accidents, so she wasn't entirely green, but nothing could have prepared her for this.

It seemed as if every police car, ambulance, and fire truck in the city had been routed to Broad and Pattison, but it wasn't nearly enough. There had been a Wasted Euth concert at Lincoln Financial Field that night, so there were crowds of gawkers to control, and the number of injured in the parking lot alone was more than they could handle. Debris lay scattered everywhere.

Most of the light poles in the parking lot were still intact, but the stadium wreckage itself was dark, an unexpected hole where once 2000-watt lights had blazed out into the night. The sky was overcast, a brooding bank of clouds that hid the stars and seemed to press down on the city.

Sandra dialed her dad's phone for what must have been the tenth time. The call went straight to voice mail, just like every other attempt. Her voice was shaking badly. "Dad, please call. Please get this. Tell me you weren't at the game."

She called her mom's phone next. No answer. She had left three messages already, but she left another one anyway. "Mom, it's Sandra. Please call. Dad was there, wasn't he? He had tickets. I don't remember when, but I think it was tonight. He invited me, but I was on duty . . ." She choked on the words and clicked off.

She weaved her way around battered blue plastic seats, strewn across the parking lot alongside unrecognizable pieces of mangled metal and concrete. There were bodies, dozens of them. Some of them were whole. Others were not. She stopped, doubled over, and vomited on her shoes.

Her sergeant took one look at her face and pointed her toward crowd control. Facing away from the stadium as much as possible, she and a dozen other cops shouted people back and strung police tape to cordon off the whole area. The first moment she could, she pulled her phone out of her pocket and called her parents again. Nothing.

"Here." Another cop pushed a water bottle into her hands. It was Nathan, from her class at the academy. She took the bottle gratefully, swished some water in her mouth, and spat it onto the pavement. It cleared some of the taste of vomit from her mouth, but not the acid taste of fear. She felt jittery and light-headed, like she was on some kind of uppers or a massive dose of caffeine.

"Thanks," she said, handing back the bottle.

"Keep it," Nathan said. He was blond and tall, with athletic good looks. The uniform fit him well. She had had a bit of a crush on him back in the day, but he had fallen for a cadet named Danielle instead, and they'd married a week after graduation.

Sandra tried her phone again, but with no result. Nathan studied her face. "You know somebody who was here?"

She nodded, swallowing hard. "My dad. He used to take us all the time, when we were . . ." Her voice cracked, and she pressed her lips together, holding back tears.

"They'll find him," Nathan said. "Don't give up hope."

She smiled as best she could and nodded her thanks. Heavy earth-moving and construction equipment rolled in, bulldozers and front-end loaders and cranes. Her sergeant pulled her back to help with search and rescue. There were people trapped under eighty-ton blocks of concrete, but no one seemed to agree about the best way to move them safely. She found herself in crews of strangers, moving what rubble could be moved by hand. She was tired, bone tired, but she knew she couldn't stop. People's lives depended on the work she was doing. And one of them just might be her father.

The FBI rolled in and added to the confusion, waving their badges and trying to preserve the crime scene at the same time rescue workers were tearing it apart. No one seemed to know quite who was in charge. Without direct orders, Sandra did whatever she could, directing EMTs with stretchers, soothing panicked family members, and checking press badges for the reporters that swarmed the site like flies.

While she did all this, she recorded everything she saw. Like most police officers, Sandra wore eyejack lenses, the raw footage feeding into a huge database that could be merged into a single, time-tagged, three-dimensional image of the site. The detectives and bomb experts would study the data for clues as to what had happened. Was it a terrorist attack? Or just a catastrophic engineering failure? Feedback to her lenses told her which views and angles were under-represented, encouraging her to aim her vision in directions that would help fill in the holes.

The news she was getting through her phone told her the media was already pointing fingers at the Turks. With American forces in Poland and Germany blocking the Turkish advance, and the Turkish navy controlling access to the Mediterranean, this was hardly a surprise. The talking heads called it a Turkish attack on American soil, comparing it to Pearl Harbor and calling for war. The Turkish president officially denied it, and it was hard for Sandra to see what they would gain from such a move. Though she supposed terrorists operated under a different set of assumptions than most people.

She hadn't seen her sergeant in hours, so she just wandered the site, joining gangs of workers where she saw a need. She queried the central database to see what views had not yet been covered and headed in those directions, trying to provide as much data as possible to the professionals whose job it was to make sense of it all. All around her, there was the horror of death, so much death that she could hardly take it in. She felt emotionally detached, floating in a protective bubble her mind had formed around the experience. Her awareness collapsed to simple tasks.

Step over the twisted metal. Help lift the concrete slab. Check GPS and shift viewing angle to forty degrees.

Her father still didn't return her calls.

"Hey! Officer! Could you give me a hand?"

Sandra turned to see a young man in a black Robson Forensic cap waving to her. He was struggling to haul two black hard cases on wheels over the debris-strewn ground.

"Finally," he said. "What's a guy got to do to get a girl to pay him some attention?"

She narrowed her eyes, not in the mood for humor. "What do you want?"

"Could you take one of these? This is really a two-person job."

One of the cases was the size of a large suitcase; the other was big enough to hold a bass fiddle. Sandra took the smaller one. "What is all this stuff?"

"ID equipment," the forensic tech said, puffing as he hauled on the larger case.

Sandra imagined a lab on wheels, blood testing and DNA, taking samples from the thousands of bodies and determining their identities. "You can do that in the field?"

The tech didn't answer. They had reached a flat area with a minimum of debris. "This will do," he said. "Open that one up, will you?"

Inside she found telescoping poles, wires, and what looked like a large security camera. "What kind of ID kit is this?" she asked.

"The best kind, I hope," the tech said. He opened the larger case. Sandra didn't understand at first what she was looking at. The case seemed to be stacked with dozens of small electric fans.

The tech circled around to the smaller case and pulled out lengths of pipe, assembling them with ease. In short order, he constructed a ten-foot tripod stand with the camera device on top. From the bottom of the case, he extracted a box with levers and a long antenna, like a remote control. "Stand back," he said.

He flipped a switch, and the larger case started rumbling. It vibrated visibly, chattering against the concrete.

"What—" Sandra started to say, but she was interrupted by a sound like the buzzing of a hundred angry bees. Out of the case rose a formation of two dozen quad-rotored helicopters, each the size of a dinner plate. They dipped in unison, shearing off to the right just as a second formation rose up to take their place. Each formation was a perfect rectangle, six copters by four, flying inches apart and moving as if locked together. At a cue from the tech, they left their places and flowed into a new formation, twenty-four wide by two deep.

He pressed another button, and the quadcopters shot off toward the ruined stadium, doing twenty or thirty miles an hour, eight feet above the ground. Several people shouted or leapt away, but the copters veered effortlessly to miss all obstacles, breaking out of formation or angling their flight as necessary. Sandra looked after them in awe. In the darkness, their LED lights swirled like a swarm of fireflies. Above her head, the device that looked like a camera came alive, smoothly slewing back and forth as if aiming at each of the receding quadcopters in rapid succession.

Some of the people nearby threw dirty looks their way. A few picked themselves off the ground after diving to avoid the copter brigade.

Sandra forgot her astonishment and wondered if she'd just been tricked. She had no idea what this guy was doing, but it wasn't forensics. Was he a reporter? Or was he a terrorist, out to destroy evidence or make a secondary attack?

She undid the snap that held her pistol in its holster. "Put the remote down," she said.

He looked bewildered. "But—"

"Now!"

He dropped the remote and held up his hands. "You don't understand—"

"What kind of stunt are you trying to pull? You said this was ID equipment." She reached for her radio to call him in.

"It is!" he said. "The copters have RFID readers on board. I told you the truth."

She paused. She would make a fool of herself if she called in a real CSI.

"Let me see your ID," she snapped.

"Honest," he said.

"ID." She held out her hand.

Sheepish, he dug around in a pocket and handed up a laminated card. It was a University of Pennsylvania student ID.

"You're a *student?*"

He looked offended. "I'm an engineering doctoral candidate in robotics and sensory perception."

"Put your hands down."

He put them down. "I'm allowed to be here."

"What about the cap?"

He took it off and looked at the logo. "Oh," he said. "Some of the forensic outfits hire us sometimes."

"And who gave you permission to loose a fleet of helicopters in a crowded search and rescue scene?" she said.

"It's a swarm, not a fleet," he said. "Look, most of the people who died out there have cards in their wallets with RFIDs in them. Credit cards, gas cards, SEPTA cards. They work with magnetic resonance; illuminate them with a burst of radio energy, and they fire back a signal with a number on it. With the right databases, those numbers can be turned into people's names. The quadcopters tag the number and the GPS coordinates, and boom: we have a map of the positions and IDs of every person on the site. Well, nearly. A lot of them anyway."

Sandra was cooling down now that he seemed to be legit. She holstered her weapon. "What's the camera for?"

"This?" he said, pointing up at the device on the tripod. "That's the radio transmitter. I have to use a pretty narrow beam to get a strong enough return signal through the rubble. The copters can't carry one, so I mount it here and coordinate them. Most RFID readers are two-way, but I had to split it up: the transmitter here to pulse the energy at each spot on the ground, and the copters at the right spot at just the right time to detect any returns."

"And you had permission to do this?"

He winced. "Sort of."

"What does 'sort of' mean?"

"The chief told me I could do whatever harebrained experiment I wanted as long as I got out of her way." He gave an awkward smile. "I guess I charmed her with my rugged good looks."

Sandra smiled in spite of herself. The tech wasn't rugged or good-looking, not by anybody's definition. He was short and soft, with a thick face, glasses, and a hint of a mustache. His skin was a light, mottled brown, and his hair could have used a trim months ago.

"Oh, fine," he said. "I see how it is. You like them tall and blond. Blue eyes, probably. Flawless skin, Swedish accent—I know the type."

"I'm just doing my job. You'd better not be lying about the chief, because I'm going to check." She glanced back at his ID card. "Your name is Angel?"

"An-HEL. The *g* is pronounced with an *h* sound." He rolled his eyes.

Her smile vanished. "What?"

"I know what you're thinking. Who would name a boy 'Angel'? Typical American. I'll have you know Angel was the fifth most popular name for boys born in Mexico last year."

"Is that where you're from?" she asked. "Mexico?"

"Born and bred." He lifted his chin high. "Spent my whole life in San Antonio, until last year."

Sandra paused. "Isn't San Antonio in the United States?"

"There you go again, with your prejudicial comments," Angel said. "Only Americans think it's in the United States."

This time she caught the sparkle in his eyes. "Are you serious?"

He grinned, breaking the tension. "I'd say about twenty percent of the time."

She wanted to punch him. She couldn't tell when he meant what he was saying and when he was just messing with her. In her current state of high tension, she didn't find that funny. On the other hand, she was having a conversation, and having a conversation meant not looking at the scene around her, expecting to stumble over her father's body at any moment.

The angry buzzing sound grew louder, and she turned just in time to see the swarm of quadcopters bearing down on her. She gasped and ducked, but the copters reined up short, breaking off into groups of four. Each group of four wheeled up to Angel, hovering around him for a few moments before banking away again. He snapped open a laptop and typed rapidly.

"It's working!" he said, the astonishment evident in his voice.

"You're surprised? Haven't you tried this before?"

"In the lab, sure, but not in real life."

"You covered the whole site already?"

"No, not even close." As the last foursome left him, the copters slid into formation and shot away toward the wreckage again. "It'll take hours to cover everything. But that's a lot better than days, maybe weeks, of dozens of techs with handheld readers doing the same thing. The information won't be conclusive; people will still have to confirm each identification, actually look at each body. But as a preliminary map, it should save a lot of effort and let family members know about their loved ones more quickly."

He rotated the laptop to show her the screen. It was an aerial map of the site, flanked by Pattison Avenue and Hartranft Street. One corner was peppered with yellow dots. Angel zoomed in on that corner, and the dots bloomed out into numbers.

"Each of those points is a person. Probably," he said. "There are RFIDs in other things, too."

"And from that you know who they are?"

"Well, I don't," he said. "I don't have access to those databases. But the police do, you can be certain, and if there are any they don't have, the feds can get them."

Sandra studied the design the dots made on the screen, swooping in zigzagging curves. It didn't look random. "Why does it make a pattern?"

Angel shrugged. "I don't know."

She thought about what her dad would say, seeing a pattern like that. "It might be important," she said. "If things were thrown around in a recognizable pattern, we might be able to determine what caused this, maybe even track down the source."

Another shrug. "I work in a robotics lab, but I'll tell you one thing; this was no bomb."

She cocked her head at him. "What do you mean?"

"There was no fire," he said. "Nothing's burned. And look at how the stadium collapsed—it looks more like it fell in on itself than like it was blown out. Most of the rubble is piled up inside, on the playing field. More like an earthquake. Or a sinkhole."

He was right. It was obvious, now that she thought about it. There was plenty of debris in the parking lot, but it looked more like it had been pushed by the force of the falling stadium walls, not like the walls themselves had been blown out. But there had been no earthquake; at least not that anyone was reporting in the news. "Maybe there were a lot of smaller charges placed at key spots," she said. "Arranged so that the walls would fall in and kill as many people as possible."

Angel nodded, thoughtful. "Hey," he said, "if we know where the people are now, and where they were originally sitting, maybe we could draw lines from their starting point to where they ended up. We could track the vectors of force."

He was getting excited, but all she could think about was the image of her father's body being blown out of his seat. She felt sick and put her hand over her mouth.

A female cop ran up to her, dark hair blown back in the wind. It was Danielle, Nathan's wife. "Sandra," she said, "you've got to come now."

"What is it?"

"I think it's your father."

Sandra's mind rebelled at the words. She wanted to punch Danielle in her pretty mouth for daring to say such a thing. "Dead?"

Danielle didn't answer, but her eyes told Sandra everything.

Sandra followed her at a run to where Nathan stood over a body on the ground. His shoulders were hunched, his eyes dead. He was holding a black leather wallet, worn and familiar. Sandra looked at the wallet, refusing to look down, terror gripping her throat.

She took the wallet and flipped it open. Her father's face stared up at her from his Pennsylvania driver's license, but she checked the name anyway. Jacob Kelley. She shook her head, trying to process what she was seeing, the information somehow failing to sink in, even though she'd been expecting it now for hours. She shook her head, trying to push the evidence away, wishing for a return to uncertainty, when it was still possible that he hadn't been here.

Finally, she looked down. Her father lay on the pavement as naturally as if he'd fallen asleep there.

"I'm sorry," Nathan began. She waved her hand to fend off his words, and he trailed off. He stood there, awkward, not knowing what to say. Danielle put a hand on her arm. Sandra turned and buried her face into the coarse, blue fabric of Danielle's shoulder. She felt like she ought to cry, but the tears didn't come. Danielle stroked her hair, while Sandra took in big gulps of air, like she was drowning.

Her phone rang.

The noise startled her. She reached for it automatically, and then nearly threw it away. She'd been waiting for it to ring all night, and now, when it finally did, it was too late. The automatic movement brought the screen up to her eyes, however, and she saw the number. It was her father's number.

She answered.

"Sandra?" Her father's voice was warm and strong and sweet and utterly recognizable.

"Dad?"

CHAPTER 2

The call came at 6:00 AM. Ryan Oronzi, chief scientist at the New Jersey Super Collider's High Energy Lab, had only been asleep for three hours, but he left home immediately, not bothering to wash or comb his hair. When he arrived, the guards at the gate recognized him and waved him through. It was an inexcusable lapse in security procedures, but Ryan didn't have time to reproach them. He parked and rushed into the building.

He walked past the bank of elevators and took the stairs at a jog. He never used elevators, and he wasn't about to start now. His colleagues thought it was claustrophobia, but they were wrong. An elevator was just a potentially lethal piece of technology that Ryan himself had not personally designed, and that made it suspect. Yes, he knew about safety brakes, as well as the more modern electromagnetic locking mechanisms, but what would happen if *those* systems failed? A quick plunge to a spectacular death, that's what.

It wasn't just elevators, of course. Ryan didn't trust airplanes, or bridges, or security systems, either. Take that baseball stadium in Philadelphia. All those people had trusted the security guards and cameras and electronic sniffers to keep them safe, but those systems had failed them. It took imagination to think of all the ways things could go wrong and protect against them. Ryan didn't trust anyone to have that much imagination but himself.

By the time he reached the eighth floor, he was breathing hard and sweating through his shirt. He made this climb every day, but it was the only exercise he got, and it didn't make up for the quantity of popcorn and Mountain Dew he consumed in the lab. He recognized the irony— his diet was more likely to kill him than an elevator ever was—but death by heart attack always seemed like a distant problem, while death by sudden deceleration could happen in an instant. Besides, he was a physicist, not a biologist.

The corridors on the eighth floor were a maze of unexpected turnings around oddly-shaped rooms, with confusing markings and uniformly painted beige walls. There weren't even any windows to provide a sense of direction. Ryan suspected the security architects had designed it this way on purpose, so that even if someone gained access to the building, they wouldn't be able to find what they were looking for. Or, Ryan thought, to find their way out again. He imagined a would-be spy wandering these halls endlessly, never finding the exit.

He hurried through the maze with the ease of long habit, pushing himself despite his exhaustion. Only four hours had passed since he had left the lab the night before. If he had known it would happen while he was gone, he never would have left. Ryan was accustomed to spending most of his time at work anyway, but lately he could hardly spare enough time to sleep. Nicole Wu, his chief lab assistant, had insisted she could handle it tonight. She said she would call him the moment there was any anomaly, and he had let her talk him into going home.

He typed a ten-digit number into a keypad, cursing as his fingers stumbled over the keys. He felt the familiar knotting in his stomach as the door opened and he was met by an armed guard. But it wasn't the guard that caused his anxiety. The guards were there to protect what was inside the lab from the public. What concerned him was whether they could protect the public from what was inside the lab.

The guard patted him down like he did every day, and Ryan submitted to fingerprint and retinal scans impatiently. His mind was already running ahead to the confrontation that was waiting for him. Nobody else understood the danger; nobody understood what they had created. Not even Nicole realized the significance. He emptied his pockets—keys, wallet, phone—and left them in a bin on the wall with his name on it. The guard typed in a code of his own, one that only he knew, and the next door buzzed open.

Finally, Ryan passed through a scanning tunnel, one sensitive enough to pick up any electronics, even smart paper. By the time he reached the other side, he felt the terror building. He was afraid to go in there, afraid of what the day might bring. But if he didn't do it, who would? At the final door, there was a combination lock, a finicky dial with a digital readout, controlling a powerful electromagnetic lock that held the door in place. It would be easier to batter through the steel-reinforced walls than to open this door without unlocking it. The walls vibrated slightly in a random pattern, defeating any technology that could reproduce voices from inside by picking up the sound waves through the walls. The whole lab was a giant Faraday cage as well, the walls threaded with copper, allowing no possibility of electronic signal leak.

He completed the combination, and the thick door swung open like the door to a safe, revealing a tiny room like an airlock. He stepped inside and swung the door shut. Only when it locked into place did the second door unlock, granting him access to the lab.

Nicole was waiting for him. "Your beta protocol kicked in, and everything held," she said, handing him a tablet.

He scrolled through the data. What he saw made a chill slide like a drop of sweat down his back. "That was close," he said. "It's never gotten that far before."

"Everything seems nominal now," she said. "Well within tolerances."

"That doesn't mean anything," Ryan said. "It's getting smarter. I'm not sure how long I can keep up with it."

He lowered his complaining body into a seat and looked at his universe. It spun gracefully in the middle of the lab, a haze of multicolored dots sparked through with a laser-light spectacle of electric arcs and flashes. It wasn't the actual thing, of course. The real universe was expanding rapidly in its own space-time, connected to theirs only through a subatomic wormhole. The display was something Ryan had invented using photoionization microscopy, a way of visualizing the quantum

n-dimensional data in an intuitively comprehensible form. It was his way of looking at his baby and watching it grow.

It was beautiful, but it was going to kill him. It was quite possibly going to kill them all.

The baby universe was an incredible scientific achievement, perhaps unequaled in its scope and implications. It had long been understood that what we called our universe was just one bubble in the quantum froth that had erupted at the beginning of time. There had been billions of other such bubbles, each one different in its physical laws, the particles it contained, the elements it could form.

Ryan had reproduced this effect, generating a bubble universe of his own. Within its own time reference, the universe was only minutes old. It had no planets or stars. It didn't even have atoms. It was just a rapidly expanding quark-gluon plasma, as our universe had been minutes after the big bang. And since its time context was so much slower, he had been able to monitor its development, pico-second by picosecond. The resulting revelations about the quantum world had led to a flurry of remarkable inventions, not least of which was the military technology demo that was supposed to take place on campus next week.

The demo. Ryan finally noticed what Nicole was wearing. She usually came to work in jeans and a T-shirt, but today she wore a black skirt, pink blouse, black jacket, and high heels. Her long hair was twisted into a knot and skewered with a silver pin. Ryan scanned the room and saw the other lab techs in suits and ties.

"You're kidding me," Ryan said. "The demo is today?"

Nicole gave him an incredulous look. "Of course it's today."

"Not anymore." Ryan waved the tablet. "Not after this. It'll have to be canceled."

He stood again, ignoring the pain in his knees, and marched back toward the lab door.

"Stan's not going to cancel," Nicole called after him. "There's too much money riding on this."

Ryan didn't answer. He knew she was right, but he had to try.

Stanley Babington's office was larger than most conference rooms. He had been the head of the New Jersey Super Collider at Lakehurst for a decade now, and his main talent was in convincing government agencies to part with their money. A job which, Ryan had to admit, he performed remarkably well. The NJSC and associated projects had grown quickly while most government spending was decreasing. The man understood politics. Unfortunately, he didn't understand physics.

"We have to cancel the demo," Ryan said without preamble.

"Oronzi, you're as predictable as a solar eclipse," Babington said. "Every time there's an important event, you start imagining the worst. Can we just get through this one without the drama?"

"This isn't like that."

"You have half an hour to get changed, and then I need you at your polite best." Babington pointed to a coat rack, where an expensive-looking black suit hung in a thin plastic sleeve. A purple tie was draped over the hanger. It looked like Ryan's size.

"You bought me a suit?"

Babington gave a wry smile. "I know you too well. You're my celebrity, Oronzi. You're my Einstein. Everybody knows you're a little eccentric; it's part of your charm. But I can't have you seen in *that*." He waved at Ryan's clothes.

Ryan had no intention of putting on the suit. He had read once, years ago, about an undertaker who stripped corpses of their clothes just before burying them and then sold the clothes on consignment. He hadn't worn a suit since. "You're not listening to me," he said. "We have to cancel. We had another incident last night. It's the closest it's ever come to breaking out."

"What are we talking about here? Worst case scenario?" Babington studied himself in a mirror and adjusted the knot of his tie.

"I don't know," Ryan said. "That's just it. It's unstable. What will happen if it ruptures? There's no precedent."

Babington sighed. "Look. This demo is everything. All our funding is riding on this. The Joint Chiefs are here already. The Secretary of Defense is on his way. I should already be downstairs shaking hands. You come in here every other day with a new Chicken Little story. Your little phobias play well in the media, and that's all fine. But your fears usually come to nothing. So tell me, should I really cancel the most important demonstration of new technology in a decade? Is it that important? Are you that sure?"

"Of course I'm not sure. This isn't something anyone has ever studied before. But hear me out."

Babington picked up a leather binder from the desk. "There's only so much Danish and coffee the Joint Chiefs can consume before they start to feel slighted. You have thirty seconds to convince me."

"There's something alive in there."

That stopped Babington short, and he made eye contact for the first time. "Alive? Is somebody hurt? One of your people? Tell me the media doesn't know."

"No, no, not like that. There's something alive inside the wormhole. Something not human."

He saw the concern drift out of Babington's eyes, replaced by annoyance. "This gets old, Oronzi. I need you to just do your job."

Babington strode out into the hallway, but Ryan walked after him. "I am doing my job. Listen, the baby universe stays connected to ours through the wormhole, but its energies are always fluctuating. There's always the danger it will detach, and we'll lose it, or else that the particle stream will increase drastically, causing widespread destruction."

Babington stopped at the elevator and glared at him. "You told me you had that under control."

"Well, sort of."

He crossed his arms. "Explain quickly. Use small words."

"I manage the baby universe by projecting energy fields through the wormhole. The shape of the fields is governed by certain equations I control. But the energy pattern mutates, so I have to change the equations all the time to keep up. At first, I thought it was just the normal change pattern as the universe grows; it's not like we've done this before. But—I know this sounds crazy—the energy pattern has been changing specifically to defeat my equations, forcing me to make them more complex. There is something *solving* those equations and shaping the wormhole accordingly. It's like I'm setting puzzles for it, rather than actually controlling it. And it's getting faster at solving them. It's so quick now that I have to have several new equations in reserve, programmed to apply as soon as one fails."

Babington's voice was disbelieving. "You're telling me the wormhole is sentient."

"No. I'm telling you there's something sentient on the other side of it. Something very intelligent. And it's trying to break through."

Babington punched the elevator's down button. "I should have seen it coming," he said to the ceiling. "I ignored all the signs, and now, at the worst possible time . . ." The elevator arrived with a ding and the doors opened. Babington stepped in and turned back to face him. "You're not going to do anything stupid like try to destroy it, are you?"

"I already tried."

"You did what?" A flash of pure anger passed quickly across Babington's face.

"I couldn't do it."

"Well, thank heaven for small favors," Babington said. "Look, I need you to hold yourself together, just for today. Don't talk to any media. Tell them you're busy or something. Tomorrow, once we get this demo out of the way, we'll talk. Maybe you should take some time off."

"I'm fine. I don't need time off," Ryan said, walking toward him. "I—" He stopped short at the elevator doorway. The floor of the elevator was a centimeter lower than the floor of the hallway, and he could see a little light through the gap. He tried to take another step, but his legs wouldn't move. The elevators doors started to close.

Babington rolled his eyes. "Right. See you at the bottom of the stairs. Remember, no media."

The doors slid shut, leaving Ryan staring at his own reflection in their mirrored surface.

CHAPTER 3

"Is that him?" Alex Kelley asked. She had only been at the NJSC for a week now, and it was her first glimpse of the famed Ryan Oronzi.

Tequila Williams looked where she was pointing and nodded. "In the flesh. Smartest guy in the world, so they say. They also say he's cracked." Tequila was tall and slender, partial to platform heels, low necklines, and neon eye shadow. When Alex and Tequila walked across a room, it was Tequila who drew all the looks. Alex didn't mind. She dressed for comfort, not to draw attention, whereas Tequila always wanted attention.

They were both physicists-turned-engineers, here at the NJSC with the Lockheed Martin contingent to demonstrate the latest technology to representatives of the military and intelligence communities. The demo would take place in the NJSC's High Energy Lab, the largest facility on the Lakehurst complex. The name was a misdirection, intentionally benign, to distract attention from the armed guards and oversized power conduits that screamed Secret Government Facility. It was an enormous building, surrounded by cameras and two layers of fencing and razor wire. Alex doubted the public was fooled by the name.

The technology they were demonstrating had been built by Alex and Tequila's company, but that the technology was possible at all was due to Dr. Ryan Oronzi. Rumor in the media was that Oronzi was on the cusp of discovering the elusive Theory of Everything, finally reconciling gravity with particle physics and finishing what Einstein had started more than a century before.

In the flesh, Oronzi was at least a hundred pounds overweight, his hair askew, dressed in a T-shirt and a pair of worn jeans that would have benefitted from a belt. "He looks like a plumber," Alex said.

Tequila stifled a laugh. "I guess if you're smart enough, you can do and say what you like, and people just call you eccentric. It's like being old."

"Or rich," Alex said.

The demo was staged in a huge, warehouse space that would give them enough room to demonstrate the new technology in dramatic style. All of the guests were milling in one corner, near a lavish breakfast spread—far nicer than anything Lockheed Martin ever provided just for their employees. Oronzi's arrival quickly attracted the attention of the generals and executives, who shook his hand and made small talk. Alex and Tequila made their way through to the tables. Tequila piled her plate high with eggs, bacon, and a Danish, but Alex just poured some coffee into a disposable cup and leaned against the wall, sipping it.

"Are you all right?" Tequila asked, eyeing her meager breakfast. "It's not like you to be nervous before a demo."

"It's not that," Alex said. "The stadium disaster has me rattled."

Tequila instantly turned serious. "You didn't know anyone there, did you?"

"My dad was at the game."

Tequila's eyes flew wide. "Was he—"

"No, he's okay. I talked to him on the phone. He left early, before the bomb went off. He was on the way home when it blew, miles away. If he had decided to stay just a few minutes longer . . ." Her voice choked, and she fought back a sudden rush of tears. She had been so close to losing him.

"What are you doing here?" Tequila said. "We can cover things without you. Go and hang out with your family. Give your dad a hug."

Alex shook her head and wiped her eyes. "We've been working on this for how long? More than a year? I'm not backing out now. I'll go home afterward."

"You're sure? You don't have to, you know. Everyone would understand."

"I'll be fine."

Tequila put a strawberry Danish in her hand. "Eat it," she said. "That's a command."

Alex managed a watery smile and took a tiny bite of the Danish. It did taste good. "Thanks."

"It's entirely selfish," Tequila said. "I was lying when I said we could cover things. Without you, we'll crash and burn, and they'll give the contract to Boeing."

"Look," Alex said. "My sister's on the Philadelphia police force, and I'll guarantee you she hasn't gone home. Probably hasn't slept, either. If she can keep working, so can I."

Tequila swallowed a large bite of eggs. "Competitive relationship, huh?"

"You could say that. Her name's Sandra. She's a twin."

Tequila whistled. "How come I didn't know you had a twin?"

"It's complicated."

"Don't I know it. Family always is."

"I have an older sister, Claire, and a younger brother, Sean, but Sandra and I are the most . . . closely linked."

"Identical?"

"In appearance? Absolutely. In personality . . ."

Tequila laughed. "Say no more. You know, I always fantasized about having an identical twin when I was a kid. I bet you pulled some crazy pranks when you were growing up together."

Alex smiled noncommittally. The truth was, she and Sandra hadn't grown up together, not until they were fourteen years old. They weren't even really twins, not in the traditional sense. But that was more than she wanted to explain right now. To change the subject, she said, "My brother's stationed in Poland. Everyone says that's where the war will break out first, if it comes."

"Army?"

"Marines. Force Recon, actually."

29

"Ooh, a real man," Tequila said, wiggling her eyebrows. "Can I meet him? When does he come home?"

Alex elbowed her. "He has two months left in his tour of duty. But that won't make any difference if Turkey attacks. Two months might turn into two years. Or he might never come home."

The speakers crackled, and all eyes turned. A Lockheed Martin functionary stood at the podium, kicking off the day's events and introducing Lockheed Martin CEO Linda Staker. Staker stood to light applause. Tequila said, "Good luck—you'll be great," and squeezed Alex's shoulder. The two of them took their places on the lower level of chairs.

Alex sat next to Vijay Bhargava, their development team lead, who knew more about the nanocircuitry in their product than any other two of them combined. Vijay was resolutely pessimistic, a glass-half-empty-and-probably-poisoned-anyway kind of guy. "And our fearless CEO takes the stage," he said. "I've never heard anyone talk as much as she does. She could put a class of five-year-olds to sleep on cupcake day."

Alex grinned and elbowed him. "She's not that bad."

"She could out-filibuster a senator," Vijay said. "She could bore a snake to tears."

"I get the idea."

"Get it? Snakes don't have tear glands, so she'd have to be really boring to bore them to tears."

She raised her hands in surrender. "Yeah, okay. I got it."

The room was large enough for a NASA convention. It was decorated like a war zone, with burned-out buildings and rubble. A special stage had been built at one end to seat the VIPs, with leather chairs and attendants to bring drinks. This was where Ryan Oronzi sat, along with the Lockheed Martin executive staff, NJSC chief Stanley Babington, two congressmen, the Joint Chiefs, and Secretary of Defense Jared Falk with his security detail. On either side of the stage were the rows of folding chairs for everyone else: the NJSC scientists, the reps from the military and intelligence communities with their science aides in tow to explain the technology to them, the Lockheed Martin executives and business managers.

True to Vijay's prediction, Staker droned on for a good ten minutes, spouting platitudes about the importance of all the people working there at Lakehurst, their dedication to excellence, ability to work together no matter their employer, and the importance of their efforts to national security. Her speech was upbeat, inclusive, patriotic, and desperately dull. Alex had nothing to do but dwell on her role in the coming demo, and the various possible ways she could botch it. At the end, Staker introduced Secretary Falk, and Alex cringed, expecting him to give more of the same.

But he didn't. He took the podium and said, "You all know what happened in Philadelphia last night. Whether Turkish terrorists were to blame or not, we live in dangerous times. The world covets our wealth and power and wants to destroy us. What we see here today might be just the edge we need to preserve our way of life for the next generation. Let's begin."

Staker nodded to a vice president, who nodded to Alex's boss, and Alex and Tequila and their team stood. It was time.

Music started, a marching drumbeat with horns in the background, probably lifted from some old war film by the Presentation Arts team. The house lights dimmed, replaced by a diffuse light from above that gave the sense of a cloudy morning. Smoke drifted across the warehouse floor. From the back, soldiers in Turkish army uniforms started working their way through the debris, slipping from wall to wall, AK-74 assault rifles at the ready.

Alex settled behind the control table with the other technicians to monitor the show. They were visible to the audience, but off to the side, not part of the action. Vijay took a back seat, monitoring them rather than actually participating. He was more familiar with the design than he was with the actual hands-on controls. That left Alex, Tequila, and their two programming experts, Rod Zeidman and Lisa Mancini. Tequila was tall, but Lisa was perhaps the tallest woman Alex had ever met, an occasional bodybuilder who climbed mountains in her free time and intimidated every man she met. Rod, by contrast, was short, red-haired, with a little-boy-cute face that make him look fifteen years younger than he really was. The five of them made up the Lockheed Martin team. Hundreds of others had worked on the program in some capacity, but the five of them were principle contributors, the ones best suited to run this demonstration. Alex was the youngest of them, but she liked to think she could hold her own.

"Do it like we practiced it," Vijay whispered.

"No problem," Rod said. "We've got this one in the bag."

"Don't say that!" Vijay said, his voice rising almost to panic. "Do you want to jinx the whole thing?"

"A little jinx never stopped us before," Rod said. "Bring it on."

He tapped a control, and the music stopped. On the warehouse floor, a single American marine stood up from where he had been hiding. He was exposed, in full view of the enemy Turkish soldiers. He had no weapon. On her screens, Alex could see what the marine could see. He wore eyejack lenses, not significantly different from those that had been on the public market for years. In his view, the scene was clearly lit, with each enemy soldier highlighted in yellow—even those still crouching behind walls. A larger screen above the VIP stage showed the audience the same view.

So far, it was standard military technology, nothing out of the ordinary. The Turkish soldiers approached, shouting at the American, who put his hands on his head, apparently docile. Then he attacked.

The American flicked his eyes at icons that overlaid his vision, an intuitive interface in a style familiar to most elementary school children. The functions he accessed, however, were a far cry from direction finders and entertainment videos. The rifles spun out of the Turkish soldiers' hands, flipping through the air and clattering to the ground far away before they could fire a shot. The Turks shouted in surprise, and then—somewhat unrealistically, in Alex's opinion—charged the American unarmed. They met the same fate as their weapons. The American didn't even move, but the Turks twisted up into the air, screaming, and were slammed into the ground or thrown over walls. The lights came up to applause. The first scenario of the day had finished without a hitch.

Alex could tell the difference between those who'd seen the technology before and those who hadn't. The "soldiers" were stunt men, hired for the occasion, and the demo was carefully choreographed, but the technology was real. There were no wires, no tricks, and the visuals had been designed to make that obvious. Those who had never seen it before were stunned, still staring out at the field with their mouths hanging slack. They had grown up taking technological miracles in stride, but this was a leap beyond, into the realm of the wizards and Jedi of their youth. This was magic. And it was only the beginning.

Stanley Babington took the podium next, describing the technology and its concept in general terms.

"The invention of the Higgs projector has brought the power of the subatomic to the warfighter's control," he said, raising his hands dramatically to either side. "The Higgs field is all around us, invisible, uniform throughout the universe. It gives matter its mass, controls the characteristics of other particles; in short, it determines all the constants that give our universe meaning.

"But what if we could change it? Science tells us that the big bang produced not just one universe, but countless trillions, all of them frothing up out of the early expansion like so many bubbles. Each has a different Higgs field, producing a different set of basic constants, a different set of fundamental particles, a completely different periodic table. Well, here at the New Jersey Super Collider's High Energy Lab, we've created a universe of our very own, and through it, learned to manipulate the Higgs field in localized areas, for very specific purposes. The Higgs has been called the God particle, and not without reason. To control the Higgs is to control the very nature of reality itself."

His speech was met with light applause, but Alex was barely paying attention. She perused logs and checked power levels, making sure everything was ready for the next scenario. The truth was, nobody at her company understood this technology completely. Alex had a master's degree in quantum physics from the University of Pennsylvania, and Lockheed was footing the bill for her to pursue her doctorate in the evenings. She could talk Pauli equations and Poincaré symmetries with the best of them. But there was a mystery at the heart of this, a black box that bridged the gap between the quantum world and the world of everyday objects. Her bosses said it was top secret, a special compartmented classification only shared on a need-to-know basis, and Alex accepted the explanation. She wanted to believe that this knowledge had been developed simply by the hard work of a very brilliant man.

In the second scenario, the same marine was trapped and under fire from multiple assailants. He cowered behind a rock, just barely protected from the bullets that rained down on either side of his position. His attackers fired through holes in a tall stone wall. The audience could see them, but the American couldn't. The American pulled his last grenade off his belt and pulled the pin. He waited. One second. Two. Through his eyejack lenses, the grenade was highlighted, a glowing arrow pointing from it. The Marine quickly adjusted the arrow's length and direction, and the grenade in his hand disappeared. At the same moment, it reappeared in mid-air on the other side of the wall—right where the arrow had been pointing—and exploded. The grenade was just smoke and light and noise, but the Turkish soldiers pantomimed their deaths admirably.

"All the miracles you're seeing rely on one basic principle of physics," Babington said. "The principle that every particle in the universe is also a wave. A subatomic particle isn't like a rock or an apple, which has a clearly defined position and velocity. A particle has a probability wave: a set of places where it *could* be, with varying probabilities. It isn't just that we don't know where it is. The particle itself hasn't decided. It's in an indeterminate state, smeared out over a region of space. And that little principle allows us to do some truly marvelous things."

The third scenario was a wooded scene. The Turks hid behind thick trees, but the American's bullets seemed to pass through the trees like they were smoke. The rubber bullets slammed into the Turks one by one, and the Turks—despite the armored vests they wore under their uniforms—did a convincing job of falling down.

Babington's voiceover continued. "Bullets don't usually have a wavelength, or not so much of one that you can tell. We've learned how to manipulate that. Our bullets are like particles, traveling in every possible path toward their target. With no obstacle, the probabilities average out to a straight path, the path we expect. But when an obstacle stands in the way, it only stops a part of the wave. The rest of the paths still exist, and so the bullet diffracts around the obstacle, just as light would diffract."

On the large screen, the audience saw a slow-motion replay of a bullet flying through space, then *blurring* as it passed through and around a tree before striking its human target, just as solid as ever.

"So far, so good," Rod said with a flip of bright red hair and a boyish smile.

Vijay scowled. "That's what people say just before everything goes wrong."

"Nothing's going to go wrong," Lisa said. "We've practiced this so many times I could do it in my sleep. I could do it with one hand while bouldering at Coopers Rock with the other."

Vijay groaned. "You guys are killing me."

Two more scenarios followed, involving Jeeps with mounted .50-caliber machine guns, and finally, a Turkish Altay battle tank. They went perfectly, despite Vijay's fears.

Tequila leaned over to Alex's station. "This last one's all you, girl," she said. "Knock 'em dead."

Alex pulled the Higgs projector from her pocket. It was a slim card, not much different than a personal phone in appearance, but it turned its owner into something like a god. She slipped it back into her pocket. Show time.

Alex stood and stepped away from her station. As she did so, the doors behind her opened, and five Turkish soldiers ran out, shouting and pointing their guns at her. She wore a dark skirt and a light blue blouse; she was obviously part of the support staff, not the show. Nevertheless, the Turks dragged her out onto the floor in front of the VIP stage with a gun to her head, while she feigned terror. The Turk closest to her tore open his jacket, revealing a dynamite vest.

Several of the audience jumped to their feet, unsure if this was part of the show or real. Secretary Falk's Secret Service detail held their ground, however; they'd been briefed on what to expect. The American marine from the first three scenarios put his gun on the ground and raised his hands. He was quickly tied and blindfolded.

She was ready for this. With a sister on the police force and a brother in Force Recon, she'd been around guns for years, knew how to handle and shoot them. Sean had even sneaked her and Sandra onto the base one evening and let them go through the MARSOC shoot house. She'd helped to choreograph a lot of this fight, working closely with the military guys who consulted for Lockheed Martin. She took a few deep breaths, willing her muscles to relax.

The Turks pointed their weapons at the stage. "Secretary Falk," said the one with the dynamite, speaking English with no trace of a Turkish accent. "Instruct your men to put their weapons on the ground."

CHAPTER 4

Ryan Oronzi was barely watching the demonstration. He was stuck in the VIP section by Babington's decree, but he had his tablet with him and was using it to study the logs from the control system around his baby universe. Energies from his universe had been used to create the Higgs projectors, and they drew a lot of their power from it. Ryan was watching to make sure the intelligence inside didn't make another break for freedom.

It was the last scenario now, the one in which the girl would escape from supposed terrorists. Everything had been stable so far, the monitor levels normal, but . . . there was a pattern. Something wrong, something that snagged at Ryan's subconscious. He had learned not to ignore the part of his mind that noticed such things.

It was Ryan's mind, after all, that made him special. He had always known, from his earliest memories, that he was different from other people. Better. He had insights they couldn't fathom, saw patterns too complicated for others to perceive. When he was young, he had even fantasized that he wasn't really human. He had imagined himself as a member of an alien race of superior intellect, who had placed his mind into a human body to guide the human race to a higher level of knowledge or achievement. It wasn't a thought he had entirely given up on, but he had learned not to mention it to other people.

Ryan brought up a modeling engine on his tablet and starting plugging in the data from the last half hour. His greatest fear was that whatever was on the other side of the wormhole would solve his latest protocol and escape. He didn't know what would happen if it did, but he didn't want to find out.

Nobody else believed his claims that the patterns in the wormhole were produced by an intelligence acting on the other side. It was a hard thing to defend. The patterns fluctuated with apparent randomness. Even Nicole thought that his equations were just failing to adequately predict and contain them. But he could tell the difference. No random fluctuations could outsmart the traps he was setting, and certainly not with increasing speed.

He studied the data. To his relief, none of the numbers he saw came anywhere close to exceeding the latest protocol. None of his proximity alarms had been tripped. This latest set of equations was holding up better. But no.

There was a pattern to the numbers. A chill went down his back as he recognized it. The numbers shadowed the solution to the equations, only an order of magnitude smaller. The intelligence was getting more clever. It was intentionally solving the puzzle in a way that avoided tripping his proximity alarms. In fact, it had already solved it. It was hiding its tracks, so that it could break out all at once, denying Ryan the chance to apply another protocol when it started to get close. Which mean that it, too, recognized that there was an intelligent being on the other side of the wormhole. It knew Ryan was there.

Ryan leaped to his feet, interrupting the scenario. "Run!" he shouted. "Everyone out, right now!"

Babington's hand closed on his shoulder like a vise. "They're not really terrorists, remember? It's part of the show." The closest member of Secretary Falk's security detail chuckled.

"You don't understand—it's the intelligence," Ryan said. "I warned you to cancel . . ."

"And I warned you to keep your mouth shut," Babington growled, trying to steer him away from the stage.

On the floor, the abducted girl sprang into action. The big screen showed her viewpoint, revealing that she, too, was wearing eyejack lenses connected to a Higgs projector. The dynamite-vested soldier was flung away over a wall. A fiery explosion on the other side cued rousing action-movie theme music as the girl ripped the guns out of the other soldiers' hands. One man pulled a backup pistol from his vest and fired at the girl's head, but it was his compatriot on her other side who collapsed. The big screen showed the bullet blurring around the girl's head in slow motion and striking the soldier behind her. In moments, all the soldiers were down, leaving only the girl, brushing off her hands. The audience erupted into applause, including the Secretary of Defense, who was beaming.

"You see?" Babington hissed into Ryan's ear.

"No," Ryan shouted over the music. "Everyone needs to get out of here. We have to shut it all down!"

Babington just glared at him, and Ryan gave up. He huddled over his tablet. His only chance was to change the protocol again before the intelligence made its move. He had no idea what it might do if it escaped, but he knew how clever it was, and how powerful. Ryan still had several backup protocols queued up, though it was getting harder to make them complex enough to hold the thing inside for more than a few days.

The lights went out. The pounding music fell suddenly silent, and the applause died away. Even Ryan's tablet, though it had its own battery source, fell black and dead. Ryan whipped out his phone. Nothing.

"Staker, what is this?" Secretary Falk asked. "Another scenario? We weren't briefed on this."

The lights came back on. The audience members breathed sighs of relief, looked at each other and smiled, but Ryan stayed frozen. Falk's security detail were on their feet, not laughing anymore, surrounding the Secretary.

Behind them, Secretary Falk stood. When Ryan saw him, he started to moan softly, uncontrollably. Falk had no eyes. Where his eyes should have been was only a flat mask of skin, as if they had never been there. Ryan knew at once that this wasn't the Secretary at all. It was the intelligence. The thing that wasn't Secretary Falk looked around with its missing eyes. It seemed relaxed, unconcerned.

One of the Secret Service agents looked back and noticed, his eyes going wide with shock. "Sir? Are you all right, sir?" Falk brushed his hand casually through the air. The agent who had spoken collapsed to the ground and lay motionless.

The other two agents drew their pistols and took shooting stances. "Sir, please sit down," one of them said. The other started talking on his radio, calling for backup.

Falk stepped toward the closest agent with an expression of curiosity. He reached for the agent's gun. "Don't do that, sir," the agent said. Falk touched the gun, which crumpled away like burning paper. The other agent fired at Falk, but the bullet blurred around him, just like in the demo scenarios, and blasted harmlessly into the wall. The first agent, now unarmed, picked up a chair and swung it down as hard as he could on Falk's head. This time, it was *Falk* that blurred, like a vibrating tuning fork, causing the chair to crash uselessly to the floor. Falk gestured and both agents fell to the ground where they lay, unmoving.

Ryan started backing away toward the exit. There was no beating this creature, not with guns or strength. There was some kind of field preventing his electronics from working. If he could get clear of it, he might be able to do something.

The creature staggered. It took Ryan a moment to realize it had been hit by a rubber bullet. The abducted girl from the scenario had one of the Turkish soldiers' rifles. She fired again. The creature blurred, but instead of passing through, the bullet blurred as well, striking the creature and knocking it back. The girl was fighting it using the Higgs projector, an incredibly gutsy move, in Ryan's opinion. She might be adept at using it, but this was how this creature *lived*. It was like trying to outswim a shark.

The Falk creature waved its hand, but the girl was unaffected. Instead, she used the projector to teleport a chunk of rubble from the floor to a position directly over the creature's head, where it fell, knocking it to the stage floor. The audience members were frozen, afraid to move. Ryan kept walking backward. He reached the edge of the stage and backed down the stairs.

The rubble exploded, and the creature rose again, its suit jacket white with concrete dust, an inhuman growl coming from its throat. Ryan decided to abandon subtlety. He turned and ran.

At the end of the room, his tablet beeped and the screen came to life. He gritted his teeth as it cycled through its boot-up sequence. Out on the floor, the girl sent one of the Secret Service agent's pistols flipping out of his lifeless hands in a graceful arc toward her. She caught it and turned it toward the creature, firing live rounds now instead of rubber. The creature blurred, but the bullets struck home anyway, ripping into its chest and out of its back. It growled, apparently unfazed, although blood streamed down its body, red tracks coursing through the white dust. It lifted its hands, and the Altay battle tank, still parked on the demonstration floor, lifted into the air and flew toward the girl.

Ryan frantically stabbed at his tablet, injecting a fresh protocol into the system controlling his baby universe. The tank lurched and fell back to the ground, shattering the floor and sending dust and debris flying, though none of it reached the girl or the crowd. The eyeless creature shuddered, and its face cleared. Secretary Falk, his eyes suddenly normal, stood amid the carnage, looking down in shock at his bloody chest. He blinked once before collapsing to the floor.

Alex stood in the shooting stance Sean had taught her years before, the Secret Service agent's Sig Sauer P229 still locked in her two-handed grip. The varcolac was gone. She didn't think she'd killed it, but at least it hadn't killed her, and most of the people in the warehouse were still alive.

Then it occurred to her how this scene would look to others. The demo area was brightly lit, but the lights over the audience were dim.

She doubted very many people could have made out Falk's missing eyes. They would have seen an exchange of gunfire, after which she was still standing with a gun in her hand, and the Secretary of Defense was dead on the floor, lying with his security detail in the growing puddle of his blood. Alex caught Tequila's gaze from the control booth. Her face was frozen in shock.

The demo was being recorded, but what would the video show? The cameras were angled to cover the stage. Who would believe that she had been firing not at Secretary Falk but at a quantum intelligence that had taken over his body? It wasn't credible. No one would understand. All they would know was that Falk was dead, and she had pulled the trigger.

She threw the gun on the floor and ran.

CHAPTER 5

"You were dead," Sandra said. "I saw your body."

She sat with both of her parents in their living room. The two of them sat on the sofa together, her father leaning forward with his elbows on his knees, her mother pressed close to him and holding him possessively. "I'm here now," he said. He opened his hands as if to demonstrate his presence. "I was tired, so I left in the eighth inning to beat the traffic."

"Show me your wallet," she said. He raised an eyebrow, but he pulled it out of his pocket. It was black, leather, and absolutely identical to the one that Sandra produced from her bag. She shouldn't have taken it from the scene, but this situation went beyond normal police procedure. She opened it and produced his driver's license. Her father pulled its duplicate out of his own wallet. Her mother took them both and held them next to each other, comparing.

"This happened once before," Sandra said. "You know what that means."

He shrugged. "Maybe. A quantum event, at the very least. A probability wave left unresolved."

Her mother gripped his arm. "Which means it could resolve again, right?"

"At some point," her father said. "Or maybe not, as Sandra knows well enough."

"You'll forgive me if I don't find that very comforting."

"There's nothing we can do," her father said. He was acting very calm, but Sandra could tell he was rattled. He was putting a brave face on it for her and her mother. "I don't know what the future will bring, and that's as much as any of us can say." He stood. "And now, Sandra needs to get some rest."

"I'm fine," Sandra said. Though even as she said it, she felt the weariness of the night overtaking her, both the long hours without sleep and the emotional strain.

"Nonsense; you're asleep on your feet." Her father wrapped her in a ferocious hug. He'd been a boxer in his youth and still had the size and strength, though he was softer than he must have been years ago. She relaxed into his embrace, feeling some of the worry and stress slip away. With no other cops to see her, she let the tears come. Her mother joined them, pressing a kiss into Sandra's cheek.

Her parents led her upstairs to her old bedroom.

"If it *is* like fifteen years ago . . ." she began, but her father put a finger to his lips. "Sleep," he said. "Then we can talk."

She lay on the bed, blue uniform and all, and let him close the door. She was so tired. From down the hall, she could hear her parents in hushed argument, her mother's tones of fear and worry, her father's of reassurance. Their voices faded away as she drifted off to sleep.

She woke, terrified, with explosions ringing in her ears. A dream of blood and gunfire, barely remembered, that faded quickly. She focused on the pink sheets, the Delia Sharp poster on the far wall, the smell of home. Her parents' house. Her old bedroom. She was safe.

A moment later, the memory of the shattered stadium and the thousands dead hit her consciousness, and she knew that no one was really safe, not ever. What time was it? How long had she slept? A Miss Kitty alarm clock on the bedside table read 11:37, but she didn't know if she could trust it. She doubted anyone had used it in years.

Her phone said 2:45 PM. She checked her mail, and found a message from her sergeant, detailing a new shift schedule for the next several days. All officers except for a tiny contingent were to report to the stadium site in a twelve-hours-on, twelve-hours-off rotation. She was due back again at 6:00 PM.

There was another message, this one from Angel Gutierrez. He had completed his survey and forwarded her a link to the raw data. She sat up in bed and started paging through it, trying to make sense of it. There was way too much to look at on the phone's tiny screen, so she shifted the output to her eyejack lenses. Her entire field of view became her output screen, as if she were sitting in a large, empty room with the data projected on all the walls.

Math had never been her strong suit—that was Alex's forte—but she *had* grown up with a physicist for a father. He'd insisted they both take calculus in high school, although by that time Sandra had known she was heading for a career in law enforcement. Not much call for math in her field, unless you were a forensics egghead, which she most decidedly wasn't.

What she wanted most was to make detective and work homicide, but that possibility was many years away. She would have to do her stints on patrol first, learning the ropes and proving herself smart enough—and hard enough—for the job. She'd made the mistake of voicing her goal out loud at the academy, prompting knowing smiles from her teachers. "Everybody thinks that as a cadet," they said. "Give it a few years on the force, and see if it changes your mind."

Sandra had no intention of changing her mind. She'd seen murder before, and she knew how it could tear a family apart. She wasn't some stream-addicted kid high on crime shows. She knew what she was asking for. And she knew she could handle it.

She surveyed the unfamiliar data spread out in front of her. It seemed to be strings of characters—the RFID keys—with geolocation points attached. Many of the keys had now been expanded into their meaning: credit card accounts, membership cards, articles of clothing, phones, entry gates. Even the baseballs, it seemed, had been tagged with RFIDs, presumably so that claims that a certain ball had been hit by a certain player in a certain game could be verified, years later. Most of the data points were connected to people's names, thousands of them. Most of those people were now dead.

What if she spotted something important in this mountain of names before the experts? Something critical that led to an arrest? That would get her noticed, no matter how young and green she might be.

The first thing to do was to visualize the data. That was easily done; she entered the geolocation points into a globe, and once she zoomed in close enough, she could see the points scattered on the ground like a field of yellow flowers. It was the same basic pattern she had noticed on site, but she was no expert. The distribution meant nothing to her.

Angel had said it was no bomb, but what he really meant was it was no *ordinary* bomb. Something had caused the stadium to tear itself apart, and no explanation seemed to fit. What she needed was to know where each point—it was easier to think of them as points rather than people— had started in the original stadium. If she could do that, then she could plot connections between where each point started and where it ended up, maybe even find the convergence point for all the vectors and discover where the bomb itself—if that's what it was—had been hidden.

Sandra thought she knew just how to accomplish that. Each seat, after all, had a number painted on the seat back and armrests. She had access to the police database of eyejack views of the wreckage, and she could easily find a map of the stadium's seating chart. The hardest part would be searching through the millions of view frames to find all the instances when a police officer saw one of the seat numbers. Fortunately, she had some experience.

She and Alex had been Life Loggers for years, making their eyejack views publicly visible and interacting with viewers. Simply the fact that they were twin teenage American girls had brought them a lot of traffic. It was something they did together, but her sister hadn't been interested in maintaining the site. Learning the practical skills, like using pattern-match programs to find and mark interesting features in vast quantities of eyejack data, had fallen to Sandra.

She downloaded the latest version of one of her favorites, and initiated a search. Finding the shapes of numbers in video streams was one of the program's built-in features, so she didn't even have to go through the process of training it to recognize a particular face or object. In moments, it started spitting out individual frames of the views in which numbers were visible. Since the views were all geo-tagged, she could tell where each number had ended up. And since she had a seating chart, she knew where each number had started.

Before long, vectors began blooming on her display, but they didn't fit the pattern she'd been expecting. She'd imagined a shape like a porcupine, lines radiating outward from some central point. Instead, she got a mess. The lines were stacked every which way, more like a spilled box of toothpicks than any kind of pattern. She sighed. This was going to be harder than she thought.

Either the programs she was using didn't operate the way she was expecting, or else each person and object in the stadium had been flung along different lines of force. Which didn't make any sense at all.

A thought occurred to her: partial numbers. The seat numbers in the stadium had three, four, or five digits. A five-digit number that was partially obscured, or at a bad angle, might be interpreted by the software as a four- or three-digit number. That would contaminate her data. Probably not enough to make it as haphazard as what she was seeing, but perhaps there were other issues as well. Now that she thought about it, there could be other numbers visible, too—numbers from signs, numbers from jerseys, anything other than seats—and that would confuse her results as well.

She posted a question about the problems she had thought of to a few of the discussion boards she used to frequent. The alternative—that she had made some fundamental blunder in setting up the software—was more discouraging. She spent a few minutes looking at example views and verifying the seat numbers, but as far as she could tell, the software was doing what she intended.

Her phone chimed, the sound of an incoming message. It chimed again, and then twice more. It continued to chime erratically, until the sounds came so quickly it sounded like an old-style telephone ring. What on Earth?

She checked and saw that there were answers to her discussion board queries. Thousands of them. That didn't make any sense; a lot of people used those boards, but not that many. She started browsing the responses, and realized that what she had written revealed the fact that she was investigating the stadium disaster. Of course. Word had spread as rapidly as it always did online, and now she was being bombarded, mostly with well-wishers and conspiracy nuts. She did a keyword search for the program name, and was able to find a few meaningful responses, one of which offered a patch she could use to cull out the false data. Another message was from someone called *TheAngelG*. The message read: *Sandra! I see great minds think alike. Angel.*

All the messages made her nervous. She could easily get in trouble for interacting with the public about an ongoing investigation, especially one of this magnitude. What if a reporter found her query and jumped to conclusions, even assumed she was a detective? They'd bury her at a desk filing paperwork for the rest of her career.

She applied the patch and checked her results again. No good. The lines were different, but just as chaotic. Could it be that seats had really been thrown in such random directions, with such different degrees of force?

Something tickled at her brain. The lines were messy, but not entirely chaotic. She thought she could discern, just at the edge of her conscious-ness, a kind of pattern, some deep part of her brain recognizing something she couldn't put into words. Or was it merely the human brain's need to make sense of what it saw, like seeing shapes in the clouds?

She turned off the eyejack display, and her old bedroom sprang back into view. She might not have the mathematics background to identify a pattern, if one existed, but she knew someone who did. She descended the stairs and found her father at the kitchen table with a mug of coffee.

"Dad," she said. "I have something I want you to see."

An hour later, Sandra got bored and went to take a shower. Her father had become totally engrossed in the data, running it through all kinds of mathematical analysis engines. The vocabulary he used to describe what he was attempting might as well have been a different language, for all she could understand it. By the time he started mumbling under his breath about M-brane manifolds and preserved supersymmetries, she had lost patience.

Clean, she put the same dusty uniform back on, not expecting to have time to get back to her own apartment for a fresh one. Her father was still in the kitchen, staring at the data. "Look at this," he said. "We've been assuming the seats traveled in roughly straight lines, as viewed from above. Simple parabolic arcs, at any rate, from their point of origin."

She sat down next to him, and he shared his eyejack view with her, so she could see the same thing he was looking at. She made his view a transparent overlay on her vision, so she could still see him and the room around her. "How else would they travel?" she said. "Without energy added mid-flight . . ." She trailed off. "Of course. If multiple blasts went off at slightly different times."

"That's one possibility." Her father was still working with the data, causing equations to fly across her vision in dizzying variety. "But I'm not finding any multiple-source solutions that work for all these paths."

A thought struck her, like doors unlocking and swinging wide. "Not any three-dimensional ones, anyway."

"Yes, that's where I'm thinking, too." Her father gave her an approving nod, a gesture that had usually been reserved for Alex. Sandra felt a small thrill of approval.

Her father attacked the data furiously, shifting and expanding it with flicks of his eyes as he applied new sets of equations. Then he stopped. "Here we are," he said, his voice soft and awed. "Supergravity, in ten dimensions."

Something like a vortex appeared in her vision. The globe view of Philadelphia was now twisted and wrapped in on itself. The lines connecting the seats from their points of origin were now complex curves forming a multi-dimensional tornado.

"It wasn't multiple blasts after all," her father said. "Just one simple equation."

Sandra didn't think "simple" was probably the right word. "Does this mean the seats traveled out of normal space before landing back in our normal three dimensions?"

Her father shook his head. "The other dimensions are paper-thin. It's not as much that the chairs themselves travel through other dimensions, as that the energies do, bending the lines of force to blast the chairs in unexpected directions."

Sandra let that go. Ultimately, she didn't care about multiple dimensions or how they worked. What she cared about was that this destruction had come from a single source, but not a traditional one.

"Could a person have done this?" she asked. "Or a government?"

Her father raised his hands in an expansive shrug. "Not with any technology I've ever heard of."

"But it's possible?"

"Anything is possible."

They traded looks, both of them thinking the same thing but

unwilling to say it. As if by speaking the word *varcolac* out loud, they would conjure it into the house and repeat the horror of fifteen years ago. As horrible as this act was, it had been better when she could think of it simply as the result of human ingenuity and hatred.

She nodded. "I have to show this to my lieutenant."

"Of course you do."

"You should come with me." Her father started to shake his head, but she pressed on. "I'm not sure I can explain it, or that they'll believe me even if I can. I need your credentials to back me up."

"I can't, sweetheart. I need to stay here." His manner was odd. Evasive.

"Why? I don't understand."

"Your mother needs me to stay. I can't just run off again, after she came so close to losing me."

He was lying. Sandra didn't know why, but she knew he was. She studied his face, trying to decide whether to call him on it. "I need you," she said.

He sighed. "Look. There's something else here, something I need to study. It's going to take me a while, but it's important. Can you come back this evening?"

"I have an all-night shift."

"Tomorrow, then. Come back here to sleep again, and I'll tell you everything when you wake up. I'll make sure Alex comes, too; it affects her as well."

"Alex won't come if she knows I'm here."

"She will if I insist."

Sandra narrowed her eyes. "Why wait? Why don't you come along with me now, and you can tell me in the car?"

"I have to do some research first. Confirm what we're looking at here." His eyes slid to the left, then purposefully came up and caught her gaze. "You can handle this. After all, you thought of the multiple dimensions angle. I'm proud of you, Alex."

He must have seen the scowl on her face, because he backtracked immediately. "Sandra, I mean. Come on, darling; it was a slip of the tongue. Forgive an old man some scrambled brain cells."

"Fine," she said. "Just stay, then. I'll do it myself."

"Sandra, I meant it. I'm proud of you. You're just as bright as—"

"I'm going to be late for work." Sandra stood and collected her phone and purse. "Goodbye, Dad. I'm glad you're safe."

CHAPTER 6

A lex ran out of the warehouse, adrenaline lighting up her senses, making everything seem bright and crisp and much too fast. She was in her car and fumbling for the keys before she could remember running to the parking lot, and driving away at high speed before she could think about where she was going. She could feel the raw power of the gun thundering in her hands, could see the bullets tearing through Secretary Falk's chest. Her own blood roared in her ears.

Who could she go to for help? Her father came immediately to mind, but, of course, that would be one of the first places the police would look. Sean was in Poland. Claire was in California. Sandra lived close by, but she was a cop herself. Alex couldn't put her in that position.

She needed a safe place. Her own apartment was obviously out, as was her parents' house, or the home of anyone she knew. She stopped at an ATM and withdrew $1000 in cash—the machine's limit—not expecting to be able to do so again anytime soon. They could track her through her bank access. She wouldn't be able to use a hotel, either, for the same reason. The enormity of trying to evade capture was overwhelming; she would need a false identification, which she had no idea how to get. She might even have to leave the country.

Or she could turn herself in. That would be the easiest thing, maybe the right thing. But there was a *varcolac* loose in the world again, and there were precious few people who knew what that meant. She had to call her father. He might not know what to do either, but at least he would believe her. At least he would know what she was talking about.

Her mother answered the phone.

"Mom," she said. "Is Dad there?"

"Alex . . ." she said, and trailed off into silence. After a moment, she realized her mother was softly crying on the other end of the line.

"Mom? What's going on? Did they already call you?"

Her mother took a shaky breath. "Did who call?"

"Never mind. What's wrong?"

"Your father's gone."

"What do you mean? You don't know where he is?"

"He was in the kitchen staring at some data that Sandra gave him, drinking his coffee. Sandra left for work, and five minutes later, he was gone. I came back, and his coffee mug was still there, but he wasn't." Her voice started to shake again. "One moment he was there; the next he was gone."

Alex looked in her rearview mirror. There was a battered green car behind her, old and rusted, a first-generation electric by the look of it. She had seen it in the NJSC parking lot. It must have left at nearly the same time she did. It was following her.

"Alex? Are you there?"

"Yes, I'm here."

"Can you come home as soon as you can? I don't know what to do."

"Mom, I'm sorry. I can't."

"Please, Alex. I know it sounds crazy. But Sandra's on shift, and I need you. I'll explain it all when you get here."

"You don't understand. I *can't*. In fact, I'm not going to be able to call for a while, either. I'm sorry."

"Where are you?" her mother said. "What's wrong? Are you in trouble?"

"Listen, when the police call . . . I didn't do what they say I did."

"Oh, Alex. What happened?"

"I have to go. I love you."

"Alex!"

Alex disconnected. She felt panicky. She needed her father, and he wasn't there. She didn't know what her mother was talking about, but she couldn't think about that right now. She needed a place to go, and a new car, and new clothes.

The green car was still behind her. Whoever it was had no subtlety. Besides which, the little electric wouldn't be able to keep up with her modern engine if she wanted to lose it. It couldn't be a cop. She stepped on the accelerator, quickly picking up speed. The green car accelerated, too, but not enough to keep up. Instead, it started honking at her.

She thought for a moment it might be Tequila, but Tequila was driving a rental, a midsized silver sedan. She slowed down again until she could see the driver in her rearview mirror, an obese man in rumpled clothes. It was Ryan Oronzi.

What did he want? He clearly wanted her to stop. Maybe he had some evidence, something that could prove that it hadn't been her fault. A recording with a good shot of Secretary Falk's face, for instance. If he wanted to turn her in, he could have done that already. And he was hardly going to overpower her in a fight. The best thing to do was to stop and see what he wanted.

Alex took the Broad Street exit into the city, and the green car followed. She pulled into the first parking lot she saw, a Dunkin' Donuts. Oronzi claimed the parking spot next to her. He hauled himself up out of the driver's seat.

She strode around her car to face him. This was the genius of Lakehurst, the man who had invented the Higgs projector. Under normal circumstances, she would have been awed to meet him. Now, she just felt impatient and annoyed. "What do you want?" she asked. "Why are you following me?"

"You've seen it before."

"What?"

"The thing that took over Secretary Falk. I could see it in your face. You've seen it before."

"Are you here to help me? Because if not, I need to go."

"I want to know what it is. Where it comes from. What it can do."

This was a bad idea. She was wasting time. "If you haven't noticed,

I'm in a little trouble right now. I can't just sit down for a little chat over a cup of coffee. The FBI and the Secret Service and the whole US military are probably out looking for me now, so if you don't mind, stop following me. Just leave me alone."

She stalked back around toward the driver's door of her car and wrenched it open.

"I can help you," Oronzi said.

She stared at him over the car roof. "How?"

"I can make you disappear."

She gave her head an angry shake. "What are you, international man of mystery? How are you going to do that?"

His eyes narrowed and darted back and forth before coming to rest on her again. "I can. Trust me."

Alex sighed. She didn't trust him. Even if he meant what he said, she didn't know if he could deliver on his promise. But neither did she have any good options of her own. She threw up her hands. "Fine," she said. "Make me disappear."

CHAPTER 7

Sandra took the results to Angel first. She messaged him on her way back up I-95, and he met her on the stadium site in the same place they had spoken before. He understood the equations immediately. "Genius," he said. "Sandra, this is incredible. It all works. What is this, some kind of new technology? A quantum weapon?"

"I don't know." She thought about taking credit for the solution herself, but that wasn't fair. "My father's a physicist," she said. "He used to work at the big collider, over in New Jersey. Now he just teaches. He's the one who figured it out."

She took Angel along to see her lieutenant, who made a few calls. An hour later, far sooner than Sandra expected, they were ushered by an aide into a nearby building to see the Inspector in charge of the entire disaster scene. The building was an office structure for the sports teams, one of several commandeered by the command staff to run operations. The FBI was on site as well, poking around and applying pressure, but they hadn't yet taken over. Sandra's stomach turned over; she had never spoken to anyone this senior in rank.

Inspector Gallagher was a study in black and white. Dark glasses framed a pale face under close-cropped gray hair, and his crisp, white uniform shirt was marked only by the silver leaf insignia of his rank. He invited them to sit, which they did. Gallagher himself did not. He peered down at Sandra with his hands clasped behind his back, and said, "Officer Kelley. I understand you've brought some intriguing information to your supervisors."

"I hope so, sir."

"Where did you get this information?"

"The raw data came from Angel here. He has a squad of quadcopters that he uses to—"

"I'm familiar with Mr. Gutierrez's work and data," Gallagher said. "What I'm interested to know is how you, Officer Kelley, came to be in possession of data that the department has paid Mr. Gutierrez to collect— even before it was submitted to us, I might add—and how you came to the conclusions you did."

Angel blushed. "She was interested. I thought, since she was police, there was no harm—"

Gallagher raised a hand without looking at him, and Angel closed his mouth. Gallagher's eyes never left Sandra's face. "Are you in a relationship with Mr. Gutierrez?"

Now it was her turn to blush. "I only met him last night."

He stared at her, impassive.

"No," she said. "No, I'm not in any kind of relationship with him."

"Do you have any relationship, formal or otherwise, with the Turkish government?"

"What? No!"

"Did you promise anything to Mr. Gutierrez in return for this data?"

This meeting was not going at all how Sandra had envisioned. She had expected, if not praise, at least a pat on the back. The information she brought had the potential to crack the case wide open. "No," she said. "I made ten minutes casual conversation with him. He sent me the data as a courtesy, and I looked into it out of curiosity. And yes, I admit it, with the hope that maybe I could discover something important, something that would help the case."

"And did you pass this highly confidential data on to anyone who is not a member of the Philadelphia Police Force?"

"Yes," she said, not hesitating. I showed it to my father. He's brilliant at that kind of thing, and I thought he might find something I couldn't."

"Did you pass the data to anyone else? Any reporters, perhaps?"

"No! Of course not."

"Are you sure?"

Sandra felt her respect for this man's rank slipping away. "I don't understand what's going on here. I brought this information thinking you would be pleased. I'm sorry if I shouldn't have shown it to my father without permission, but have you seen his conclusions? It makes sense of the patterns; it may even pinpoint the exact location the explosion originated from."

Gallagher nodded gravely. He pursed his lips slightly, seemed to wrestle with himself for a moment, and said, "In fact, it has pinpointed the origin of the blast, to one particular seat. Section C, seat 5F, as it happens."

He stared at her, apparently watching for a reaction. She shrugged. "That's good, right? You can at least find out who was sitting in that seat, and follow that lead."

Gallagher's expression didn't change. "We already have. The person sitting in that seat was Jacob Kelley. Your father."

Sandra gaped. "But my father left, before . . ."

"Exactly. He was, apparently, one of the last people to leave the stadium alive. His seat was the center point of the blast. And he has specialized knowledge about how one might create such a blast."

She tried to answer, then closed her mouth again. Finally, she said, "But he *gave* me the equations to make sense of the data. You wouldn't even know about it, if not for him."

Gallagher raised an eyebrow. "Perhaps our forensic specialists are smarter than you give them credit for. In any event, you have revealed critical data about our investigation to the man who is now our chief suspect."

Sandra remembered how evasive her father had been, and how unwilling to come along with her. Had he realized that the data pointed to him? "He's at home," she said. "He's not running. He's not acting like a suspect."

"For your sake, I hope he's still at home when the arresting officers arrive."

Her heart pounded. "You're arresting him?"

Gallagher gave a small cough. "Of course, Miss Kelley. I think it would be wise if you didn't attempt to contact him. And please don't leave the Philadelphia area."

She stood to face him, pulling herself together, and tried to match his frosty tone. "Sir, I have no intention of leaving the area. I'm an officer of the Philadelphia police department, and I have a job to do here. I believe my father to be innocent, and I expect that to quickly become clear. But I have no intention of interfering with the process in any way."

"One more thing, Miss Kelley. Have you heard from your sister?"

"My sister? Which one?"

"Your twin sister, Alex."

Her mind raced, but she could make no sense of it. "No. Not recently. Not for a few days, anyway. She's in New Jersey; she had some kind of big presentation at work today."

"May I please examine your cell phone?"

Sandra's breath caught. She remembered all the responses from the discussion boards on her phone that she hadn't even reviewed yet. She hadn't provided any data to them, but she doubted Gallagher would see the distinction. She was being treated like a suspect, and it was making her angry. She was one of the good guys.

"Why? Do you think my sister is involved in this, too?"

He pursed his lips again, another internal battle. "We received an APB for your sister's arrest an hour ago from the Secret Service."

"The Secret Service? As in . . ."

"Yes, Miss Kelley. Your sister is wanted for the murder of four people, one of them Secretary of Defense Jared Falk."

It was too much. This whole meeting was surreal. It was a test of some sort, or a dream. She must still be at home, in her old bed. She pulled out her phone and handed it to Gallagher, who caught it in a Ziploc evidence bag and sealed it shut.

"I would like to think that you are as innocent as you seem," Gallagher said. "But I will not assume it. These two crimes are clearly connected, and they're connected through your family. As a result, you are forbidden from taking part in this investigation in any way. Furthermore, you are to be given a leave of absence, starting today—"

"I don't need a leave, sir. There's so much work to do, and—"

"A mandatory suspension, then. Miss Kelley, you are relieved of duty until further notice. Now, I have other matters to attend to. You will now report to Detective Messinger, who will question you about your family connections and your movements over the past several days. Then you will return home and stay clear of this crime scene. You are dismissed." Gallagher swiveled his head to stare at Angel. "Mr. Gutierrez, you will stay. I have a few questions for you about how you share the data you collect."

Sandra left Angel behind and followed the aide down the hall. Cheeks burning, she followed an officer down the hall to a conference room. He left her there, and she heard the click as the door locked behind him. It wasn't a proper interrogation room—no mirrored one-way glass—but she guessed they had it bugged. She scanned the ceiling for hidden cameras and saw none, but that didn't mean much.

If her experience was any judge, it would be a long time until anyone came back to question her. They would let her sweat, put her off guard. It's what they did with everyone. She thought about her father's strange refusal to come with her. What had he been hiding? She tried to imagine him devising a high-tech bomb to kill thousands of people, and she just couldn't do it. There was no reason in the world that might prompt him to such an act. But then why had he lied to her?

When Detective Melissa Messinger finally came in, only about a half-hour had gone by. Sandra was surprised, having expected at least an hour. Messinger was short, stocky, with a hard expression and tired eyes. She was everything Sandra admired and aspired to: a full detective, trusted with some of the department's most serious and public cases.

"Where is your father, Miss Kelley?" she asked without preamble.

"He wasn't at his house? That's the last place I saw him."

"We sent officers to question him, but he was gone. Your mother claims to have no idea where he is. We need to understand the nature of this conspiracy between your father and your sister, why they committed these crimes, and what they hope to gain."

"There's no conspiracy—"

"Where is your father?"

"I honestly don't know."

"Where is your sister?"

"I don't know that, either. She's not a killer, though; I can tell you that."

"Over a hundred people saw her shoot Secretary Falk in the chest. So either she did it, or it was her twin sister." Messinger smiled, but there was no humor in it.

Sandra didn't take the bait. "I haven't talked to Alex in days. I haven't seen her for weeks."

Messinger was meticulous. She walked Sandra through every part of her conversation with her father: exactly what he had said, whose idea it had been that the destruction had followed a multidimensional pattern. She asked for every detail Sandra could remember about recent conversations with Alex, including dates and times, and wrote it all down in a notebook. Then she went through the same questions all over again.

"Fifteen years ago, your father was charged with murder, and then acquitted. How much do you remember of that experience?"

Sandra frowned. "Very little, actually. It was Alex who spent a lot of time with Dad during that time." In fact, that had been the main difference between them, from the beginning. Alex had been there with Dad, had hunted the varcolac with him, while Sandra had not.

"Would you say, then, that Alex and your father shared a special relationship?" Messinger said.

"Yeah, you could say that." It came out with more emotion than Sandra had intended.

"More special than his relationship with you?"

"Yes."

"So there might be secrets he and Alex have together. Things they think about and talk about that you wouldn't necessarily know."

"I can see where you're going," Sandra said. "Yes, they were close. No, I don't think either of them are capable of the crimes you suspect them of committing."

Though she wondered. Not whether they would intentionally kill. She was certain they wouldn't. But a ten-dimensional explosion? It had to have been done by someone—or something—with a deep understanding of quantum physics. Alex and Dad wouldn't have been so stupid as to try to bring back the varcolac, would they? Could they actually have been so foolish as to tamper with those forces again, after it had nearly killed their whole family fifteen years ago?

"If you had to guess where your sister is, if you wanted to find her, where would you go?"

Sandra shook her head. "I honestly don't know."

It wasn't exactly true. She didn't know where Alex was, but there were places she could look, places from their history. But Alex was her flesh and blood. More than that, really. Alex was *her*, what she might have been if things had been different. There wasn't anyone else in the world who shared the same kind of bond that they did. She couldn't just betray her.

And yet, Sandra was a police officer. It was her duty to report what she knew, sister or no. She felt angry at Alex for putting her in this position. If she was innocent, why had she run? And if she was guilty, why should Sandra cover for her?

Fifteen years ago, Alex had very nearly given her life to save Sandra's. Alex had been in a wheelchair for months, and ever after, Sandra had felt the imbalance between them. Alex had saved the family when the varcolac would have killed them all. In truth, she had always resented Alex a bit for it. For the special bond she had formed with their father during that time, for the hero status she had enjoyed ever since. For the sense of inferiority Sandra always felt. It sometimes seemed like Alex was the real daughter, while Sandra was just a fluke of nature. A mistake.

Even so, she stayed silent. She owed Alex, and she couldn't rat her out, not even if it meant her job. On the other hand, she knew the resources the police could bring to bear to track down murderers, and this case would be their first priority. Alex would be caught eventually, whether Sandra helped or not. If she was innocent, it was better for her to come forward and tell her side of the story. If not . . . Well, if she wasn't innocent, she would have to accept the consequences.

A sharp knock on the door made Sandra jump. Three men in black suits came in, wearing serious expressions. Two of them were just what Sandra would have expected: tall, well-muscled, dark-suited, with bulges that spoke of lethal weaponry. The third was skinny and balding, with a pockmarked face and an easy, salesman's smile. Messinger seemed profoundly irritated that they were there.

The third man introduced himself as Sanford Liddle. "Everything I'm about to tell you is classified and protected under the Espionage Act," he said. "As a United States citizen, you are bound not to share this information with anyone else, no matter what their nationality. Failure to obey this law is punishable, depending on severity, with sentences up to and including life imprisonment or death. Do you understand this restriction?"

Sandra nodded numbly. She wondered if that would actually hold up in court, or if it was just something he said to intimidate people. If so, it was working.

She heard a ping, indicating that Agent Liddle was trying to share a view to her eyejack. She accepted the view, and suddenly she was in a building like a huge warehouse, watching her sister tearing guns out of soldiers' hands and diffracting bullets around herself. She gasped. She knew that technology, had seen it fifteen years ago, and had thought it destroyed. Was Alex working to revive it? Was she out of her mind?

Then she saw her sister firing into the crowd. What was she doing? She saw a blur that at first seemed like a problem with the video, but no. She had seen that before. Her sister's bullets tore into the Secretary of Defense and he toppled, but at just that instant Sandra could see his face in the light reflected from the more brightly lit demonstration area. He had no eyes.

By the time the clip was over and her awareness returned to the room around her, Sandra was tight with anger. "She didn't murder anyone. She probably saved all those people's lives."

Liddle held up a hand. "We're inclined to agree with you," he said. "But there are two points against her. One, she ran. That doesn't look good. Two, we're dealing with technology that not many people understand." He shrugged. "And your sister appears to be one of them. Whoever made this happen must have been one of those people, and the list is pretty short."

The two big agents stood on either side of the doorway, flanking the exit. Messinger still sat with her arms crossed, a mutinous expression on her face. She didn't like her interrogation being taken over.

Liddle sat down across from Sandra. "We have some pieces of the puzzle," he said. "We know your father was involved with the illegal use of similar technology fifteen years ago." Sandra tried to protest, but Liddle held up a hand. "And we know that before your fourteenth birthday there was no record of a girl named Sandra Kelley living in your home."

The silence stretched. Sandra finally broke. "Okay," she said. "I'll tell you the whole story. But it's going to take a while."

"I've got all day," Liddle said.

Sandra sighed and cleared her throat. "Alex and I aren't really sisters. We were born as Alessandra Kelley, the second daughter of Jacob and Elena Kelley."

"I don't understand."

"We're not twins," Sandra said. "We're the same person."

CHAPTER 8

They abandoned Alex's car at the Dunkin' Donuts. Alex climbed into the green electric next to Dr. Oronzi, who gunned the little engine back toward I-95. She would have been forced to ditch the car anyway; the police would be looking for it, and she wouldn't last long if she were still driving it. She worried about security cameras in the parking lot; if there was a record of her getting into Dr. Oronzi's car, then this escape would be over quickly. For that matter, the fact that Dr. Oronzi had left the building before the police had arrived would put him under suspicion. She wondered if it had been wise to go with him.

But what other options did she have? It wasn't like she had planned ahead for this. There was a friend of her uncle who sometimes helped abused women hide from the men who had hurt them, but it wasn't a great option. Even if the friend had been willing to help her evade the authorities—which was a big if—the US government was a lot harder to fool than one angry husband.

The little engine whined as Oronzi coaxed it up to speed. Alex noticed that the speedometer, odometer, and fuel gauge were independent devices, bolted, and in one case duct-taped, to the dashboard rather than integrated as part of a single instrument panel. Wires showed under and behind the steering column. In fact, very little about the car seemed to have been designed to fit together, at least not in any aesthetic way.

"What did you do, build this car from a kit?" she asked.

Oronzi pulled an unfamiliar lever to his left, and the car jerked into a slightly higher rate of speed. "Nobody sells car-building kits," he said, apparently oblivious to her sarcasm. "I built it from the ground up, from first principles."

She couldn't hide her surprise. "Seriously? Why?"

He stole a glance at her before returning his attention to the road.

"That sleek little computerized bullet you drive—do you know how many moving parts it has? With every independent component, the probability of failure multiplies. Thousands of parts, each from a factory production line. And who was on duty when *your* part was audited for quality? What was his IQ? Was he having a bad day? Was it his first week on the job and he was afraid to make a fuss?"

Alex eyed the rattling contraption around her, which looked like it was held together with bits of twine. "And you think you can do better?"

"Don't confuse polish for quality," Oronzi said. "I know every part of this car. I know its design tolerances, its life expectancy, its performance over time. I personally designed every piece of it. I trust it."

She held up her hands. "Okay. I guess it hasn't killed you yet."

They pulled back onto I-95, heading north, back the way they had come. Oronzi had insisted on going into the Dunkin' Donuts before they left—for sustenance, as he called it—and he juggled a double latte and several glazed doughnuts as he drove.

"So, how are you going to hide me?" Alex asked.

"First things first," Oronzi said. "You have to tell me about that creature."

"The varcolac."

"Whatever you want to call it. Tell me what you know."

Alex looked out the passenger side window and saw a long-legged bird flying over the river. She wished she could fly away like that, unconstrained by gravity and unnoticed by the world. "Look, I'm running for my life here. You said you could hide me. Before we talk, I want to know where we're going."

Oronzi swallowed another bite of doughnut. "Back to the High Energy Lab."

She whipped around to face him. "What? You're turning me in?"

"No. I told you to trust me."

"When you're taking me right back again?"

"That's what trust means. If I handed you a new identity and a plane ticket to Australia, you wouldn't have to trust me. You'd know."

Alex was starting to think this had been a very bad idea. "Fine. Then I don't trust you. I barely know you. For all I know, you're planning to turn me over to the police. Or maybe you're a Turkish spy. So if you want to know what I know about varcolacs, then you'd better explain."

Oronzi looked at her, considering. He kept eye contact long enough that she glanced nervously at the road, afraid he was going to veer out of the lane and crash into another car. Finally, he said, "I'm going to make you invisible."

She wasn't sure whether to write him off as a madman or take him seriously. This was, after all, the man who had made possible all the quantum technology in their demo. Those things were impossible, weren't they? What made invisibility any different?

"Okay," she said.

His eyebrows rose. "Okay? You believe me?"

"Should I?"

"Yes."

"Fine, then. I'll believe you." She laughed nervously. "Though I may be just as crazy as you are."

They were quiet for a time, the road rumbling by under the car. "The varcolac," Oronzi prompted.

"They're intelligent beings," Alex said. "They're living all around us, existing through the quantum interactions of particles, in the molecules that make up our air and food and our own bodies. The surfaces of things aren't as important to them as they are to us, and things like gravity and electricity are just one more kind of particle interaction. They're aliens, of sorts, but not from outer space. They live here, with us. They've been here all along."

"*We* exist through the quantum interactions of particles, too," Oronzi objected. "Everything does."

"Not the way they do. They're not biological, or even material. They're more like artificial intelligences, only their computer is the whole universe."

Oronzi's face pinched in confusion. "What do you mean?"

Alex took a deep breath, trying to clear her mind. The conversation was helping her forget the horror of the demonstration, and so she welcomed it. "Okay. You know the argument that compares the universe to a quantum computer? It stores a finite number of bits for each particle: the type, spin, momentum—"

Oronzi waved his hand, dismissive. "It's not a comparison. The universe *is* a quantum computer. Since you can simulate any set of particle interactions with a quantum computer made of the same number of particles, then there's no practical difference between the universe and a quantum computer simulating the universe."

"Exactly."

"But what's the point?" Oronzi asked around a big bite of doughnut. "It's just a self-referential definition."

"The point is, the universe is a computational device with sufficient complexity to generate consciousness. Life springing out of complexity."

The car was silent except for the sound of Oronzi eating the last of his doughnut. Finally, he said, "You're telling me the universe is conscious."

"No. But varcolacs are. They're intelligences that live in the universe—through all the universes—and are composed of the complex quantum interactions of the particles."

Oronzi gave a short nod, accepting the explanation. "Why do you call them varcolacs?"

"A Romanian friend of my father's named them that. After demons in Romanian myth that live on the mirror side of the world."

"How do you know so much about them?"

"They almost killed my whole family fifteen years ago. They communicated with a colleague of my father's, taught him things, but ultimately got him killed." Alex narrowed her eyes and studied Oronzi for a reaction. "Have they communicated with you?"

"What? No. Of course not."

"How did you discover all this technology?"

"I figured it out." He cast a belligerent look at her. "I'm a smart guy."

"Of course you are. But you knew what the varcolac was when you saw it today. You called it an intelligence from another universe. You've communicated with it, haven't you?"

"Not communicated, no. But interacted? Maybe. I've always known there was *something* on the other side of the wormhole. Something intelligent, trying to get out. I designed barriers to keep it out, but it kept finding a way through. I made the barriers more and more complex, like mazes made from energy patterns, defined by complex equations. It always solved them. I had to use layers of them, continually adding new ones to the outer layers while it broke through the inner layers with increasing speed. Finally . . ." A dawning horror spread across his face. "Oh, no."

"What is it?"

"I started using equations I didn't have the answer for. Equations I didn't even know were solvable. It would solve them for me."

"And did these equations have anything to do with the technology you've been inventing?"

"They were crucial to it."

Alex nodded, taking no pleasure from the revelation. "So you did communicate with them. They gave you the key to the technology."

"I guess they did." Oronzi nodded glumly.

"The technology which ultimately gave them entrance into the world."

"They manipulated me," he said.

"Don't worry about it. You weren't the first," she said.

"They're pretty clever."

"When it comes down to it, they're probably smarter than you are."

CHAPTER 9

"That," Agent Liddle said, "is the most preposterous story I've ever heard."

They were still in the same conference room, an hour and a half into Sandra's explanation. She was tired and thirsty and getting annoyed at Liddle's unrelenting skepticism.

"Believe me or not," Sandra said. "I don't care. I'm trying to help you understand what you're up against."

"So your—what did you call it—your *probability wave* never resolved?" Agent Liddle said. "Which makes you some kind of clone of Alessandra?"

"I'm just as much Alessandra as she is," Sandra said. "I remember growing up in that house. I remember when my brother, Sean, was born. I remember losing my teeth, and learning to ride a bike. I *am* Alessandra Kelley. The problem is, Alex is, too."

Detective Messinger had been quiet for a long time, standing against the wall while the feds took over the investigation. Now she spoke up. "What you're describing took place years ago. What about now?"

Liddle glared at Messinger, but didn't say anything.

"I have no idea," Sandra said. "I haven't talked to Alex. My dad didn't seem to know anything about it. I just showed up for work today."

"What if you had to guess?" Messinger pressed.

Sandra sighed. "I suppose I would say, on the basis of the viewfeed you showed me, that Alex has been playing with the same technology that caused our family so much trouble years ago. If so, I think she's an arrogant fool. Her demo must have given the varcolac access to our universe again. But even if that's the case, Alex didn't kill anyone, at least not directly. It was the varcolac that killed Secretary Falk and his bodyguards. Quite possibly, it was the varcolac that destroyed the stadium, too."

Liddle shook his head. "The stadium was destroyed twelve hours before your sister's demo."

"So maybe it broke out before the demo. I don't know what you want me to say."

Liddle put a finger to his ear. "You'll have to excuse me," he said. He stepped out of the room, followed by his two silent shadows.

Messinger stepped out as well, returning moments later with a chilled bottle of water that she slid across the table to Sandra. Sandra popped the cap and drank it gratefully.

Messinger slipped into the seat across from her. "You understand how all this looks, right? Two major terrorist actions on the same day, your father and sister present at both of them, and both of them now on the run."

Sandra didn't try to hide her worry. "You haven't found either of them yet?"

"Disappeared without a trace. Your father left his car behind, so he's apparently found some other means of transportation. We've checked buses, trains, taxis: so far, nothing. Do you know which of his associates might be willing to lend him a car?"

"Associates?" Sandra ran her fingers through her hair. "My father has *friends*, not associates. Might one of them lend him a car? Sure, I don't know. But there's no conspiracy. He's not a terrorist."

"Then why is he running?"

Sandra pictured her father leaving the house suddenly without telling her mother, heading down the street on foot, and tried to imagine what he would do, how he would get transportation. It didn't make any sense. There was no reason for him to suddenly run away without a word and without a car. An itching fire grew behind her eyes and a lump formed in her throat. She knew what this meant. There was only one way her father could have suddenly disappeared from his house without warning. His probability wave had resolved.

"What is it?" Messinger said.

"My father," Sandra said. "He's not on the run."

"What do you mean?"

She swallowed hard. "I'm pretty sure he's dead."

Detective Messinger took Sandra for a drive in her cruiser. Liddle had been called away, probably to harass some other innocent person, and Sandra was just as glad he was gone. Messinger drove haphazardly for ten minutes, and then parked illegally in front of a Mexican restaurant.

"Like Mexican?" she asked.

Sandra suddenly realized how hungry she was. "Sure. Anything," she said.

Inside, they settled into a corner booth and ordered a plate of quesadillas. "So now you claim your father died in the stadium disaster," Messinger said.

Sandra nodded.

Messinger nodded back thoughtfully. "And yet, you testified earlier to having spoken to him after the explosion. That you shared Mr. Gutierrez's data with him, and that he provided you with the key to understanding the pattern of the blast and determining the source."

"Also true," Sandra said.

Messinger stopped nodding and waited.

"It's hard to explain," Sandra said.

Messinger opened her hands wide, indicating the empty table on which their food had not yet been served. Plenty of time.

"In high school, you might have learned about something called Heisenberg's uncertainty principle."

"Sounds vaguely familiar," Messinger said.

"My father always complains that they teach it wrong—that kids memorize it without a clue as to what it means. The gist is that subatomic particles—protons or electrons or photons—can't be entirely known. If you pinpoint where they are at a given moment, then you can't know how fast they're going. If you determine their velocity, you can't know where they are. And the weird thing is, it's not just a matter of our ignorance. The proton itself isn't in just one place. It's smeared out across a range of possible places, with a certain probability. It's called superposition. It really is in more than one place at one time."

"So, your father . . ."

"One step at a time," Sandra said. "The varcolac is a quantum creature. It carries with it a quantum probability wave that affects the things around it. It makes large things, like people and cars and houses, behave in the crazy way that subatomic particles can. The technology you saw my sister using is the same."

"I didn't see the video," Messinger said, her tone bitter. "Need-to-know classification, according to Mr. Black Suit. I'm just running this investigation. Why would I need to know?"

The quesadillas arrived, and Sandra paused to take a bite. It was delicious, piping hot, with lots of melted cheese. She wiped her mouth before responding. "An encounter with the varcolac can put a person in a state of superposition, like a subatomic particle, so that he exists as a set of possibilities rather than a single reality. It happened to my father fifteen years ago, and it happened to me.

"When I spoke to my father this morning, he said he had left the game early, in the eighth inning. I think the varcolac must have appeared there at that time, splitting my father into two possibilities—one of which left the game early, and the other of which stayed and died."

Liddle had seemed to find her story farfetched, but Messinger listened attentively, and Sandra found she could explain herself better. It also occurred to her that perhaps Liddle and Messinger were working together more than they appeared to be, manipulating her with a classic good-cop, bad-cop routine, but she didn't care. She was glad to talk to a willing listener, and she didn't have anything to hide.

"So you're saying your father split into two versions of himself, before the explosion," Messinger said, her tone a little skeptical, but not mocking. "The first version went home early. The second version stayed."

"Yes."

"So you think there are two versions of your father, one dead and one alive?"

"There were."

"Not anymore?"

"I don't think so." Sandra heard her voice wavering, and willed herself not to start crying. "Usually, probability waves don't stay unresolved for long. I think my father resolved back into only one version of himself, and the version he resolved to was the dead one."

"And why do you think that?"

"Because my living father is gone, apparently vanished into thin air without even a word to his wife, while his dead body is still very much here."

She sent Messinger a link to the view of her father's body from Nathan's viewfeed. Messinger studied it, her face grave.

"Has the body been positively identified?" she asked.

"My father's wallet and keys were found in the pockets," Sandra said. "I doubt DNA is back at this point, given the number of people to process."

"Perhaps we can expedite that," Messinger said.

CHAPTER 10

The whole facility was locked down. Alex had no idea how Oronzi was going to get her in the building. Even if he could hide her, what about himself? He had also fled from the crime scene before police arrived. They had probably been looking for him, would certainly want to question him. He wouldn't be able to get through security without attracting notice.

Oronzi drove past the front gate without turning. "So much for that plan," Alex said. "I can't believe I trusted you. Now get us out of here before somebody notices us."

Oronzi didn't answer. His eyes darted around, and she realized he was accessing his viewfeed. Without warning, the view through the windshield changed abruptly, and Alex was thrown violently forward against her seatbelt. A moment before, they had been moving slowly along the road outside the facility; in the next moment, they were parked in a secluded parking spot between two of the buildings.

Alex drew in her breath sharply, breathing hard. "What did you . . . ?" But she knew. It was the same trick the American marine in the demo had done with the grenade and the stone wall. She didn't know it was possible to do with an entire car—while riding inside it—but apparently it was.

"Quickly, now." Oronzi heaved himself out of the driver's seat and out of the car. He beckoned to her. "Hurry, before we're seen."

She ran around the car to him. He grabbed her shoulder, flicked his eyes, and just as abruptly, they were inside, in a large room Alex had never seen before. Instead of a normal door, there was a thick metal slab on huge hinges, like a bank vault. The room had no windows. There were rows of computers and workspaces on one side of the room, and a large clear space with charts and graphics on the wall on the other. In the center, flashing colors like a Times Square advertisement, was a spectacle of light points and shifting beams, spinning gracefully around a vertical axis.

"This is your lab," she said. "On the eighth floor."

Oronzi nodded.

"Ryan!" said a shocked voice. A pretty Asian woman in a short black skirt and jacket strode toward them. Her hair was pinned up, but a strand had fallen loose around one ear. Alex recognized her from the demo as Nicole Wu, Dr. Oronzi's chief lab assistant.

"What are you doing here?" Nicole asked. "Don't you know everyone is looking for you?"

"That's exactly why we're here. So that no one will find us."

Nicole's eyes widened when she recognized Alex. "So you *are* together, just like everyone is saying. Ryan, what happened down there?"

"You were there," he said gruffly.

"Yeah, I was there." She pointed a finger at Alex. "I saw her shoot Secretary Falk."

"And did you see how he didn't have any eyes? How he was killing his own security agents?" Alex said. "Did you see the part where I saved the lives of everyone else there, yours included?"

Nicole waved a hand in dismissal. She looked at Oronzi. "You'd better get down there and tell your side of the story, if you don't want to be a suspect. Right now, it looks like you're harboring a criminal, maybe even conspiring with her to commit murder."

"And what about me?" Alex asked.

"You can do what you like," Nicole said. "Just leave Ryan out of it."

"We need her, Nicole," Oronzi said. "She knows about the intelligence. She's seen it before."

Nicole raised an eyebrow and said nothing.

"I'm going to go down there and be seen," Oronzi said. He took a deep breath and let it out. "I'll tell them I've just been up here in the lab, working. You need to keep her safe, Nicole."

"And why should I do that?"

"Because if you don't, I'll tell them all who you really are."

Nicole glared. "You know that's not in your best interest."

"Nicole, it's important. She's not guilty, and we both know it. Now make sure she stays safe while I go put in an appearance."

Nicole looked mutinous, but didn't object. Alex was seriously regretting coming here. She should have gone to her uncle's friend. She wouldn't last an hour in this place.

A panel above the door buzzed and flashed red. "Too late," Oronzi said. "Somebody's here." He turned to Alex. "Hold still," he said. "Don't move, don't speak. Don't even breathe."

Alex opened her mouth to protest, but the look in his eyes silenced her. The bank vault door swung slowly open. Five men came into the room, all of them wearing dark suits.

"Dr. Oronzi," one of the men said, a quiet menace in his voice. "We've been looking for you for some time."

"I'm a busy man," Oronzi said.

"I'd like to talk to you about that."

"And you are?"

The man gave a thin smile. "Agent Clark, FBI."

"This is my colleague, Dr. Wu," Oronzi said, indicating Nicole.

"We've met," Clark said.

To Alex's astonishment, no one looked at her or seemed to notice her at all. She obeyed Oronzi's instructions, standing as still as possible. Clark asked Oronzi to accompany him downstairs. Oronzi went out with him, leaving Alex alone with Nicole.

Nicole smirked at her. "Not as eye-catching as you thought, are you?"

"He made me invisible," Alex breathed, hardly believing it. "He teleported me up eight stories, through solid walls, and then made me invisible."

Nicole shrugged. "If you say so."

"How many more tricks are you hiding up here?"

"You're not cleared for that."

"Don't play games with me. I shot someone today, and that might not have happened if you weren't keeping so many secrets. I think I've earned the right to a few answers."

"You've put our whole operation in jeopardy, and now you've gotten Ryan tangled up in it," Nicole said. "You haven't earned the right to anything."

"How long have you known about the varcolac? The intelligence, I mean?"

Nicole rolled her eyes. "That's Ryan's crazy theory. I never put much stock in it, and neither should you. Complex phenomena do not require malicious intelligent aliens to explain them. If you ask me, the best thing you can do is turn yourself in."

"And if you ask me," Alex said, "the best thing you can do is stop lying to yourself to protect your precious lab, or your career, or whatever it is you're afraid of losing if you admit the truth to yourself. This creature is real, and it isn't going to stop here. Your boss might be a bit crazy, but he's right about this."

As she spoke, Alex brought up her eyejack display. She queried the available local networks, and found only one. Of course—the lab was a Faraday cage, so no signals were getting in any more than they were getting out. It was an entirely isolated network, closed to the outside world. Which meant that the security from inside the lab was minimal— all the efforts had been expended toward keeping people out. The network followed the same interface that her team at Lockheed had designed, and her eyejack system connected to it without objection.

"I'm just helping you for Ryan's sake," Nicole said. "It doesn't mean I have to listen to your little rants."

"Little rants?" Alex said, pretending to be offended, though she was mostly paying attention to what she was doing. She still had the

Higgs projector from the demo in her pocket. The lab's network had the software that ran it, but it was a different version than she had. A later version. How was that possible? She initiated the software upgrade service. A spinning icon appeared in the upper right corner of her vision, indicating that the latest software from the lab's server was being downloaded to her system.

"In fact," Nicole said, "I'm not sure I'm up for conspiracy to commit murder. If Ryan's not back here soon, I'm going to call the feds, and you can tell them it was the aliens that did it."

The download completed. Alex flicked through the new icons that had appeared on her display. As familiar as she was with this interface, it was easy to identify the right one. The same glowing arrow with adjustable length and direction appeared in her vision, only this time it was annotated with a few numeric parameters and a drop-down list of locations. Alex chose "parking lot" and saw the numeric parameters change.

"Don't worry," Alex said. "I'm not going to wait around that long." She didn't have time to experiment. She flicked her eyes, and the lab disappeared.

Without any transition, she was back in the parking lot. She stumbled and fell headlong into Oronzi's car, disoriented and feeling sick. This would take some getting used to, but oh, was it glorious. She didn't know whether Nicole would sound an alarm or not, but she didn't want to wait around to find out. Examining her reflection in the window, she initiated the invisibility module, and was gratified to see her reflection disappear.

She knew she had to get away from the NJSC grounds as quickly as possible, but she didn't want to risk another teleport before she knew what she was doing. The possibility of ending up underground, or inside a wall, or thirty feet above pavement, was just too great.

She sat down on the hood of Oronzi's car, trusting that no one would be able to see her, and brought up the teleportation interface. There were a few preset locations, but the arrow could be oriented in any direction, and the numbers set arbitrarily. With a little experimentation, Alex realized that the numbers were in ECEF coordinates, making the arrow a vector from the center of the Earth to a precise point. Not only that, but the program had been hooked up to a map locator with terrain and altitude data, allowing her to determine what vector would actually put her on the Earth's surface, instead of over or under it.

Was it really possible? The interface implied that she could teleport from here to Beijing, if she got the coordinates right. More than that, if she set the magnitude of the vector high enough, she could teleport to *anywhere*. Of course, the fact that the interface could support a teleport to Jupiter didn't mean that the underlying technology could actually do it, any more than a speedometer with numbers up to 200 mph meant the car could actually drive that fast.

Oronzi's warning about believing technologies you hadn't designed yourself came starkly to mind. Where did the map and terrain data the program was using come from? How accurate was it? It included the locations of buildings as well, but was it up-to-date with new construction? And what about moving obstacles like cars? Not to mention that this was beta software, probably written by physicists, not professional software engineers.

In the end, however, she couldn't not use it. It was too powerful, too amazing a technology to resist. She chose Marsh Creek Lake, a place she had been many times as a child, in an area that she knew was likely to be isolated. She figured teleporting over water gave the best chance of the elevation data being reasonably accurate, and gave her the best protection in case it wasn't. She chose a point twenty feet from the shore and two feet over the surface of the water, then yelped when it was more like five feet over the water. She splashed under and came up spluttering and treading water.

She was glad that she'd tried it over water first; that fall would have been rough over land. The disadvantage, of course, was that now she was wet. She swam to shore and sloshed through the mud to dry ground. She didn't care. She had just traveled from Lakehurst, New Jersey, to Lyndell, Pennsylvania, instantaneously. She wanted to go back and do it again. It was incredible, world-changing technology. Elated by her success, she tried again, this time to Blue Marsh Lake, a larger body of water in Berks County that she had visited once, years ago. The elevation data was better this time, and she slipped into the water with a little more grace.

She wondered what happened to the air when she did this. Could it be displaced that fast? Trying to move air molecules the width of her body instantaneously was impossible; even if they moved at the speed of light, the force of it would start a fusion reaction and annihilate her. Perhaps the air was traded, ending up back in the position she had left behind. Or perhaps she didn't really appear instantaneously, as it seemed to her, but a little at a time, slowly enough that the air could move out of the way. If so, what would happen if she appeared *in* the water? Could the water molecules move away fast enough, or would the friction tear her apart?

The technology was incredible, but the obvious risks she was taking started to sober her. Not only that, but she knew that this was no purely human-invented technology. Fifteen years earlier, such a technology had been the means by which the varcolac entered the world. For all she knew, she was calling the creature to her by this unrestrained experimentation.

The sky was darkening. She needed to find a place to stay, and teleportation couldn't conjure her a bed or a fake ID. Her older sister Claire lived in California. The thought of going to Claire for help filled Alex with a sudden hope. Claire always knew what to do. She was never rattled, never without a plan, never with a lock of beautiful blond hair out of place. It was sometimes infuriating, but if Alex was in trouble, Claire was the one who could help. She wouldn't judge or ask embarrassing questions; she would just take care of everything. Besides, the police wouldn't be looking for her so far away, at least not yet.

But she couldn't go to Claire. She didn't know California, for one thing, so she would be teleporting to an unfamiliar place. Besides, she didn't know how far away teleportation would work, or what would happen to her if she went too far. She had been lucky so far, but she was starting to think she shouldn't push her luck stretching the limits of this technology.

There was only one place nearby where she thought she would be safe. She risked one more teleport, this time into the Schuylkill River where it twisted its way through Philadelphia. She was tiring of these blind dunks under water, but it was better than risking materializing eight feet above a parking lot. She clambered out at Grays Ferry Road, still a good ten city blocks from her destination.

It was a long walk in wet shoes. She almost took the risk and teleported there instead. What she needed was someone standing at her destination who could confirm the coordinates and guarantee her a clear zone. For this to become a usable technology, there would have to be teleportation stations established around the world, measured and adjusted to maintain a constant vector, with coordinated transition times between stations. In fact, all that could be automated, so that a traveler in Philadelphia could enter a booth, choose a location—and pay the fee—and then reappear in a similar booth in Australia. Cross-Atlantic travel could be as easy as riding an elevator.

But she was getting ahead of herself. This technology came with strings attached, and those strings could get her, and anyone involved with it, killed. She'd been stupid. Stupid to have believed that the wonderful technologies she had been working with had come merely through the brilliance of a man. She had known, at some level, that this was the same basic technology her father's colleague had "invented" fifteen years before, and that, just like then, it involved a deal with the devil.

She finally arrived, exhausted and disheveled, at the gate of Salt and Light, a religious outreach that her uncle had founded twenty years before. Her uncle had died suddenly of a brain aneurysm a year earlier, but Alex knew the woman who had taken over the work, Marta Gonzales. She rang the bell.

After a few minutes, Marta herself came to the gate. Salt and Light was a little bit of everything: orphanage, school, homeless shelter, and Marta herself was part schoolteacher, part counselor, part mother. She was short and overweight, but stern, and she carried a presence about her that commanded politeness and respect from anyone who came through her gates.

She peered out at Alex, and Alex was struck by how the lines in her face seemed more deeply drawn than the last time she had seen her. "Alex Kelley?" she said.

Alex shrugged. "It's me. I need some help, Marta."

"That you do," Marta said. She unlocked the gate and swung it open. She ushered Alex inside, up a stained staircase, and down a narrow hallway. The walls were covered with bulletin boards with photographs pinned to them in a haphazard array, the newer ones obscuring the older. Marta found a large cardboard box at the end of the hall and rifled through it, eventually emerging with a pair of jeans and a T-shirt. "Can't help you with the underwear, honey, but these are dry, which is more than you've got."

She opened a bathroom door and practically pushed Alex into it. "Just hang your wet stuff in there. When you're dry and dressed again, we'll talk."

Alex did as she was told. When she came out again, she followed the light to Marta's cramped office.

"It's so quiet," she said.

Marta looked up from a paper she was reading. She took off her glasses and set them on the table. "It's after curfew. Everyone's in bed. Now, what's your trouble?"

Alex told her. When she tried to talk about the technology at the demo, Marta shook her head. "Cut to the chase, honey."

"A man was killed. They think I did it. I can't reach my dad, and anyway, I don't want to involve—"

"Enough said." Marta stood. "You need a bed to sleep in and a plan for the near future. The bed we can do tonight; the plan will have to wait until tomorrow."

"Okay," Alex said, her eyes filling with tears. She had known Marta would help her, but at the same time, she had still half-expected to be turned away. Marta led her up to another floor, down another hallway, and opened a door. The room contained a small bed, made up neatly with white sheets, and a battered dresser.

"Thank you," Alex said.

"We'll talk more tomorrow," Marta said.

Alex stepped into the room and closed the door behind her. When she turned around again, Ryan Oronzi was sitting on her bed.

"Are you done playing games now?" he asked.

CHAPTER 11

Halfway through their quesadillas, Messinger's phone rang. She made a terse reply, and hung up. "We've got to go."

"What is it?"

"They found your sister's car." Messinger stood. "Are you coming?"

"Yes. Absolutely."

"Not as a cop," Messinger qualified.

Sandra frowned. "If I'm a suspect, you can't hold me. You can't make me go anywhere."

"I'm not making you," Messinger said. "I'm asking you to come, as an expert witness, to help with the investigation."

"Okay," Sandra said. "I'm in."

They abandoned the rest of their meal and got back into the cruiser. It had grown dark outside while they were eating. Sandra thought Messinger might just leave her, or else drop her at the station first, but she turned south instead. Messinger was choosing to trust her. It meant that she believed her story, at least to a point.

They stopped outside a Dunkin' Donuts that was already crawling with cops. The CSI van was there, and cops were routing traffic away from the block. Sandra's stomach turned over. What if Alex was dead? Messinger hadn't said very much on the drive. What if she had brought her here to identify Alex's body?

They approached the car. There were floodlights on it from several angles, and a man was laser scanning the steering wheel for fingerprints.

"Does this belong to your sister?" Messinger asked.

Sandra nodded, not trusting herself to speak. Finally, she asked, "Is she dead?"

Messinger looked up, confused. "What? Oh—no. At least, not that I know of. We haven't found a body."

Sandra felt a rush of relief, and at the same time, a flood of pure anger at Alex for putting her through this. What on earth had she been thinking, to help reproduce the same technology that had nearly killed them before?

"Were there any cameras?" Sandra asked.

Messinger made a sour face. "No. The cameras in the Dunkin' Donuts are just fakes to deter thieves. We're tracking credit cards to find customers who may have been here at the time, to see if they have view-feeds, or just remember seeing something. Anyone paying in cash will be practically impossible to track down."

Sandra thought about the route her sister would have taken driving here from the NJSC. She would have crossed over to Pennsylvania on either the Walt Whitman bridge or the Commodore Barry bridge, either one of which would have brought her to I-95. She could have been heading home to their parents' house, but that wouldn't have required getting off at this exit. It seemed unlikely she would have stopped just for a doughnut.

"She was meeting someone," Sandra said.

"What makes you say that?"

"She ditched her car here. If she wanted public transportation, she could have gotten off at the airport instead. It would have taken us a lot longer to find the car, and she could have taken a bus, train, or taxi practically anywhere. There's no public transportation here, so either she's on foot in a poor neighborhood where she knows no one, or else she left in someone else's car."

Messinger nodded. "Can you think of any friends for whom this would be a likely meeting place?"

"Not at all. It doesn't make any sense."

Sandra peered into the back seat of the car, careful not to touch anything. It was pristine, without a receipt or gum wrapper or discarded grocery bag in sight. That was typical Alex, neat to a fault. For a moment, Sandra's vision swam. She could still see the car in front of her, but at the same time, she saw a stern woman, short and overweight, peering through a gate. She recognized her: Marta Gonzales.

The sensation of having seen Marta was strong. Years ago, before the two copies of her father had resolved into one person again, each of his selves had seen glimpses of what the other was seeing. Was that what was happening? Was she seeing through Alex's eyes?

The thought was terrifying. It was an unwelcome reminder of the fact that she and Alex were two versions of the same person and might someday resolve again into a single individual. No satisfactory explanation had ever been made as to why their probability wave had never resolved, and that meant there was no reason she knew of why it might not collapse at any moment.

Neither of them knew exactly what would happen if their wave collapsed. Their father had spent weeks split into two people, and when they combined again, he retained many of the memories from both versions, but not all. The real problem was not just the memories, however, but the personality, the sense of identity, the sense of self. Sandra was *not* Alex, and she didn't want to become her, not even a little bit. It was part of what had prompted her to spend less time around Alex, to minimize the overlap in their experiences.

But the vision had been clear, and she was pretty sure it wasn't just her imagination. It made sense, now that she thought about it. Alex wouldn't have wanted to leave her car at the mission, because the police would be looking for it. From here, it was a long walk to Salt and Light, but it was doable. And Marta would certainly take her in.

"Do you see anything else?" Messinger said. "Anything missing or out of the ordinary?"

Sandra shook herself, as if waking from a dream. "No," she said. "Nothing jumps out at me."

"All right. I'll drop you back at the station, and you can take a cruiser home."

They drove to the district station in silence. Halfway there, Messinger took a call. She listened for a while, and then said, "That was confirmation from DNA. The body found at the stadium was your father."

Sandra nodded, unable to speak. Tears stung her eyes, and a hard ball formed in her throat. The last time she had seen him, she had walked out in irritation because he had called her Alex instead of Sandra. It seemed so petty now. All she had ever wanted was his approval. For him to look at her in admiration like he did Alex, or to get that excited gleam in his eyes when she suggested some new physics conundrum.

Despite that, she had always known he loved her. She would miss him desperately. She would have to call Claire and tell her, and somehow they would have to get the word to Sean in Poland. She imagined him in that distant country, hearing such dreadful news without any family members nearby. Would they give him leave to fly home for the funeral?

They pulled into the parking lot of the police station. Messinger pointed to a black sedan and made an exasperated noise. "Mr. Black Suit got here ahead of us," she said.

"You mean Liddle?" Sandra said.

"That's the one."

As they drove past the sedan, Sandra could see Liddle himself standing there, and another cop helping a woman out of the back seat. It was her mother.

Sandra opened the door, heedless of the fact that it was still moving, and jumped out. Messinger called after her, but she didn't stop. "Mom!" she called.

Her mother turned. Her beautiful long hair was loose, curling around her shoulders and arms, and her face was red and streaked with tears.

Sandra went to embrace her.

"Keep them apart," Liddle barked, and the other cop, a man Sandra knew and had talked Philadelphia sports with over coffee, stepped forward with a cold expression to block her way.

"She's my mother," Sandra protested.

Messinger jogged up to join them, and Liddle glared at her. "Detective, get this woman away from here."

Messinger took Sandra's elbow, but Sandra shook her off. "I just want to see my mom. There's no law against that."

"The easy way, or the hard way," Messinger said in low tones.

Sandra growled in frustration. "I'll be back soon, Mom," she called. "It's going to be all right."

She allowed Messinger to lead her away. "Sorry about that," Messinger said. "But you know we can't have you talking to her."

"I don't know any such thing. She's not under arrest, and as far as I know, neither am I. We should both be free to walk out of here if we want."

Messinger shrugged. "Maybe. But practically, we can hold you for twenty-four hours if we feel you're interfering with the investigation or withholding crucial evidence. And we need to talk to your mother before you do."

"What do you think I'm going to do, threaten her to keep her mouth shut? Feed her a story?"

"I don't know you, Miss Kelley. I don't know what you're going to do. But we need to talk to her before she talks to anyone else."

The clouds were low, and a strong wind was picking up. "My father is dead," she said. "You saw his body for yourself. Isn't that enough?"

"That doesn't stop the investigation. The blast originated from his seat. We have to question everyone who knew him or saw him recently. Besides—his car was found at his house, not at the stadium. Somebody must have driven it home."

"I told you—"

"I know what you said," Messinger said. "It doesn't matter. We have to investigate."

Sandra thought about Alex and the Salt and Light mission. Was she afraid? Did she have a plan? Sandra didn't know why she hadn't told Messinger to look there for Alex, but she realized now that she didn't trust the Philadelphia police department to investigate this mystery. There was too much going on, too much that was beyond their ability to understand. Even if the police did find Alex, they might not believe her story, and they certainly wouldn't let Sandra talk to her. The only way Sandra was going to understand what was going on was if she found Alex herself.

She stopped walking. Messinger kept going for a few steps before turning to look at her.

"Am I free to go?" Sandra asked.

Messinger hesitated. "You are. But don't go far."

"I won't," Sandra said. But she didn't mean it. She planned to go as far as it took to get some answers. She was on her own now. They didn't trust her to be a cop, and she didn't trust them with her family. Sandra didn't know what next steps the police would take, but she knew one thing. She would find Alex before they did.

CHAPTER 12

"Dr. Oronzi!" Alex said. He was just sitting there on the bed, as if it were the most natural thing in the world.

"Please, call me Ryan."

"Fine. But how did you find me here?"

"The module you stole uses an unclassified map server that we host outside of the lab. Whenever you teleport, it logs your location. We didn't want anyone to teleport and not know where they ended up." He chuckled. "You chose a pretty wet itinerary."

Alex narrowed her eyes. "I didn't want to die. How did you teleport in here so precisely?"

"I had your actual location to key off of. Normally, we have to do the same thing—either aim for water, or, more commonly, have someone waiting at the destination already to make more accurate measurements. I wasn't mocking you; it was smart not to trust the data."

Alex still stood with her back to the door. Though she supposed it would do no good to run from a man who could track her location and teleport to wherever she went. It was a disturbing thought. Though if she simply powered down her eyejack lenses, he would lose his track. And she was pretty sure she could outrun him.

She stepped into the room. There was no chair, but the dresser was low and bare, so she hopped up to sit on top of it. "You've been keeping secrets," she said. "This technology can do more than you've been letting on."

He shrugged. "It's unproven research. Not ready for prime time."

"Yeah? Or did you just want to keep it to yourself?"

"The government pays the bills. They know what I'm doing."

Alex shook her head, still amazed. "I get the teleportation thing, at least partially," she said. "We were already using tunneling concepts to shift the location of objects. But invisibility? How is that remotely possible?"

"Not that hard, really," Oronzi said. "The Higgs projector makes it possible, but it's just a matter of recalculating Maxwell's equations for each photon that comes into the field, so that a new photon is released on the other side with the same direction and energy, as if the first had never been captured. There's actually a small time delay, but not so much that anyone would ever notice."

Alex crossed her arms and examined him. "So what do you want from me?"

"You promised you would tell me what you know about the varcolac. I did my part: if not for me, you would have been caught by now for certain."

Alex felt a sense of indignation rising up in her, although he was probably right. "Maybe you underestimate me."

He shrugged, acknowledging the point. "It doesn't matter. What matters is that I need to know everything I can about this thing. I need to know how to beat it."

Alex's eyes were adjusting to the dim light, and she saw how haggard he looked. "Haven't you been sleeping?"

"I've been fighting this thing for weeks. I barely go to sleep, because I'm afraid it might break through my equations during the night. And now you tell me that it's just been playing with me all this time, tricking me into doing what it wants."

"I don't know that 'tricking' is the right word," Alex said. "It's so different from us, so alien, that I don't know if it can understand why we do things. It doesn't intentionally deceive. I think it's just solving the probability equations to make what it wants the most likely outcome."

Oronzi pursed his lips. "I don't know about that. It's been pretty deceptive."

"Has it? Can it really put itself in our place and predict what we would do with certain stimuli as opposed to others? Maybe it can to some extent, but I would guess it's more in a mathematical way than by sympathy or imagination."

"What does it want?"

"I don't know. We never did know. It kills casually, as if death means nothing to it. And yet it knows we're there. It nearly electrocuted my mother and my brother, but was it trying to kill or torture them? Or does its kind communicate through electrical energy? Or feed off of it? We don't know if it meant us harm or not, but it harmed us all the same."

"How did you get rid of it?"

"We shut down the super collider."

Oronzi blinked. "Seriously?"

Alex pulled her feet up onto the dresser and hugged her knees. "The collider powers hundreds of huge electromagnets at thousands of volts per second. It has a huge electric potential, and the varcolac was tapping into that. We think it was also feeding off of the exotic particles the collider produced. At any rate, once we shut it down, the varcolac was gone."

"Only this time, it's got its own universe to draw power from," Oronzi said. "Thanks to me."

"Can't you shut down the universe? You created it, after all."

Oronzi shook his head. "I've tried. It's self-sufficient now. It may be small by universe standards, but it's a *universe*. It's expanding in its own space-time, generating its own exotic particles by the trillions. Thousands of years from now, when it spreads out enough, it may form its own stars. Maybe even its own form of life. Right now, though, it's just an incredibly hot ball of energy. There's no way I can destroy it."

"Fifteen years ago, the varcolac was tied to the collider. It couldn't go very far from it. This varcolac may be tied to your lab in the same way."

"Unless its range is a factor of the amount of energy available," Oronzi said. "We're talking 10^{23} times more energy than the collider. That might give it a little more room to wander."

"We should talk to my father," Alex said. "He studied it before. He might have a better idea."

A soft tap sounded three times against the door. Alex froze. It was probably just Marta coming back to give her a blanket, or to ask why she could hear a man's voice in the room. The police wouldn't rap softly; they would shout to announce themselves, or else just break down the door. It didn't matter. If need be, she could simply teleport away and then find a new place to hide.

Alex opened the door. When she saw who was on the other side, she almost did teleport away.

"Sandra?"

Sandra stood at the door in her police uniform, radio and gun strapped to her belt. "Hi, Alex."

Alex crossed her arms. "Are you here to turn me in?"

"No. Though I really should. I risked my career by not telling them where you are."

"Then why didn't you tell them?"

Sandra paused. "Look, are you going to let me in, or what?"

Alex stood aside to let her into the room, and Sandra stepped inside. Oronzi looked back and forth between the two of them. "Wow, you two really do look exactly alike, don't you?"

"Sandra, this is Dr. Oronzi, chief physicist at the super collider," Alex said.

Oronzi stood. "Please call me Ryan," he said. He extended a hand, but Sandra ignored it.

"Ryan Oronzi," Sandra said. "I should have known."

"And what is that supposed to mean?" Alex shut the door, already struggling with the fury and inadequacy she always felt when her twin was around.

"It means, I should have known you would be hanging out with your partner in idiocy."

Alex couldn't believe it. Sandra had met the man for ten seconds, and she was already insulting him. "Ryan is no idiot."

"Maybe not, but you are. What were you thinking?" Sandra stood with her arms crossed in the middle of the room, glaring at Alex. "The last time somebody played with that technology, it nearly got us all killed."

"I know that. Don't you think I know that?" Alex said.

"Then why on earth did you do it? You brought the *varcolac* back, and for what?"

"I didn't know that's what we were doing," Alex protested. It sounded weak, even to her ears. True, she hadn't known, exactly. But she had realized how similar the technology was to what Brian Vanderhall and Jean Massey had been playing with years before.

"Didn't know? For heaven's sake, Alex. I knew what it was the first time I saw a video of your demo."

"You saw a video?" Ryan asked.

Sandra waved a hand in dismissal. "The feds played one for me."

"That's supposed to be classified," he said. "You don't have a clearance for that."

"Hardly the greatest of our concerns. Have you two figured out what we're going to do?"

"Do?"

"To kill the varcolac. Or at least to send it back to where it came from."

"It is back where it came from," Ryan said. "At least for the moment. Though I don't think I can keep it there for long."

Alex took a deep breath. "I was just saying how we should get Dad involved. He might have some ideas."

Sandra shook her head, and all the bellicosity drained from her face. "You don't know, do you?"

Alex could see it in her eyes. She could see it, and she knew, but she couldn't bear to hear it spoken. It was some trick, some malicious prank of Sandra's to teach her a lesson. It couldn't be true. "No," she said. "Don't say it. No."

"He's dead."

The word hung in the room. Alex kept shaking her head, willing it away. It was not possible. Finally, she whispered, "How?"

"In the stadium."

"No," Alex said, and there was force behind it now. "No, that's not true. He was alive this morning. Mom said he had just been there, sitting in the kitchen. She said *you* were there with him."

"He split. I did see him at the house this morning, but I also saw his body at the stadium. So there were two versions. Then the second version—the one sitting in the kitchen—disappeared with no trace. You know what that means." Sandra seemed to lose all her energy. There were no chairs, so she sank down to sit on the floor. "The varcolac killed him."

"I don't understand," Alex said. "You're saying it was the varcolac that destroyed the stadium?"

"Yes," Sandra said.

Ryan cleared his throat. "Not possible. The creature broke out for the first time at 11:08 this morning."

"Are you sure of that?"

"Absolutely. I've been tracking its progress for weeks. I have alarms set to tell me when it solves another equation and breaks through another layer. This morning was the first time, and it lasted only six minutes before I got it back under control."

"In that case, I have some data for you to look at," Sandra said.

Alex heard a ping, indicating Sandra was trying to share a viewfeed to her eyejack. She accepted it automatically, but her head was spinning. Was this all their father's death meant to Sandra? Data? She knew Sandra had never been as close to Dad as she was, but she wouldn't have expected this coldness from her.

"This is force vector data from the stadium site, connecting known objects to their final positions," Sandra said. "And here is an overlay using an equation Dad suggested before . . ." She swallowed. "I mean, when I was with him this morning. The pattern only makes sense using a ten-dimensional construct."

Ryan stood up from the bed and spun in place, examining the data through his own eyejack. "Extraordinary."

"Parabolic solutions didn't work," Sandra said. "We couldn't figure out what kind of single or even multiple force would have caused the objects to end up where they did. It wasn't until Dad suggested trying a ten-dimensional equation that we could nail down a single point of origin."

"This was definitely not accomplished by any human being," Ryan said.

"Why not?" Alex asked.

"Because *I* couldn't have done it."

"I told you," Sandra said. "The varcolac destroyed the stadium."

Alex couldn't believe it. Sandra was trying to blame their father's death on *her*. After all that had happened in the last twenty-four hours, all she could think of was assigning blame. "It wasn't the varcolac. Ryan just told you it didn't even break out until this morning."

"I don't know what to say, then," Sandra said. "Is somebody *else* out there releasing multidimensional quantum creatures into the world?"

"Hang on," Ryan said. "Think about it." He stretched his pudgy fingers back, cracking them loudly. "I think we need to consider the possibility that the varcolac, while free in our universe from 11:08 to 11:14 this morning, initiated the destruction of the stadium at 9:35 last night."

Alex knew exactly what he meant, but it was ridiculous. Impossible. "Time travel?" she said, letting the scorn drip from her voice. "That's pure fantasy. I can't believe you would even suggest it."

"Actually, it explains the nature of this data," Ryan said. "It could have used a reverse-time Higgs singlet. The time parameter would require this kind of dimensional complexity . . ."

"No. Absolutely not." Alex felt angry at him for even suggesting it. "There is no way we caused that stadium to blow. It happened *the night before*."

"It's not your fault," Sandra said.

"You'd better believe it's not my fault! I was just doing my job. I didn't know there was a varcolac involved. I didn't let it get free. That was him!" She jabbed an accusing finger at Ryan. "And I certainly didn't send it back in time to kill my father and thousands of other people!"

Sandra stood and held out a tentative hand as if to pat Alex on the shoulder. "You couldn't have known."

Alex didn't want to cry, but once she started, she couldn't stop. "Yes, I could," she said, the tears running freely. "I could have known. You were right. I should have said something. I didn't want to believe it."

Sandra slowly wrapped her arms around her. "It's not your fault," she said. "But we'll make it right." Alex sank her head against her sister's shoulders. She didn't say anything, but she knew that Sandra was wrong. Thousands were dead, her father among them. It could never be made right again.

CHAPTER 13

Sandra wanted to disapprove of teleporting, but she just couldn't manage it. The thrill of choosing a new location with her eyejacks and then just *being* there was so electrifying, she couldn't hide her enthusiasm.

"I told you you'd like it," Alex said.

The three of them stood on an outcropping at Hawk Mountain Sanctuary in Kempton, Pennsylvania, watching red-tails ride the thermals in search of prey far below. The mountain had been recently surveyed, its location data verified via GPS, making it an ideally safe teleport location.

Sandra wanted to protest that just using the technology at all was daring the varcolac to reappear, but she had enjoyed the experience too much to want to object. "Where does the power come from?" she asked instead.

"The power?" Ryan asked.

"The energy, I mean. We're transporting mass across a distance, instantaneously. It has to take a tremendous amount of energy to accomplish that, doesn't it? Where does the energy come from?"

"Through the wormhole," Ryan said. "There's a whole universe full of energy that we're tapping."

"But the universe is—"

"In my lab? No. You can't keep a universe in a lab. My baby universe is outside of our universe entirely. Parallel to it, if you will. Think of it like this: the other universe is rotating with respect to ours. That's not exactly accurate, because there are more dimensions involved, but it's close enough. When we teleport, we're slipping out of our normal dimensional space and using the spin of the other universe to shift position. Which means every time we teleport, we're slowing down its rotation with respect to us by a tiny, fractional amount. Stealing its energy."

"What happens if it stops rotating?"

Ryan snorted. "Not going to happen. The moon has been robbing Earth's rotational energy for years, but none of us feel the difference. Your tiny mass is nothing to a universe. The effect is just too small."

"It seems wrong," Sandra said. "It seems like it shouldn't be possible."

Ryan shrugged. "Ever seen an airplane take off? That seems impossible, too."

"But there's already mass in the spot we teleport to. Air can just move out of the way, I guess, but what happens if you teleport to a place where something already is?"

"I'll show you," Ryan said. He picked up a small rock from the ground and hefted it. He looked out toward the view, then walked to the other side of the outcropping and looked out again.

"What are you doing?" Sandra asked.

"I have a rangefinder on my eyejack system," Ryan said. "It needs two points to triangulate."

"What are you triangulating on?"

He pointed. "See that hawk?"

Alex spoke up. "No. Don't you dare."

"Your sister wants to see what will happen."

"It's a beautiful creature. It's probably endangered. Don't—"

Ryan held the rock up between two fingers. "Bye-bye," he said. The rock disappeared. Out over the valley, high above them, the hawk he had indicated puffed outward suddenly, like a bag of popcorn in the microwave. The bird plummeted, wings spinning free, until it fell out of sight among the trees far below.

Sandra watched in silence, horrified.

"It didn't explode," Ryan said. He sounded disappointed. "The skin is pretty strong, I guess."

Sandra didn't say anything. She stared at Ryan. The casual cruelty with which he had killed the hawk made a chill run down her spine. The media presented him as charmingly neurotic, the caricature of an eccentric scientist, but this was something different. It didn't even seem to occur to him that the hawk's life mattered, or that anyone else might find the action upsetting.

"I can't believe you did that!" Alex said. "You just killed it, for no reason."

"I was demonstrating the principle," Ryan said. "When you teleport something, it reenters our space at a single point, then rapidly expands outward until it reaches a pressure equilibrium. If I teleported you into a haystack, you'd be fine. The hay would shift. But if I sent you into, say, a block of granite, you would be crushed. The granite wouldn't expand to accommodate you. If I teleported the block of granite into you, however, you would expand just fine to accommodate it."

"You're a monster," Alex said. "You could have used another rock instead of a living thing. You just wanted to see it blow apart, didn't you?"

"Wasn't it you I saw demonstrating this technology on people?" Ryan said.

"They were actors. It wasn't real."

"You work for Lockheed Martin," he said, annoyed now. "What, you think the military is paying you billions so they can put on stage performances? This technology is meant to kill people—quickly, efficiently, and from a distance. It's made to make our soldiers invincible. So don't get all high and mighty on me."

"The bird didn't have to die."

They kept arguing, but Sandra wasn't looking at them. She was still staring at the empty space where the hawk used to be. No wonder the military was so interested. Ryan had basically just snapped his fingers and the bird had died. He could have done the same to *her*. For that matter, she now had the same power, to kill or destroy at a distance and then disappear from the scene. What would happen if this ability went public? If anyone could kill with a thought and then escape the consequences? It could tear the whole fabric of society apart. Never mind the varcolac—it was this technology they should fear.

"Shut up, both of you," she said.

Alex and Ryan stopped arguing and looked at her. Sandra was surprised; she hadn't expected that to work.

"Well?" Alex said. "What do you want?"

"Arguing won't get us anywhere. We're supposed to be talking about how to defeat the varcolac. Or at the least, discussing what we think it's capable of."

"Right," Ryan said. "Time travel."

"So you keep telling us," Alex said. "Though I don't know how we're supposed to defeat it if it can just go back in time and change anything we do."

"How does that even work?" Sandra said. "I thought time travel was impossible."

"Einstein was the first to suggest that it might really be possible," Ryan said. "We always say that Einstein's theory of general relativity sets the speed of light as a limit for travel, but that's not exactly true. His equations do allow for velocities faster than the speed of light, but only if you use negative values for time. Einstein himself recognized that, at least in theory, relativity meant time-travel was possible. But it wasn't until more than a century later that M-theory was experimentally proven and gravity was successfully incorporated into quantum mechanics."

Sandra sighed. "I knew this was how this conversation was going to go. What's M-theory? Though really, I'm afraid to ask."

"It stands for Membrane Theory," Alex said. "Think membranes in multiple dimensions."

Ryan frowned. "That's not what it stands for."

"What, then?"

"I don't think it stands for anything. I know it doesn't stand for membrane, though."

"Matrix?" Alex said.

"Look, I don't care," Sandra said. "Just tell me what the Muffin Theory says, and why I should care."

Ryan laughed. "Okay, here's how it works. You normally live in four dimensions, right?"

"The fourth being time?"

"Yes. But space-time is actually composed of eleven dimensions. There's the four you usually think about, and seven more that are all curled up where you can't see them. The four dimensions we generally experience are what we call a 'brane'—they're roughly fixed in reference to each other, and they float around in the other dimensions, which we call the 'bulk.' Most particles, and thus most matter, are confined to the standard four dimensions, but there are some exceptions."

"Like gravity," Sandra said.

Ryan raised an eyebrow and whistled.

"I did grow up with a physicist as a father," Sandra said. "I picked up a few things."

"Well, you're right." Ryan threw a pebble over the edge of the ridge and watched it fall into the wooded valley below. "Gravity—meaning, of course, the gravitons that communicate the force of gravity—bleeds out into the other dimensions. It's what makes gravity the weakest of all the standard forces."

"And the varcolac lives out among those other dimensions," Sandra said.

"That's what we think," Alex said.

"So, I'm losing the thread a little. What does this have to do with time travel?"

Ryan scooped up a handful of pebbles and started throwing them over the edge, one at a time. "It has to do with a very special particle called the Higgs singlet."

"The God Particle," Sandra said.

"Nope," Alex said. "That's the Higgs boson. This is a different one."

"The Higgs singlet's remarkable, special property is that it is affected only by gravity, and not by any of the other forces," Ryan said.

Sandra wrinkled her forehead. "So . . . it can travel into those other dimensions?"

"Exactly. If there's a sufficiently high velocity collision of protons in the super collider, then Higgs singlets will also be created that travel backward in time, through those other dimensions. That is, their decay paths appear in our universe before they're created in the first place."

Sandra sat down on a rock, enjoying the fresh breeze blowing her hair back. A large golden eagle caught a thermal and emerged over a ridge, dwarfing the smaller red-tailed hawks circling below it. "Why does going into other dimensions mean going back in time?"

Ryan stood on the edge of the cliff. "You see that eagle out there?"

"Don't kill it," Alex said.

"I'm not going to kill it." He turned back to Sandra. "Why can't the eagle instantaneously travel over here, to our ridge?"

"It can't fly that fast."

"What if it was a really good flier?"

Sandra rolled her eyes. "It couldn't fly faster than the speed of light, so it still couldn't do it instantaneously."

"Exactly. Alex, I think your sister's smarter than you."

Alex stuck out her tongue.

"So, we could describe the places the eagle could theoretically fly with a sphere, expanding as time passes. In the first nanosecond, it could reach no more than about a foot in any direction, even flying at the speed of light. In two nanoseconds, two feet in any direction."

"Okay, with you so far."

"We call that a light cone, and I'd show you how we draw it if I had some paper."

"Why doesn't that bother you?" Alex said.

Ryan turned, confused. "What? Not having paper?"

"No. You're afraid of taking the elevator, yet you crouch at the very edge of a cliff, and you don't blink an eye."

Ryan glared at her. "I'm not *afraid* of taking the elevator. I just don't trust the people who built it. This cliff is a different matter. It's solid stone. It's not going anywhere."

"If you say so."

Ryan turned back to Sandra. "As I was saying, our expanding sphere image isn't quite accurate."

"Why not?" Sandra asked.

"The planet," Alex said.

"Two points for the ugly sister," Ryan said.

Alex rolled her eyes. "Nice."

"The point is, the sphere will be slightly deformed toward the Earth," Ryan said. "Our speed-of-light eagle can fly farther toward the Earth than it can away from it."

"Because of gravity?" Sandra asked dubiously.

"That's right. Earth's gravity isn't a pulling force, like a giant magnet attracting things toward itself. Gravity deforms space-time. Even a beam of light, which has no mass, will bend when it passes by a massive planet. So our speed-of-light eagle will actually travel farther if it flies toward the Earth than if it flies away from it, though by only the tiniest amount. Our sphere is deformed, but not noticeably. So, what would happen if we made the Earth more massive?"

"The sphere of possible places it could go would deform more," Sandra said.

"Right."

"Wait a minute, though. You're talking about the places the eagle could theoretically fly in a given amount of time. It could fly here, but not to China. But haven't we been breaking that law all day? Haven't we been teleporting to places outside our own light cone? Traveling faster than the speed of light?"

Ryan grinned. "Sort of. It's all part of the puzzle. One thing at a time: what if we put a black hole near the eagle? How would that affect its light cone?"

Sandra looked at Alex, but they were both looking at her, waiting. "I don't know," she said. "It would deform the sphere even more, I guess."

"That's right," Ryan said. "In fact, it would deform the sphere so much that it couldn't fly away from the black hole at all. Even flying at the speed of light in the other direction, it would still end up traveling toward the hole. It wouldn't be able to escape the hole's gravity, any more than light itself can. Space-time is warped so badly that the bird is unavoidably sliding down the slope toward it. But let's keep going. What if we keep adding mass to the black hole?"

"The slope increases. The bird slides toward it faster."

"Yes. And if we keep on going?"

"Um . . . faster still?"

"Eventually the slope becomes vertical. At that point, the bird isn't sliding toward the black hole; it arrives there instantly. What if we add even more mass?"

Sandra shrugged. "You're going to tell me, I bet."

"Space-time becomes so warped that the slope is backward: the only solution to the equation is negative. Now, instead of a black hole, we call it a wormhole. Unlike the wormhole that connects my baby universe to ours, this one connects our universe in the present to a point in the past. The eagle is sucked through the wormhole and arrives before it left. Of course, it's been ripped apart into its constituent atoms, but besides that, it's fine."

"What do you have against birds?" Alex asked.

"The point is, the topography of space-time allows time travel. Not for eagles or humans—the process would completely destroy us. But for single particles, yes. The NJSC, in fact, has successfully demonstrated time travel for Higgs singlets."

"I know you're a genius and all, so you probably know what you're talking about," Sandra said. "But there's a paradox here, right? If something goes back in time, there's always the possibility that it can interfere with its own creation. Like going back in time and killing my own grandfather. What if the Higgs singlets, traveling back in time, get in the way of the protons that were about to collide to create them? Or what if you use the singlets to send your past self a message, warning you not to perform the experiment in the first place?"

Alex spoke up. "The universe won't allow it."

"The universe?"

"That's right." She looked at Ryan. "May I?"

Ryan made a mock bow.

"All right," Alex said. "I think we've exhausted the eagle analogy. Let's move on to billiard balls."

Sandra crossed her hands in her lap and looked up with an attentive expression, as if in class.

"The problem you raise is called Polchinski's paradox," Alex said. "Say you roll a billiard ball through a wormhole, so that it goes five seconds back in time."

"Okay."

"Only, you roll it through the wormhole at such an angle that it hits its earlier self, thus preventing itself from rolling into the wormhole in first place."

"That's what I'm saying. It's a paradox."

"And that's why it can't actually happen," Alex said.

"*Can't* happen? Who says? Is there a referee that cries foul and takes you out of the game?"

"Not exactly. But the universe can't contradict itself. There's a natural law that says self-consistency is always conserved. If you roll the ball through the wormhole at its past self, then either it will miss entirely, or else it will deliver itself a glancing blow that will knock it into the wormhole at such an angle that it will give itself that glancing blow," Alex said.

"You're kidding," Sandra said. Then she made a connection in her mind, and without thinking, said, "It's called the Novikov self-consistency principle, isn't it?"

Ryan's surprise was obvious on his face. "You really did grow up with a physicist father, didn't you?"

Sandra shrugged, surprised herself. "I guess so."

"Well, you're right," he said. "It's the only way the math works out. In fact, this specific case, with billiard balls, has been studied."

Sandra raised an eyebrow. "People have been sending billiard balls back in time?"

"No, I mean mathematically. Echeverria and Klinkhammer set up a computer simulation with billions of variations. They showed empirically that, not only do most conditions have multiple solutions, but that there are *no* initial conditions for which no self-consistent solution exists. It's actually where my work started." Ryan's excitement grew as he spoke. "The universe is a giant quantum computer, remember? It takes these complex consistency problems and solves them. It's doing it all the time."

Sandra grew sober. "And the varcolac fits into that somehow, doesn't it?"

"It's a sentient manifestation of that quantum computer," Alex said. "It's like an artificial intelligence, only on a vaster scale."

"You're saying the varcolac *is* the universe?"

"No. Or at least, I don't think so. It's an intelligence born out of the quantum complexity of the universe. We don't even know if there are many of them, or only one. Or if that distinction even has meaning to a being like that."

"And it can travel in time?"

"*I* can travel in time," Ryan said. "At roughly the rate of one minute every minute."

Sandra made a face. "At some other rate than the usual," she clarified.

"No. Not travel, exactly, not like you're thinking. It wouldn't be able to send its intelligence back to a point in the past; that would be like rewinding the particle interactions of the universe. But could it send a Higgs singlet back in time on exactly the right trajectory to cause a chain reaction that destroys a baseball stadium? Yes. I think it might very well be able to do exactly that."

Sandra felt suddenly tired and sad, overwhelmed by the conversation. It wasn't just a distracting intellectual exercise anymore. She spoke quietly. "Why? Why would it do such a thing?"

"I don't know," Oronzi said. "Maybe your father would have found a way to stop it, and it could see that somehow."

Alex stood up and stretched. "This is all a possible explanation, but how do we test it? How can we know if that's really what happened, or if it's just a wild fantasy?"

"We go back to the lab," Oronzi said. "We pore through the logs, double-check the math, look for anomalies. See if we can find when such a thing might have happened."

Sandra shook her head. "You two go. I need to be alone for a while."

"Are you okay?" Alex asked.

Sandra smiled wanly. "Not exactly." In truth, she wasn't okay at all. Her father was dead, and she had hardly even paused to let that truth sink in. Her mother was all alone, and instead of helping her when she needed them the most, they were worrying about murder charges and time-traveling quantum creatures. "Has anyone even told Claire? Or Sean?"

"I'm sure Mom called them."

"There's going to have to be a funeral, you know. They'll arrest you, if they see you there."

Alex shrugged. "That's all right. I don't need to go."

"We could switch. We'll wear the same dress. I'll go into the bathroom with a GPS, then I can teleport out, and you—"

"No." Alex took Sandra's shoulders. "You go. I don't want to see him like that."

Sandra nodded. "All right."

"I need to get back to the lab," Ryan said. "If we're right about the varcolac changing the past, we need to understand how it works."

"I'll come, too," Alex said.

"Okay," Sandra said. "I'll see you later then."

"What are you going to do?"

"I'm going to walk down the mountain. I just need some time to think. Then I'll go find Mom."

"Later, then."

"Later. And Alex?"

Alex turned. "Yes?"

"It's not your fault."

Alex made a tiny shrug, noncommittal, and frowned. "Thanks."

Ryan and Alex made eye contact and then teleported away, leaving Sandra alone on the mountain. Sandra took the trail leading from the peak back down to the road. She was still wearing her police uniform, which attracted looks from the other hikers, but the slope was an easy one, and the walk pleasant. She soon settled into a comfortable pace. The pretty, wooded surroundings and the sound of birdsong increased her melancholy.

In truth, it was more than just her father's death that was bothering her. She was certain, quite certain, that she had never heard of the Novikov self-consistency principle, and yet she had come up with the name in an instant. She wanted to tell herself that she must have heard of it a long time ago, when she was a child, and it just came bubbling to the surface of her memory at that moment. But she knew that wasn't true.

It was Alex's memory. Her sister knew very well what the Novikov self-consistency principle was, and Sandra had accessed that knowledge as if it were her own. It was what had happened fifteen years ago to her father, shortly before he resolved into a single person, after having been split in two for months. It made her afraid that their probability wave, after all this time, was in danger of collapsing. Maybe the reason they had remained two individuals for so many years was because the varcolac was gone. Now that it was back, maybe they would resolve into one person again.

And what if they did? Who would Alessandra Kelley be? She and Alex were such different people now, with different skill sets, different desires, different relationships, different lives. Would either of them survive in any meaningful sense? Or would one personality dominate, and the other, for all practical purposes, die? Sandra was afraid that if it came down to strength of personality, there wouldn't be very much of her personality left.

She thought of her father, and his brief split before death. How awful for her mother, to have him home, to think him safe, and then to have him so suddenly gone. She ought to visit her. Sandra checked her phone and found the GPS log. She had made calls when in her old bedroom, and the data was still there. No one would be in her room.

On her eyejack system, she brought up the menu of quantum functions that Alex had copied for her. There was a professional-looking menu with a military feel and a tiny Lockheed Martin logo. The options were tagged with unfamiliar icons and words like State Spin, Diffract, Tunnel, Attraction, and Probable Split. The only one she was familiar with was Teleport, and it didn't seem very safe to experiment with the others. She accessed the teleport function, and her bedroom materialized around her.

She grinned. It was such a rush, doing that. She barely understood how it was possible. She didn't even have as much as a battery on her to provide the power. There was so much energy bound up in the basic structure of the universe. Technology like this would make primitive techniques like burning fuel a thing of the past. If they could learn how to tap it without calling murderous alien creatures out of the space between the atoms, that is.

Sandra heard talking from her parents' bedroom; it sounded like a comedy show on the stream. She didn't want to startle her mother by walking in on her, so she sneaked downstairs and out the front door, and then rang the doorbell. A few minutes passed before her mother opened the door. Her normally pale face was leached of color, except for the skin around her eyes, which was red and raw. She wrapped her arms around Sandra without a word and buried her face in Sandra's hair. Sandra remembered her mother as such a strong presence in her life, but her thin body felt fragile in Sandra's arms.

They went inside. Her mother went through the mechanical actions of pouring Sandra a cup of coffee. The forensics crew must have been through, looking for evidence to support the claim that her father had been here after the explosion, but the kitchen had since been cleaned to an antiseptic shine. Sandra had last seen her father right there, sitting at that table, poring over the data she had given him.

"Is Claire here yet?" Sandra asked. She knew without asking that Claire would take care of the arrangements for the funeral. Claire was the planner in the family, the organizer of all details, and always had been. Even from California, Sandra had no doubt she was already making calls and writing lists of what needed to be done.

"Her flight doesn't come in until nine-thirty."

"And Sean?"

"He called." Her mother's voice sounded dead, devoid of emotion. "You know the military."

"Will they let him come home?"

"You mean, was it his choice or theirs for him to stay in Poland? I don't know. He said something about a special mission."

Considering the current friction with Turkey, talk of a special mission was a frightening thing. Turkey's influence had been spreading across the Balkans for years, and now Greece, Bulgaria, Romania, Serbia, Croatia, Hungary, and Slovenia had all been quietly assimilated, either through military threat or economic pressure. Allied with an increasingly powerful Iran, Turkey maintained a strong source of oil and a secure southern border. The growing Turkish navy now dominated the Mediterranean. Worse, they had apparently recovered a stockpile of Soviet nuclear warheads left over in Romania from the Cold War. The Romanian government had previously declared the weapons disassembled, but Turkey now claimed they were operational.

American politicians were anxious to restore balance in the region before Turkey grew into a world power, so they were pouring troops and money into Poland and Germany. War seemed inevitable. As a Force Recon marine, Sean wasn't trained for a back-row seat. Sandra didn't know how her mother would survive if the next funeral was his.

"I'm sure he'll be okay," Sandra said.

Her mother forced a smile and squeezed her hand. They sat there for a while, their hands clasped across the table, not talking about war, or her father, or varcolacs, or what the future might hold. Memories flashed through Sandra's mind, cued by this so-familiar kitchen. The memories that came from both before her split with Alex and those that came after merged seamlessly together in her mind. It was as if at fourteen years old, she had suddenly gained a twin sister. It felt to her like Alex was the new one, and she the daughter who had always been there. Of course, it would have felt just the same to Alex.

Sandra wanted to share some of these memories with her mother. They were good memories, on the whole. Her father had loved them all, though imperfectly, and they had loved him. He had been a father who was present in their home, for whom family, rather than work or friends or other ambitions, was the highest priority. She said none of these things to her mother. There would be time for such remembrances. For now, she just held her hand.

A ping told Sandra that someone was trying to contact her. She checked her phone, and saw that it was Angel Gutierrez. "Hello?" she said.

"Sandra. It's me. Do you have some time to talk?"

"Yeah, sure."

"I mean, in person? I don't think this should be going over the airwaves."

"Sure. Where are you?"

"At the robotics lab at U-Penn."

Sandra turned to her mother. "I need to go meet someone."

"Go ahead," her mother said. "I'll be okay. I'll have to pick up Claire from the airport soon anyway."

Sandra left the house and closed the door behind her, then spoke into her phone again. "Is there anyone else there at the lab with you?"

"No. Why?" Angel said.

"Send me the GPS data from your phone."

"Um, okay. Done." She could hear the confusion in his voice. "Does that mean you're coming?"

"Yeah. One more thing. Can you clear away anything within about five meters of where you're standing?"

"Um, it's pretty clear already."

"Pretty clear?"

"Nothing but a folding chair, which I just slid out of the way."

"Great. Now walk five meters away yourself, and don't move."

"This is really weird, Sandra. Are you watching me or something?"

"Did you do it?"

"Yes. How long do I have to stand here?"

Sandra smiled. "Not long at all."

CHAPTER 14

Sandra materialized in the University of Pennsylvania robotics lab. Angel, standing five meters away, leaped back with a shriek and crashed to the floor, knocking over a folding chair with a clatter. Sandra shrugged. "Sorry," she said. "Did I startle you?"

He looked up at her from the ground with an expression of utter astonishment. "Where did you come from?"

"My parents' house. It's about twenty miles west of here, in Media."

"No, I mean, just now. Were you hiding in here?" He looked up, examining the ceiling tiles above her.

She laughed. "Nope. I just teleported right in. That's why I needed the coordinates. And why I asked you to stand aside."

"You . . ."

"Teleported." Sandra was enjoying this, despite the seriousness of the situation—or maybe even because of it. "I'll tell you all about it. But you wanted to tell me something, too, right? Which should we do first?"

Angel stood shakily to his feet. "I think we'd better start with you explaining how you just did black magic in my science lab."

The lab's interior was two stories high, and most of the space was taken up by a central cage, no more than a wooden framework wrapped with tightly stretched mosquito netting. The inside of the cage was entirely empty, except for a series of cameras and motion sensors affixed at regular intervals. Outside of the cage, the room was cluttered with metal folding chairs, ladders, scraps of wood and piping, tablets, wiring, and card tables piled with random electronics. Sandra saw a few surprising items as well: hula-hoops, brightly colored beach balls, and marching-band batons.

"Okay, fine. Watch. This is the technology my sister was working on." It was supposed to be super-classified, Sandra knew, but she wasn't a government employee. No one had sworn her to secrecy. If she wanted to show off for Angel and tell him all about it, she'd do as she pleased. Sandra looked inside the wood-and-mesh cage and estimated the distance. Teleporting this close, she wasn't too worried about making a mistake. She disappeared and reappeared in the middle of the empty cage. To her, it seemed as though the entire room had suddenly shifted. Angel was still staring at the spot she had been standing a moment earlier. "Hey," she said. "Over here."

Angel turned and saw her, his face incredulous and a little frightened. "Is this really happening?"

"There's more. Soldiers with this technology can walk through walls, dodge bullets, even rip an enemy's gun out of his hands from across a field. They'll be practically invincible."

"What's the catch?"

Sandra teleported back so she was standing right next to him again. "The occasional massacre of a stadium full of people." She kept her tone light, but she felt a pain in her throat like she was swallowing a rock. "You asked if it was a quantum weapon that destroyed the stadium. You weren't too far off. Only it wasn't a person who pulled the trigger."

She told him the whole story. She hadn't intended to go into her whole childhood and the events of fifteen years ago, but he was such an intent listener that she just kept talking. Besides, he seemed at least somewhat familiar with her father's murder case and the public claim made in court that there had been two versions of him. And he nodded at everything she said, no matter how outlandish.

"You're really taking this in stride," she said.

He laughed, a little nervously. "This isn't the first crazy thing to happen to me today."

She wrapped up her story with an explanation of how she had split into two, and the probability wave had never resolved. "So, my sister is really me," she concluded. "There are two of me."

Angel shook his head, dismissive. "That's ridiculous."

"Ridiculous, but true," she said.

"No. Ridiculous and false."

"Angel, I—"

"I'm not talking about your story. I'm talking about your claim that your sister is really you. That's observably false, and to claim otherwise is just semantics. Even identical twins of the normal stripe start out as a single zygote. No one says they're really the same person. As soon as you split, you became two people. Different."

"But we share the same memories of growing up. I'm one possibility of how I turned out; she's another. She's what I would have been if just the slightest things had been different. And . . . well, there's always the possibility that the probability wave could resolve, and we would become one person again." She said it lightly, but the dread of considering that possibility gave her a sick feeling in the pit of her stomach.

"Yeah, well, that's really odd," Angel said. "I admit it: you're a weirdo. You're not the only one, though. I have six toes on my left foot. That's like one in three thousand. Very odd, but I've learned to cope. Want to see?" He reached down as if to untie his shoe.

She laughed in spite of herself. "I'll pass."

"You're different people," he said again. "It's who you are now. The past doesn't matter."

She was quiet for a moment. "You had something you wanted to tell me," she said.

"Right," he said. "Well, it's kind of less impressive than teleporting around the lab."

"Let me hear it."

"I'll have to show you instead."

Angel scooped up a tablet and tapped a series of commands. The lab filled with a whirring noise like a swarm of bees, the same as Sandra had heard from Angel's cases in the stadium parking lot. "Come with me," he said.

She followed him through a gate in the mesh wall into the cage. He opened a black case, and six quad-copters rose out of it in eerie precision. "These weren't at the stadium," he said, raising his voice to be heard over the hum. "I'll show you these first, so you can see the difference."

At commands from his tablet, the copters snapped into various formations: a horizontal line of six, a two-by-three stack, a rotating ring. They moved to their new positions quickly and precisely, often only inches apart, with no collisions, or even last-minute swerves. Each seemed to know exactly where the others were going to move, which she supposed made sense, since it was surely the same software controlling all of them.

"Now watch this," Angel said. He went out of the cage and returned with a handful of hula-hoops, batons, and tennis balls. He tossed a hula-hoop in the air, and all six copters flew through it, quick as lightning, before it fell back into his hand. He threw two at once, and they did the same. Then he tossed a baton in the air, end over end, and one of the copters *caught* it, balanced vertically on top of a portion of its frame that extended up between the rotors. It hovered there, adjusting its position back and forth slightly to keep the baton balanced, for all the world like a vaudeville performer with a push broom on his nose.

"Impressive," Sandra said.

"I like to think so," Angel said. "But I just want you to know what's normal, before I show you what's abnormal." He tapped the tablet, and the copter jerked suddenly higher, lofting the baton in a slowly twirling arc. Another copter caught it vertically again, dipping to cancel out the baton's spin and momentum. The copters began a game of catch, flipping the baton to one another and catching it perfectly. Angel started throwing the hula-hoops into the game, and the copters again responded seamlessly, sometimes dashing through a hoop to catch a baton on the other side. Finally, he began hurling tennis balls at the copters, trying to disrupt their rhythm, but they dodged the balls effortlessly without interrupting the game with the batons.

Sandra knew the hard part of this performance was designing the copters in the first place with the ability to move precisely and know their exact position at any moment. The tricks themselves were just mathematics; the encoding of position and velocity and spin and momentum into a simulated model of reality. Even so, it was remarkable to see.

Angel touched the tablet, and the baton and hula-hoops dropped to the floor. "One more thing."

He left the cage and wheeled in a stand with a wooden wall and a window. The window was adjustable; it could be made wider or narrower in both horizontal and vertical directions. Angel demonstrated the copters diving through the window in different configurations. When he made the window into a narrow vertical slit, the copters would actually hurl themselves sideways, momentarily losing control of their flight as they flew through the window at a ninety-degree angle, before regaining control on the other side.

"Watch what happens when I do this," Angel said. He closed the window even farther, making it impossible for the copters to fit through the gap, no matter how they oriented themselves. He tapped the tablet, but the copters didn't move. "They can detect that there's no way through," he said. "But watch this."

He sent the copters back to their case, and opened a new case. A new set of six copters flew out. "These are from the set I used at the stadium," he said. They hovered on one side of the too-small window, the same as the others had. This time, however, when Angel gave the command, all six copters dove, following each other in tight sequence. When each one reached the window, it *turned*, a rapid twisting motion like the first set had done, and reemerged on the other side.

It was less impressive than it might have been, considering all that Sandra had seen in the last twenty-four hours, but it was still dramatic. The opening was no bigger than her fist; there was no room for the copters to pass through it.

"They turned into another dimension," she said. She had seen the varcolac do essentially the same thing, and given Ryan's explanation on the mountain, she felt confident in assuming that a few of his extra curled-up dimensions were involved.

"Is this normal for you?" Angel asked. "Flitting in and out of other dimensions like taking a cab?"

Sandra smiled. "Not exactly. But I guess I've had an interesting life."

"How did this happen? This is the same hardware and the same software I've been working with for years. They clearly picked up this ability at the stadium site, but I don't see how that's possible. Even if your varcolac used some weird quantum magic to destroy the stadium in the first place, my copters weren't even there at the time."

Sandra thought about it. "It must be in the data."

"You mean the RFID data? That doesn't make sense."

"There aren't too many options. I'm going to go out on a limb and assume your copters aren't smart enough to learn a new behavior of this magnitude. So, either there was some magic quantum pixie dust at the scene that stuck to their rotors, or there was something in the data they picked up at the scene that altered their operations."

Angel returned the copters to their case. Their engines quieted, making the empty room ring with the sudden silence. "I'm going to vote for the pixie dust. We're not talking about altering their behavior to fly in figure eights. We're talking about behavior that should be impossible. I don't care what software or data you load into their onboard computers; you won't be able to make them do *that*."

"I'm not so sure." Sandra said. Her throat was dry. "Do you have anything to drink?"

"Sure." They exited the cage, and Angel led the way to a mini-fridge on a cluttered tabletop. "Coke okay?"

"Perfect." Sandra popped the tab and took a long swallow of cold sweetness. She sighed and wiped her mouth. "The only thing I can think is that your copters are somehow accessing a Higgs projector, the same as the software in my eyejacks."

"How does that work?"

"There's a wormhole in the High Energy Lab in New Jersey that's connected to a bubble universe. Somehow, Ryan Oronzi has figured out how to tap the power from it to affect the Higgs field in our universe, allowing quantum effects in the macro world. I have a copy of Oronzi's software modules from my sister that accesses that projector, allowing me to create certain quantum and probabilistic effects." She accessed a method from her eyejack display, and let go of the can of Coke. It hovered there, untouched, until she grasped it again.

"That's really freaky," Angel said.

"The point is, it's the Higgs projector that's causing the effect, not the software. I don't know how far its reach is. Considering it's another universe, though, the distance may not matter."

Angel shook his head. "It doesn't make any sense. Even if someone stored such a method on a chip, it would have to be written as a self-executing virus, and the virus would have to know how to plug in to the specific maneuver interfaces in my software. In this *version* of my software. And the only way that could happen is if I did it myself."

Sandra grinned. "Is there something you're not telling yourself?"

Angel rolled his eyes. "I'm not that crazy."

"I don't know what to tell you," Sandra said. "Maybe my sister or Dr. Oronzi would have a better idea."

"I'm sticking with the magic pixie dust theory, until you can prove it wrong."

CHAPTER 15

Ryan was ready for the drop when he and Alex materialized on the top floor of the High Energy Lab. Alex wasn't. She yelped and nearly fell over as they dropped six inches to the floor.

He laughed, and she glared at him. "What was that? We just teleported in here yesterday, and we didn't fall then. I thought you had a pretty good lock on this place."

"There's some error drift with the distance you travel," Ryan said. "Yesterday we teleported from the parking lot."

"Error drift? So we could have ended up two inches under the floor instead of over it?"

Ryan found his favorite chair—a tattered recliner they had lugged up here at his request, and sat down. "Nope. The drift is always up. The module uses a tangent plane to shortcut some of the math."

"So if I had tried to teleport to California . . . ?"

Ryan shook his head. "Disaster."

Alex's face soured. "That's a bit dangerous, isn't it? Shouldn't you adjust for the curvature of the Earth?"

"I did. That's why we came in so close."

"I mean adjust in the software, not in your head. I thought everything you designed was supposed to be oh-so-safe."

"Not safe for you. Safe for me." That was the whole point, after all. He had written the software, so he knew exactly what it would do and how far to trust it. If he hadn't written it, he wouldn't be using it at all.

Alex stared at the glowing universe in its laser-light display. She muttered something under her breath. He caught the word "hubris."

He didn't bother asking her to repeat herself. Sooner or later, everyone he got to know started treating him like he was either stupid or crazy. He liked to think it was because his intelligence was so much greater than theirs. He should call it Oronzi's Law: *Any sufficiently-advanced intelligence will be indistinguishable from insanity.* But he knew that wasn't all there was to it. The truth was, he didn't like other people very much, and they could probably tell.

"So, you don't think I should teleport, because I didn't personally write the code," Alex said.

"I didn't say that. I just said that I wouldn't, if I were in your place."

"What kind of world would that be, if nobody trusted anything they didn't make themselves? No one could build on anyone else's work. No one could even ride in the same car together. It would be ridiculous."

"You're hardly the first person to call me that."

She looked at him with an odd expression, making Ryan think he had probably let a little too much of his bitterness leak into his tone of voice. To cover his embarrassment, he took a tablet from a nearby desk and started manipulating it. "Take a look," he said.

He sent a link to her viewfeed, which she accepted. Their shared vision was overlaid with stacks of log data organized in a traditional file-system display, like a rotating carousel of file folders.

"Did you write your own operating system, too?" she asked.

Ryan ignored her. Of course he hadn't, but then, an operating system wasn't likely to kill him, either. He cycled through the files until he found what he was looking for. "Here's the log data from the morning of the demo. I'm going to graph the Higgs particle count over time." A graph appeared in the air, showing a high quantity of Higgs activity, peaking suddenly from 11:08 to 11:14. The rest was empty except for a little random noise near the bottom, like a sandy beach with a mountain peak suddenly jutting out of it. "This matches the time that the varcolac was loose. Just as we would expect."

"What about the previous night?"

Ryan found the appropriate log and updated the graph. The peak disappeared, leaving a nearly empty graph.

"No activity at all?" Alex asked.

"Just background radiation. Nothing out of the ordinary," Ryan said. "But look at this."

Ryan stabbed the tablet, and the graph changed. He filtered out the peak from the morning of the demo, and graphed just the background radiation over the whole time interval, between the stadium explosion and the demo the next morning. He zoomed in on the bottom of the graph, taking a closer look at what had previously appeared to be random. From this perspective, there were two clearly-defined spikes. One was at 11:14 in the morning, in the last moment before the varcolac disappeared. The other was at 9:35 the night before, when the stadium had imploded.

Alex whistled. "I see it. That's consistent with a singlet sent back in time from the demo on Monday morning to the stadium the previous night. You were right." She cast a fearful look at the spinning universe display. "Are you sure that thing's still contained?"

"Of course I'm not. I've been telling Babington for weeks that I can't keep it contained indefinitely."

The reminder turned Ryan's attention back to the tablet with a sudden stab of fear. He had been checking on it frequently, at least once an hour, but it didn't make him feel safe. He had updated his alarms to detect the kind of subtle strategy the varcolac had used to escape last time, but it was clever. What if it had breached the barrier so subtly that it had escaped without him even knowing it?

He reviewed the latest logs. Everything seemed to be in order. His protocols were still in place, with no indication that any of the values he was measuring from the wormhole had so much as hiccupped. It didn't make him relax, exactly, but there was no immediate reason for alarm.

"It's still contained," he said. "For now."

"Can I see?" Alex asked.

Ryan regarded her, suspicious. She was asking to see the foundation of all his research; the equations and concepts behind his control over the baby universe. How well did he know her, really? She didn't have clearance even to be in this room, never mind to look at the technical basis of his work.

"Why do you want to see it?" he asked.

She raised an eyebrow slightly. "I just want to understand what we're dealing with. I want to help, and the more I know, the better I can help."

It occurred to Ryan just how young and pretty she was. He had never much liked pretty women; he always felt like they were laughing at him behind his back. She was manipulating him, trying to make him give up his data. "It's classified," he said.

She took a step back and gave him a sideways look, the one people gave him when they thought he was acting crazy. "You brought me in here."

He shook his head to clear it. What was wrong with him? "You're right," he said. "I'm sorry. I'm just not used to working too closely with other people."

"You run a lab full of people."

"Well . . . when it comes down to it, Nicole runs the lab. I like to concentrate on the math. I get my best work done here at night, when no one else is around."

"I have to go now," Alex said. Her pretty face showed confusion and pity rather than anger. He hated her for that.

"Okay," he said.

"I'll see you tomorrow." She disappeared.

Ryan collapsed back on his chair and held his head in his hands. What was wrong with him? Alex wasn't trying to steal anything from him. He had followed her in his car and practically insisted she come with him. It wasn't her fault the varcolac had broken out while she was on stage. Or was it? Could she have planned it that way, so as to kill Secretary Falk?

Ridiculous. He shoved his fists into his eyes and rubbed them. He wasn't thinking clearly. He wasn't getting enough sleep. To distract himself, he brought up the logs again. They were quiet; barely any movement in the measured values at all. Had the varcolac given up? That didn't seem likely.

Ryan tried to put himself into the varcolac's perspective. What did it want? Why was it trying to break into their world? Just to kill people? Or was it trying to learn something? He knew the varcolac was intelligent, incredibly so. He knew now that it had been manipulating him even as he kept it contained, influencing him through the equations it solved for him. But had it really been manipulating him, or simply communicating to him? What if it had recognized him as the one human truly capable of communicating at its level of intelligence?

His mind returned again to his childhood dream, that he was in fact the progeny of a superior alien race, planted here in this human body. He had always known it was a ludicrous fantasy, but it seemed to explain so much—not just his intelligence, which was so far beyond anyone else's, but also how awkward and isolated he felt, and how incomprehensible human social interaction so often seemed. Only in lecture mode, when he was explaining his ideas to others, did he feel remotely comfortable.

But what if it wasn't so ludicrous? What if Ryan's mind was in fact not a human mind, but a varcolac's? He had never belonged with the people surrounding him; he was something different, something greater. Maybe he was destined for something far beyond the simple fame of a smarter-than-average scientist.

The varcolac wasn't evil, after all. It was just intelligent. Now that he thought about it, it had been the Secret Service agents that had attacked first, not the varcolac. It had only defended itself. When Alex started firing, it fought back, but it wasn't the aggressor. It had just been trying to communicate. Though there was the baseball stadium. If the varcolac really had destroyed that, as seemed to be the case, it could hardly be considered self-defense.

He returned to the logs surrounding the time of the stadium explosion, scrutinizing the data for anything he had previously missed, looking for some indication that it had been an attempt by the varcolac to communicate. How would a quantum creature know what destruction it had caused from a human perspective? Did it understand the concept of human life and death?

Ryan grew lost in the work, drinking Cokes from his fridge and eating potato chips when he got hungry, barely aware of the taste as they slid down his throat. He studied the times right around the Higgs singlet spikes, filtering by frequency. And then he found it: a barely discernible pattern at the edge of the EHF band.

But it wasn't quite what he was expecting. Two hours *before* the Higgs singlet spike that had destroyed the baseball stadium, the wormhole had registered a burst of EHF energy. The more he looked at it, the more he was sure that it wasn't just a random fluctuation. It looked purposeful. He couldn't say why, exactly, but he trusted his intuitions where mathematical patterns were concerned. To be certain, he ran it through a Shannon entropy plot to measure its randomness. No question. It wasn't just some natural phenomenon; there was information encoded there. It *meant* something.

He worked all night, and by the morning, he had the answer. Encapsulated in the tiny burst of data was a representation of the location of the blast and its exact time. Direction, distance, and time were encoded in terms of Higgs particle wavelength, amplitude, and frequency, and measured from the wormhole and the time of the varcolac's escape the next morning. It hadn't been easy to crack the code, but once he had worked it out, it was irrefutable. It was a signal, or possibly just a measure of the varcolac's own thought process, but it was there. If he had known all this ahead of time, he could have actually *predicted* the place and time of the stadium blast two hours before it had happened.

Ryan searched the rest of the data that had been gathered from the wormhole in the days since, looking for similar patterns. He found only one. It had appeared in the logs an hour earlier, just a tiny packet of energy at the same EM frequency as the first signal. He decoded it using the same method, and came up with a location, sixty-two miles away, and a time, 11:26 AM. He checked his watch. It was already past 11:00.

Ryan's body surged with adrenaline. Did this mean what he thought it did? He identified the location using an online mapping program: Chelsey Funeral Parlor, in Media, Pennsylvania. He didn't recognize it. He had been expecting another large population gathering, like a sky-scraper or a sporting event. A funeral parlor? Why would the varcolac target that?

Whatever its significance, it wasn't going to be there for much longer.

CHAPTER 16

Alex hated funeral parlors. All the furniture and decorations were unreal, larger than life, like a magazine photo instead of a real place. The flowers were too bright. The tables and divans along the walls were so polished they looked like plastic. The staff, too, seemed fake, sympathy rolling automatically off their tongues in practiced, meaningless phrases. Even the air seemed dreamlike, free of dust and speared with artful beams of sunlight.

Alex wasn't technically there at all—she was watching through Sandra's viewfeed—but her brain couldn't tell the difference. If she weren't so accustomed to it, it would have been disconcerting to be trapped in someone else's point of view, unable to change the angle with a flick of her eyes. But Alex had been watching viewfeeds since elementary school, and her eyes tracked with Sandra's by habit, moving so quickly that it gave her brain the impression that she was the one in control.

She was, in reality, sitting in Sandra's apartment, staying away from the windows. Teleportation meant she could come and go secretly, and she would be able to escape quickly if anyone showed up at the door, but she still didn't want to be seen. Besides Sandra's place, she'd been spending a lot of time in the woods at Ridley Creek State Park, a few miles away from her parents' house, staying off the main paths and using the invisibility module to stay out of sight. Being invisible was a liability in any more public place, since people would try to walk through her, close doors in her face, or even drive their cars right at her. Which was why Alex wasn't at the funeral right now—it would be too crowded. The chance of her accidentally being discovered was too great. Besides, she didn't want to be there.

Alex could disconnect from the funeral feed at any time, but she knew she wouldn't. It was hard to bear now, but if she didn't at least watch her own father's funeral, the loss of it would haunt her forever. It made her feel trapped. Maybe she should have gone after all, stayed invisible and tried to keep to empty corners. If she had been there in person, she could have decided on her own where to look, where to sit, how to respond, instead of being caught in Sandra's viewpoint.

Sandra stood in a line with their mother and Claire, greeting the guests, accepting their platitudes with good grace. Their mother shook hands and endured kisses with stiff resignation, her polite expression clearly strained. Claire, on the other hand, greeted each guest with the same poise and practiced gravity as the funeral director, her shining blond hair flowing over the shoulders of her expensive black dress.

The two sisters seemed to fit together: Claire and Alessandra, one blond and the other dark. Watching through Sandra's eyes, Alex felt like an outsider. The truth was, she had always thought of Sandra as the real sister, the original Alessandra. She, Alex, was the interloper, the girl who had suddenly appeared when their father was accused of murder. She was the one who had hidden away with her father, had fought the varcolac, and had been forever changed by the experience. When Sandra—the real Alessandra—returned, Alex had felt like a stranger in her own home. A freak of nature. A quantum mistake.

On second thought, maybe it was better that she wasn't there at the funeral in person. She might have snatched a too-perfect vase from a too-perfect table and smashed it on the too-perfect floor.

Two uniformed police officers, a man and a woman, came through the line, friends of Sandra. Sandra greeted them with hugs and called them Nathan and Danielle. Their sympathy seemed sincere. Alex supposed police officers grew used to funerals and knew how to talk and act. Another woman, also in uniform, hung back and didn't go through the line. Sandra kept glancing at her nervously.

"Who's the woman in the back?" Alex asked.

"Detective Messinger," Sandra said under her breath, after accepting yet another well-meaning hug by a distant relative. Their mother's family was large and mostly lived in the area, though their father had never gotten on very well with them.

"Is she the one who's been interrogating you?"

"Yes. I think she half-believes me about the varcolac, but she could just be trying to gain my confidence."

Alex suspected there were probably other officers and agents there in normal clothes, blending into the crowd. Watching to see if she would make an appearance, perhaps. Alex had no experience on the street with identifying cops, and there were enough of her parents' friends she didn't recognize that she couldn't be certain.

The greeting line seemed endless. Alex didn't know how her mother and Sandra could stand it. Finally, everyone filed into the small chapel.

While the organ was playing something somber, a ping notified Alex of an incoming call. She ignored it at first, but it kept pinging over and over, evidence that whoever it was was calling over and over. She checked and saw that it was Ryan Oronzi. She rolled her eyes and answered it.

"Ever hear of just leaving a message?" she said.

"Alex? This is Ryan."

"I know who it is. There's this new invention—you might have heard of it. Instead of calling over and over, you can just send me a message, and I don't have to interrupt my father's funeral to answer you."

"Listen to me. The varcolac . . . wait. Did you say funeral?"

"Yes. My dad's funeral is going on as we speak."

"At the Chelsey Funeral Home?"

"Yes."

"In Media?"

"Yes! Did you just call to check the address? If you were planning to go, you're a bit late."

The organ music stopped, and the minister walked toward the front. His hair was long and gray, drawn back into a leather tie. He wore ecclesiastical black with a traditional white collar.

"They have to leave," Ryan said. He sounded agitated.

"What are you talking about?"

"I found some data. It points to that funeral home. The varcolac is going to destroy it."

"What? I thought you said the varcolac was contained!"

"It *is* contained. It sends particles back in time, remember? Sometime in the future, it's going to break out and send a Higgs singlet back in time to this moment. Can you imagine the precision and understanding it takes to create the effect you want through the chain reaction of a single particle? It's incredible."

"I'm not interested in how incredible it is! Is there anything we can do?"

"We can . . . well. Never mind."

"What?"

"There's less than a minute left. Not much we can do, at this point."

At the funeral, the minister turned to face the assembled guests. He had no eyes. Where his eyes should have been was just blank, featureless skin.

Alex leaped to her feet. "Sandra!" she shouted, just before her viewfeed went black.

She flicked the viewfeed aside, revealing her true surroundings: the front room of Sandra's two-room apartment. She frantically tried to reconnect to Sandra's vision, but she couldn't. The varcolac's presence must be interfering with the signal. The alternative—that the varcolac had already destroyed Sandra and her system with it—didn't bear thinking. Alex had to get to that funeral home, and she needed to do it now.

She brought up the last image she had received from Sandra, the horrible, eyeless face of the minister staring out at the guests. She knew Sandra's precise location as of seconds before, but she might have moved by now. If she teleported there, she might appear right in the middle of someone else's body. Or she might arrive just as the building exploded.

It didn't matter. Her sister was in danger. She had to do it, and she had to do it now.

Sandra stared into the eyeless face of the varcolac, at first too startled to react. It was happening again. She would be captured or killed, and all these people with her. She thought of her mother losing another loved one, or else dying herself. She was not going to let that happen.

The varcolac swiveled its head toward her, seeming to stare at her despite its lack of eyes. It opened the minister's mouth and groaned.

It was an awful sound. It was as if someone had taken the mouth and throat of a corpse and played air through it with a bellows. It was the most terrifying sound Sandra had ever heard. The funeral director approached the minister, solicitous as always, but clearly disturbed by the varcolac's face. "Sir, is everything all right? Do you need help? Should we call 911?"

The varcolac didn't even look at him. It raised a hand, and the director cried out and clutched at his chest. He collapsed to the floor, shuddered once, and then lay still, his eyes staring out at nothing. The room erupted then, guests scrambling over one another and trying to push out the doors. Sandra stood, but she didn't run. She was a police officer, sworn to protect the people of Pennsylvania. Besides, it couldn't be a coincidence that it had shown up here, of all places. It had come for her.

She didn't have her firearm—she was suspended, and besides, it hadn't seemed appropriate for a funeral. She didn't think it would do much good against the varcolac anyway. She had seen how Alex had fought in her demo, and knew she had some of those same capabilities available through the software Alex had copied for her, but by the time she figured any of them out, she could be dead.

Her mother still sat in her seat, staring frozen up at the varcolac. Claire was tugging at her arm, looking panicked. "Mom, you need to leave," Sandra said. "Leave now."

Suddenly Alex was there next to her. "Keep moving!" Alex said. "Don't stay in one place." She disappeared and reappeared across the room.

The varcolac advanced and raised its hand toward Sandra. No time. Sandra chose a spot on the other side of it and teleported. To her, it seemed as though the room had suddenly spun around. Across the room, where she had just been standing, a young woman that looked just like her clutched at her chest and fell to the floor.

"Alex!" Sandra screamed. But no, it wasn't Alex. The woman was wearing the dark dress that she herself was wearing, and her hair was put up in the same style. The woman on the floor was *her*.

Disoriented, Sandra looked around and saw Alex, still very much alive. Then who had just died?

Suddenly, Sandra understood. The varcolac was a quantum creature, a probabilistic being. Like a quantum particle, it acted at more than one time and place at once, as part of a probability waveform. It had attacked her both before and after she teleported, and so just like her father, she had split. One version of her had teleported and appeared here. The other version had died.

Sandra flushed with horror and rage. She wanted to tear the varcolac to pieces, but she didn't know what to do. How could such a creature even be harmed? It could kill every person here with a gesture.

For that matter, why was it even here? If it had the power to destroy a baseball stadium, why didn't it just destroy the whole building, or the whole block? Why weren't they already dead?

Nathan and Danielle, both in uniform, advanced on the varcolac, spreading out and drawing their sidearms. "Police!" Danielle shouted. "Hands on your head!"

"No!" Sandra yelled. "Get out of here! It'll kill you!"

They either didn't hear or didn't listen. Danielle raised her weapon and fired three shots at the varcolac, center mass. It blurred, and the bullets passed through it, punching holes in the paneling at the back of the room. The sound was deafening in the enclosed space.

The varcolac raised its hand toward Danielle, but suddenly Alex was there, standing between them. There was a brilliant flash of light. Alex fell back a step, but stayed on her feet. She pointed at the wall, and the varcolac flew toward it as if gravity had suddenly been turned on its side. The minister's body hit the wall with an audible crunch. It fell to the floor, and for a moment, Sandra thought the fight was over, but the minister stood again. One of its arms was twisted at an angle, and it dragged one leg behind it, but it came at them, eyeless and terrifying.

Then Sandra saw something that took her breath away. She called her sister's name and pointed. Behind Alex, Nathan and Danielle's faces were also covered with blank skin where their eyes had been just a moment ago. All three varcolacs advanced, surrounding them.

Ryan could see what was happening in the funeral parlor through Alex's viewfeed, but there was nothing he could do about it, not directly. If he teleported there, he might be killed. Then who would devise the next equation to trap the varcolac? He was like a general, too valuable to be risked on the front line. He wanted them to survive, but when it came down to it, his life was worth more than theirs.

The crazy thing was, as far as he could tell, the varcolac was still trapped in the wormhole. The creatures attacking Sandra and Alex at that moment had somehow been manufactured by the varcolac in the future, through the Higgs sequence it had sent back in time. Or that it *would* send back in time. Ryan had underestimated the complexity of the sequence of particle interactions the varcolac could initiate with a Higgs singlet. He had imagined it doing the equivalent of sending a billiard ball back in time with exactly the direction and spin to impact each of the other balls and win the game—a difficult enough concept. Instead, the particle it had sent back in time had initiated a sequence that had created an instance of the varcolac itself, an extension of its own intelligence and physical presence.

Ryan was in awe. This creature had such mastery over time and space that it could recreate the pattern of its own existence with the chain reaction of a single, precisely aimed particle. Which meant that it understood its own configuration down to every quark and gluon. It could replicate some portion of itself, and these replications were mere extensions of its mind. Could it be that it was a species of one, communicating itself across the universes and the ages? Its awareness and experience must be vast.

But it wasn't invincible. It was no god, free to rewrite the laws of nature as it saw fit. It was confined by the wormhole, at least to some extent. It had been banished from the world when its source of power was removed. There was still some chance that they would be able to defeat it.

On the other hand, they couldn't hold it back forever. They had to come to terms with the fact that varcolac would, eventually, win. If it was sending particles back in time from some later date, that meant it was going to escape from the wormhole—something that had been seeming increasingly inevitable anyway. It occurred to Ryan that perhaps, instead of fighting it, he should be helping it. If there was no way to win, wouldn't it be better to join the winning side?

But no, that was ridiculous. He didn't even know what the varcolac wanted. He couldn't trust it to reward him for helping it, if it even noticed that he had. He had to keep it contained as long as possible. In the time that remained, he would study it, collecting as much data as possible about how it worked and what it could and couldn't do. That way, if there was some way to defeat it, he would find it. And if not, he would at least know better what he was dealing with.

Sandra shouted her friends' names, but it was no use. They were varcolacs now, or at least its puppets. Danielle pointed her gun at Alex and fired. Alex blurred, just like the varcolac had, but Nathan disappeared and reappeared behind Alex, trapping her between them. Alex blurred again just as he fired.

Was it three varcolacs? Or was the same creature inhabiting all three bodies? It hardly mattered. The varcolacs advanced on Alex from all sides. Two of Sandra's friends were going to kill her sister, or else her sister was going to kill them. Though she supposed her friends were probably already dead.

The varcolacs raised their hands, firing shot after shot of whatever invisible energy they used to stop people's hearts. Alex blocked with some kind of energy field of her own, producing more of those blinding bursts of light. "Sandra!" she shouted. "Get Mom out of here!"

Their mother still crouched next to Sandra's body, watching the fight with an expression of terror and rage. Claire was there, holding her back. Whether their mother was foolhardy enough to try to attack the varcolacs, Sandra didn't know, but she might risk anything if her children were in danger. Sandra teleported to her and wrapped her arms around her. She didn't know for sure that this would work, but so far the software governing the teleportation seemed to be able to account for her clothing and anything she was carrying. Sure enough, the room around them disappeared and was replaced by Sandra's old bedroom, in her parents' house.

"I'll be back soon," Sandra said. Her mother started to protest, but Sandra teleported away without listening. She reappeared in the funeral parlor and grabbed Claire, teleporting her away, too. It was the best she could do for them. When she returned again, Alex was still fighting hard, a sheen of sweat glinting from her forehead. Sandra spotted a familiar person hiding behind a table, cowering with her head in her hands.

"Detective Messinger?" Sandra said.

Messinger looked up. Her eyes were wild. "Did you see it?" she said. "Did you see what it did to those people?"

"Stay down," Sandra said.

"I'm a *cop*," Messinger said. "But I couldn't . . . how can anyone fight such a thing?"

Sandra didn't answer. She was watching Alex, who was now sending folding chairs flying at the varcolacs. The varcolacs flickered and teleported around the room, avoiding the attack. Alex was amazing, but she couldn't keep it up forever. And how could they win against a creature that could simply find more bodies to inhabit and press into service?

Sandra felt something cold and hard being pressed into her hand. She looked down. Messinger was holding out a Glock 19, her service weapon. Sandra snatched it up. She teleported and reappeared next to Alex, immediately firing at the nearest varcolac. The varcolac blurred to avoid it.

"How do you block their attacks?" Sandra shouted.

"Turn your automated system on!" Alex shouted back, just before teleporting again to a spot behind one of the varcolacs.

Sandra quickly paged through the menu options on her eyejack system. There it was—Automated Defense. It made sense. A human couldn't react fast enough to choose the "diffract" function after a bullet was fired; they needed software to detect the attack and react to it. She toggled the option on, just in time. A varcolac appeared in front of her and a flash of light sparked through the air as the system blocked its attack.

"We have to get out of here," Sandra shouted. "They'll just keep coming."

"It'll find us, wherever we go," Alex said.

"Then what do we do?"

Alex didn't answer. She clutched at her chest, and fell to her knees, her face pulled back in a rictus of pain.

"No!" Sandra shouted. But then she saw that there was another Alex standing next to her, and another, and another, until there were at least a dozen.

"Surround them," one of the Alexes said. "Grab hold of them."

The Alexes teleported into positions surrounding each of the varco-lacs—Nathan, Danielle, and the minister—and wrapped their arms around them. Bright light flashed and sparked, like lightning arcing through the spaces between their bodies. Sandra understood what she was doing—using the shield as a weapon, disrupting whatever energy pattern allowed the varcolacs to inhabit and control these material forms. It worked, after a fashion. The two officers and the minister writhed in the flashes and fell to the ground. All three of them now had eyes again. They looked like their original selves. They were also dead.

Sandra rushed to Danielle's body, touching her, listening for her breath or some indication that she might still be alive. She was warm, flushed even, but had no pulse.

"We need to leave," one of the Alexes said.

Sandra looked up at her, furious. "These were my friends!"

"I didn't kill them," Alex said.

"They're still dead! Don't you even care?"

"I care about keeping you alive. I care about letting Mom know we're okay."

"You call this okay?" Sandra waved her hand, indicating the multiple Alexes. But there were fewer of them now, only five or six. As she watched, another Alex disappeared.

"I'm converging again," Alex said. "It doesn't last long."

"You've done this before?" But even as she said it, Sandra knew Alex *had* done it before. She could remember the lab at Lockheed Martin when they had first gotten that particular module to work, the thrill of dis-covery, the promise of a bright future for their department. It was still under development, and so hadn't been included in the demo. But Sandra hadn't been there. Those were Alex's memories she was seeing.

Sandra felt the blood rush to her face. Alex had been a fool to experiment with such things, knowing what she knew. Didn't she know what was at stake? Just because something could be done didn't mean it should be.

But no. She wasn't a fool. That's what Sandra didn't understand about science. It wasn't an option to leave a discovery hidden, like a treasure buried in sand. The truth was out there. You couldn't know that things like teleportation were possible and do nothing about it. If you did nothing, you had no power—not over other people who didn't have the same moral standards, and not over varcolacs who could appear without warning out of nowhere. It was much better to have the power and knowledge and decide what to do with it than to wring your hands and hope nobody else would discover what was possible.

For a brief moment, Sandra could see the room—and in fact, the world—through Alex's eyes.

"No!" Sandra yelled the word out loud and jumped to her feet. She was Sandra, *Sandra*, not Alex. Those were not her memories, and they were not her thoughts.

Alex's probability wave had collapsed, and all the other versions of herself had converged back into the whole. Sandra took a step back, away from her sister. *She* had almost converged with Alex as well. In truth, she was like those others, wasn't she? Simply a probability split that had stayed unresolved a lot longer than it should. But she didn't feel disposable. She didn't want to cease to exist as a separate individual.

Sandra clenched her teeth. "Never do that again," she said.

Alex looked bewildered. "Do what? Save both of our lives?"

"That splitting thing. It's unnatural. You'll only make it worse."

"If you had a better idea for fighting off three varcolacs, you should have mentioned it a little earlier." Alex gave a small laugh. "In fact, if splitting wasn't possible, you wouldn't even be here."

There it was. Sandra felt tears rising and fought them back down. Alex was staking her claim as the real Alessandra, the true daughter. She had been the heroine, the sister everyone loved, certainly the one her father had loved best. Sandra was nothing more than an inconvenient copy, not quite as good as the original.

"You might as well just assimilate me now and get it over with," Sandra said. "You could do it if you wanted to, couldn't you?"

"I didn't mean that. We wouldn't either of us be here, if splitting weren't possible. I wasn't trying to say . . . and no, I couldn't do it. And I wouldn't want to." Alex stepped forward and took Sandra's hands. Sandra flinched, but her sister didn't let go. "We're different people," Alex said. "We always will be."

"And if getting rid of this varcolac for good means that we converge to a single person again?"

"It won't come to that," Alex said.

Sandra traced her eyes over Alex's familiar features: the same height, the same hair, the same build, the same face. People without a twin didn't know what it was like, to look across the room and see yourself looking back. To have a constant, living example of what you might have been if your choices had been different. Just by being alive, Alex was a subtle judgment of who Sandra was. Even real twins didn't know that experience like she did, when the person across the room really *was* her. No matter where she went, no matter how far from Alex she ran, her entire life would always be defined in some way by the inescapable presence of her sister. Her other self.

CHAPTER 17

Alex lay on her bed in her old room in her parents' house, shaking uncontrollably. The adrenaline that had flooded her through the battle with the varcolacs had drained away, and now the terror threatened to overwhelm her. She had come so close to death. And she wasn't safe now. Far from it. The varcolac was so alien, so implacable, and she knew she hadn't killed it. What if it appeared, right now, in her room? She didn't think she would have the strength even to rise from her bed.

The way it possessed human bodies like that, killing them and using them like macabre puppets, was the stuff of nightmares. A familiar friend, an ally and a source of safety, turned suddenly evil. Like a child looking up at her father's face in a crowded room, only to discover that it wasn't her father at all.

Downstairs, Sandra talked with their mother and Claire, providing encouragement and comfort. Sandra was good at that. Alex never had been. She would find her own way to help.

They couldn't just stay here and wait for the next attack. They had to find a way to go on the offensive. The varcolac was so powerful, with abilities so far beyond theirs, that it would eventually kill them if it kept trying. And then what? Would it stop with them, or would it go on killing? If they couldn't stop it, would anyone? What if it wanted to remove all potential for intelligent competition? She didn't think there was a limit to how many it could kill. They had to find a weakness, a way they could actually defeat it instead of just barely staying alive.

Ryan was brilliant, but unpredictable. She wasn't sure she could trust him anymore. He claimed not to be able to destroy the wormhole or keep the varcolac contained there, but from the way he talked, she wasn't even sure he wanted to. He seemed to admire it. They needed help from someone better than that, someone who had defeated it before. They needed her father.

The thought drove a swell of tears that felt like it started in her stomach and forced its way out through her mouth and eyes. She cried helplessly for a while. The lives of her family, maybe even the whole world, were depending on her, and she didn't have a clue how to do it. Every physicist who had studied the varcolac the first time was dead. Her father, his colleague Brian Vanderhall . . . and one more.

There *had* been another person involved, Vanderhall's partner in science and in crime. And she was still alive.

When Sandra came upstairs, she found her sister lying on her old bed, staring at the ceiling. Sandra collapsed on the other bed and let out a breath. It felt surreal to be lying there together, in their old room, as if it was fifteen years earlier and they still lived there, sleeping in the same room and sharing each other's clothes.

They lay there in silence for a long while, alone with their thoughts. Finally, Sandra said, "Why are we still alive?"

"What do you mean?" Alex asked.

"That thing destroyed the entire baseball stadium. If it can do that, why didn't it just snap its fingers and kill the lot of us? Or destroy the whole funeral parlor?"

Alex considered this. "It's not all-powerful," she said. "We don't know what it's capable of, so we tend to treat it like it's omnipotent. We think it must have been easy for it to destroy the stadium, but it might not have been. It may have required a lot of energy that wasn't easy to collect, or else it took advantage of a particular opportunity that it can't always duplicate. We don't know its limitations, but it must have them. The important thing is that we find out what they are."

Sandra nodded, but it was all just speculation. How could they ever know the varcolac's limitations? Finally, she voiced the issue that was troubling her the most. "I died back there," she said. "A copy of me. When the varcolac attacked, I tried to teleport, and I split into two. Part of me got away. But it killed the other one."

"I saw that," Alex said. "But it was the copy that died. Not you."

"The copy *is* me," Sandra said. "She didn't live very long, but she was me. She and I could just as easily have been swapped, and it would be her lying here with you, and me lying dead on the floor."

"You can't think that way," Alex said. "The copy was someone else, just like *I'm* someone else. Just be glad you're not the one who's dead."

Sandra frowned. The copy's body had disappeared shortly after it died, but she couldn't dismiss it so easily. She wanted to forget it had ever existed, but the memory of it haunted her. That version of her had tried in vain to teleport, fumbling with the interface, and had died where she stood, feeling the varcolac's energy rush into her and stop her heart. Had she felt pain? Did she know she was dying? Did she realize that another version of herself had survived? If so, it would be scant comfort. Maybe Alex was right, and that other person didn't matter, but it didn't seem that way to Sandra.

"Is that how you feel about me?" Sandra asked quietly.

Alex had opened her bedside table and was rummaging through its contents: magazines and gaudy teenage jewelry and half-finished crafts. "What?"

"If I died, would you dismiss me as easily? Just a copy of yourself gone bad?"

Alex looked up. "Of course not. Sandra, you have a life separate from me. You're a person in your own right. That copy was never its own person, not really. Forget about it."

A person in her own right. There was an achievement. "Nice," Sandra said.

"What are you upset about?"

"Nothing."

"No," Alex said. "You're angry, and I want to know why."

"Why? You think I should be dancing with joy that you deign to consider me a real person?"

"What are you talking about?"

"Does it even occur to you that *I* may have some claim to be Alessandra Kelley? That just because you're the one who followed in Dad's footsteps doesn't make me the unnatural clone?"

The words rang in the small room as the two sisters stared at each other. "All the time," Alex said.

The silence stretched.

"Well, then, what now?" Sandra said. "If we're just supposed to move on with our lives, what do we do? I'm going to go out on a limb and guess that your little duplication trick didn't actually kill the varcolac. Which means it'll be back."

Alex waited a moment before answering, but then she seemed to shake herself. "The first thing we need to do is copy the Higgs projector interface over to Mom and Claire."

"Why? You expect them to fight?"

"No. But the varcolac possessed three people in the funeral home, all of whom are now dead. If its goal is to kill you and me, then why didn't it just possess *us*?"

"Because the Higgs projector package protects us?" Sandra asked.

"That's what I think. Regardless, I want them to have it, and I want them to know how to use it."

"Shouldn't we tell Ryan what happened?"

Alex's expression soured. "I don't know how far we can trust him."

"I didn't trust him in the first place," Sandra said. "What has he done recently?"

"He knew the varcolac was going to attack," Alex said. "He called and warned me."

"He *warned* you?"

"Yeah, like five seconds before it showed up and started killing people. He knew it was there, and he knew what it was doing, but he didn't come and help. He didn't fight with us."

"Maybe he was trying to stop it from where he was, in the lab," Sandra said.

"Or maybe he was helping it."

"What? Why would he do that?"

Alex shook her head. "I don't know. But you should have heard him. He was talking really weird. All about how amazing and smart the varcolac is. Like he admired it."

"But Ryan's the one who knows the most about it," Sandra objected. "He's the only one who knows how to contain it. We have to work with him."

"Maybe," Alex said. She looked pensive.

"What do you mean? Who else is there?"

"What we need is another physicist. Someone with experience building a Higgs projector. Someone who understands splitting and has experience with trying to make changes backward in time. Someone who might be able to understand the varcolac and what it wants."

Sandra shook her head. "There's no such person. Dad is gone. He's not coming back."

"Not Dad. Someone like him."

"You mean Ryan's lab assistant? Nicole something?"

"No way. I'm not sure how much she knows, but regardless, I don't think she'll be inclined to help us."

"Then who? Nobody besides Dad and Ryan has any experience with . . . oh." It hit her. "You mean Jean Massey."

Alex nodded slowly.

"But Jean's in prison. A lifetime sentence for murdering her colleague and trying to murder her own baby girl."

"Doesn't mean I can't visit her," Alex said.

153

Sandra considered that. Jean Massey was, to a large extent, the reason that she and Alex were different people and her father was now dead. It had been Brian Vanderhall who had first discovered the Higgs projector, and through it, the varcolac, but Jean had been his partner. According to her, it had been mostly his work that had accomplished it. She had killed him, however, sparking a sequence of events that resulted in their father being arrested and tried for the murder, while Sandra and Claire and Sean and their mother were kidnapped and nearly killed by the varcolac.

If not for Jean, their father would still be alive. If not for Jean, however, Alessandra would never have split, and either Sandra or Alex would never have existed. Though she supposed neither of them would have existed, when it came down to it. Alessandra would have, but she would have never heard of a varcolac, and her life would have been very different. Sandra sighed. Did other people have so much trouble defining their own selves? She couldn't even say with certainty that she was the same person she had been five minutes ago. Who exactly was Sandra Kelley?

"I guess it doesn't hurt to talk," she said. "But Alex, you can't go. Every policeman and federal agent in the state is looking for you."

"But they're not looking for you. I'll take your ID and call myself Sandra."

Sandra frowned. "It'll raise red flags. They'll want to know why I was there."

"So? Is it a crime to visit someone in prison?"

"They think you and Dad were part of a conspiracy. They'll think I'm part of it, too."

Alex raised her hands and then let them drop. "I don't believe this. You're still trying to preserve your reputation here? What part of 'a creature from another universe is trying to kill us' are you not understanding here?"

Sandra felt a flush rise to her cheeks. She wasn't being selfish; she was trying to be practical. "Fine," she said. "Do what you want."

"Excellent," Alex said. "I'll go first thing tomorrow."

Ryan hated his body. He was tired, his eyes hurt from studying log files and pattern data, and he felt sick from all the Coke and chips he had consumed. The physical body was so weak and needy, a hindrance to the true life of the mind. It had to be fed, and it had to be rested—several hours out of every day, wasted—and it had to be coddled with nutrients and vitamins and exercise to keep it in working order. It was an obstacle. Worse, it would someday betray him completely, snuffing out the bright candle of his true self. It was a failing of the body, not of the consciousness. He envied the varcolac's unencumbered existence. If the technology had existed to upload his mind into a computer, Ryan would have done it in an instant.

He wondered if the varcolac had ever had a physical body. He still wasn't clear if there was a race of varcolacs, or just a single intelligence. Had it been born out of the complexity of the particle interactions of the universe? Or had there once been a physical race of creatures, living their sad, short little lives and then dying, their consciousnesses dragged screaming into the void? What if one of these creatures, a scientist and inventor, had discovered a way to imprint his consciousness on the fabric of the universe? That might have been millions, even billions of years ago. And now it was here, at the edge of his world, trying to make contact. What if the varcolac knew the secret to doing this and could teach Ryan? What if he could project *his* mind onto the universe and live forever?

Ryan brought up the module that controlled the energy pattern keeping the varcolac contained beyond the wormhole. It felt somehow wrong to keep such an amazing creature confined. There was so much he could learn from it, if he could only communicate with it. In fact, as Alex had shown him, there was so much he already *had* learned from it. So many of the Higgs projector applications—teleportation, invisibility—had been made possible through the equations the varcolac had solved for him.

Ryan loaded a simple pattern on his tablet, one of the earliest he had used to shape the wormhole when he had first created the baby universe. If he replaced one of the incredibly complex patterns he had been forced to devise with this simple one, the varcolac would escape in a moment. Just a push of a button, and it would be done. The varcolac would be out, free to do as it pleased. It apparently wanted the Kelley family destroyed, but that didn't mean it would destroy him. Ryan was a kindred mind, practically a varcolac himself in spirit.

It was going to escape anyway. It was inevitable. It had sent the singlet back in time from the future to cause the attack on the funeral parlor. It must, therefore, at some time in the near future, be free to act outside the wormhole. And if the varcolac was going to escape anyway, wouldn't it be better for Ryan to let it loose on his own terms? He could establish himself as an ally, rather than an enemy.

But he wasn't going to do it. It was foolish, an insane choice that couldn't be taken back again. The varcolac might communicate with him, but it might just as soon kill him the moment it was out. Ryan sat with the pattern on his tablet, however, unable to set it aside, as the minutes ticked by toward evening. It was like looking over the edge of a cliff and thinking about jumping. Just imagining how easy it would be to simply vault over the railing. He had no intention of setting the varcolac free. But his hand hovered over the controls anyway, flirting with the idea. Of course, he wouldn't do it. He drew his hand away.

Or at least, he tried. He *intended* to pull it away. But there was his hand, touching the button, pressing it. Releasing the varcolac into the world.

He stood frozen with his finger still on the button, staring at his hand like it belonged to someone else. He couldn't believe what he had just done. He wanted to go check the logs, to see if the complex patterns of equations had really been replaced by the simple one, but he was finding it hard to move.

He hadn't meant to just let it out. It was stupid. Suicidal. His childish dream that he was a superhuman seemed insane now. He was a human being, the same as everyone else, only with an intelligence that had isolated him from others and stunted his social development. Was that so hard to accept? It had been true of many scientists and thinkers before him. Maybe his problem was worse than simple social awkwardness; maybe he was going insane. Or maybe . . .

Could the varcolac have influenced his mind? It had been manipulating him all along, using the solutions to the equations he had designed to get him to do its bidding. What if his immersion in its technology, or just his proximity to the wormhole, had given it access to his brain? Why else would he have done such a cataclysmically stupid thing?

Finally, by inches, Ryan forced himself to move. He brought up the logs and saw what he already knew to be true. The patterns were broken. The equations compromised. There was nothing stopping the free quantum flow of particles from one universe into the next.

It wasn't too late, though. He could fix this. In the warehouse, during the demo, he'd been able to stuff the genie back in the bottle by introducing a new equation to control the shape of the wormhole. The energies that gave it life and power in their universe came from the baby universe; if he reblocked that path, the varcolac would be recaptured. His fingers flew over the touch screen, fueled by adrenaline.

It didn't take long. He already had several equations saved off that he had worked out previously. Each was deviously complex, patterns that would require years of effort by high-level mathematicians to solve, if they could solve them at all. He chose one of these, a tricky piece of work based on a generalized form of the Riemann zeta function. He loaded it into the software that regulated the wormhole and initiated the procedure. In his photoionization display, the laser-light arcs shifted and reformed, representing the invisible quantum reality. The pattern held.

Ryan took a deep breath and let it out. Nothing was going to get through that barrier for quite some time. He had done a foolish thing, an insane thing, but no harm had been done. No varcolac had appeared, and no one had been killed. No one would ever know.

His smile faded as the pattern unraveled in front of him.

CHAPTER 18

The Muncy State Correctional Facility for Women stood at the end of a picturesque gravel drive lined with old, full-growth maple trees. The main building looked like a courthouse or a prep school, solid limestone and brick architecture with two chimneys and a central tower topped with a white cupola in classic American Renaissance style. In the 150 years since its construction, however, the prison population had grown twenty times larger. Alex had already seen the place from satellite photos and knew that behind the charming, old-school facade was a dull, white monstrosity of a building that might have been mistaken for an enormous warehouse or distribution facility, except for the twelve-foot fence topped with razor wire.

Alex walked up to the front entrance, surprised by how quiet it was. She could hear the wind brushing through the leaves and birds chirping in the distance. She walked through the open doors and was stopped by a turnstile with interlocking steel teeth that reached from floor to ceiling.

"Name and business?" said a woman through a small grating set into a piece of glass.

"Sandra Kelley, to visit Jean Massey."

She passed her ID through a drawer. The woman studied it and her face carefully, and then pressed a button. The turnstile buzzed. Alex walked through, feeling an odd sense of entering a place from which few returned easily. A female guard met her on the other side and frisked her thoroughly. She indicated a bench. "You'll have to wait here while I call a block warden."

Alex sat, taking deep breaths to calm her nerves. As Sandra, she had every right to be here. At the first hint of any trouble, she could teleport away. The guard ignored her. Alex regarded her: middle-aged, Hispanic, a solid strength and no-nonsense expression. She wondered what sorts of things the guard had seen and how it felt to come to work at such a place every day.

Ten minutes later, a light-skinned woman with African features and short-cropped hair bustled into the room and smiled at Alex. "You must be my visitor."

Alex cocked her head. "Warden?"

"That's what they tell me, hon. You can call me Aisha. You ready?"

"I guess so." Alex stood up.

"It's a bit of a walk, I'm afraid. The Charlies don't get many visitors. Follow me."

Alex followed her through a locked set of double doors, which the warden opened with a key card. A sharp smell hit her, institutional and antiseptic. "Charlies?" she asked.

The warden pointed. "A-block is that way, the Alphas; they're in minimum. The Bravos are in B-block. Our maximum security ladies, they're in C-block. Our Charlies."

She navigated through a bewildering maze of corridors, through multiple gates and checkpoints, some of them electronic, and some of them with human guards. Alex noticed that the warden didn't carry any weapons, but the guards, sitting in glass-enclosed booths, were holding automatic rifles in clear view. Alex assumed that the people who actually came in contact with prisoners were unarmed to avoid the possibility that a prisoner might take the weapon and use it against them, while the glassed-in guards, protected from easy assault, could fire on prisoners through the glass if needed. It was a simple, low-tech solution to the problem of arming guards without tempting prisoners.

They passed above an open mess hall, crossing on a balcony. Below them, rows of women in rust-colored jumpsuits ate at tables, served by other women in the same clothes. On seeing the warden, several called up to her with various complaints. "Hush now, ladies," she called down to them without breaking stride. Alex followed, careful not to meet anyone's eye.

"I apologize for this," the warden said. "They didn't think things through when they built the guest area for C-block. As I said, we don't get many. The first year, sure, but when someone's on the mile, or put away for life, it doesn't take long for family and friends to write them off. What's the point of visiting someone who's never going to get out anyway? They think they will, and they promise to, but after a few months, maybe a year, they start to move on. Are you related to Jeannie?"

"She was a friend of my father's." Alex heard screaming, faintly, through one of the doors.

"Will you accept my signal?" the warden asked.

A ping told Alex of an incoming feed to her system. "Um, sure," she said.

"Then here we are," the warden said.

She unlocked a side door with her keycard. They entered what looked like a small conference room, with a central wooden table and several chairs. To Alex's surprise, Jean Massey was already sitting in one of the chairs. She was dressed in one of the same rust-colored jumpsuits as the women in the mess hall, with a large D.O.C printed on it in white. She wore no handcuffs.

The warden squinted at Alex. "Can you see her?"

"Of course."

"Good. You must have a modern kit; sometimes we have to adjust for older models, or lend people one of our own."

Her response confused Alex momentarily, until she realized: *Jean isn't really here.* The room was configured to project Jean's image to her eyejack display, creating the illusion of a face-to-face meeting without actually putting people together. Jean was probably sitting in a similar room somewhere else in the prison, seeing Alex the same way.

It made sense. Without true physical contact, there was no fear of an inmate attacking a guest, or vice versa, nor any concern that a guest would try to smuggle contraband in to a family member. It did, however, put a wrinkle in Alex's plans to teleport Jean away. She had to touch her to do it, and she didn't even know where in the prison Jean was. Alex almost gave up and walked away right then, but she had come this far. She could at least talk to the woman. She pulled back a chair and sat down.

Fifteen years earlier, Jean Massey had been an amazing young woman. In her thirties, she had been a recognized expert in her field, published in top journals, and employed at the New Jersey Super Collider, the largest scientific instrument in the world. Together with her boss, Dr. Vanderhall, she had pioneered dramatic new processes and made discoveries that could have revolutionized human experience. She had been, in short, everything that Alex herself now aspired to be. That is, until she had killed Dr. Vanderhall and tried to kill her own daughter.

Jean had a daughter named Chance, who had Down Syndrome. Thanks to a twist of fate, the random dice roll of a pair of genes, Chance would never reach the heights of her mother's brilliance and achievement. But who was Chance Massey, exactly? Was the Down Syndrome her identity? Jean hadn't thought so. She had tried to use the Higgs projector to change the past, to alter the fall of the dice, and resolve her unborn daughter's probability wave as a healthy, able child. She didn't see it as murder, but as choosing a new life for her daughter. Alex and her father had seen it as the destruction of one person in order to create a different one.

It was confusing to Alex. How did morality work, when nonlinear time came into play? A birth was just the accident of a particular sperm implanting in an egg at a particular place and time, causing a particular set of genes to come together. At the time, it wouldn't have been immoral to avoid that genetic combination, if the power existed to do so, or to choose not to allow that sperm and egg to combine at all. There was no human being created yet, and so no one to harm. But later, when the child was almost a year old, it seemed like murder to go back in time and make a different choice.

But what about the other version of Chance, the one that had never been given an opportunity to live? For that matter, what about the thousands of other possible Chances, the alternate combinations of genes that would have yielded different people? Why were they any less valid than the one who lived? Alex supposed that, morally speaking, there had to be a distinction between choosing not to create a life and killing one that already existed. But it wasn't always so simple. What if Alex were to send a particle back in time to affect her own life? To, say, change a choice she had made yesterday? That would make her a different person, of sorts. Would that be the same as killing herself in favor of someone else?

Jean stared off into space, her eyes focused on some distant point far beyond the walls. Alex remembered her as a friend, a beautiful and energetic woman, always cheerful and kind, with a mind like a knife with an atom-thick blade. Now her face was gaunt and deeply lined, giving the appearance of a much greater age. Her face was loose and expressionless. She didn't acknowledge Alex's presence.

The warden left the room. "Knock when you're finished, and I'll escort you back," she said before closing the door.

Alex turned back to Jean. "I'm Alex Kelley," she said. "You knew my father, Jacob."

Jean registered this information with a quick flick of her eyes toward Alex's face, and then returned to her thousand-mile stare. Alex felt intimidated. She hadn't anticipated the possibility that Jean would be completely uninterested. Surely after fifteen years in prison she would welcome a conversation about physics? Perhaps it was too painful a subject.

"The varcolac is back," Alex said.

That earned her another look. "I never understood why you called it that," Jean said.

"It's what destroyed the stadium in Philadelphia. It killed my dad."

Jean shrugged, a slow and barely discernable gesture. The empty expression on her face didn't change. "You expect me to weep for him?"

"I thought you could help me understand it. Specifically, how it changes things in the past. I know you once used a Higgs projector to do that, but we don't know the principle behind it. I need to stop the varcolac before it kills any more people."

"Are you a physicist?"

"Yes," Alex said. "I work for Lockheed Martin, but I'm assigned to a project that runs in the NJSC's High Energy Lab."

Jean sniffed, an ambiguous expression that could have been grudging respect, but was probably disdain. "In that case, you already know more than I do. I've been out of the field for fifteen years. I spend my time washing laundry and scrubbing floors now."

Alex leaned close to the table. "Are they treating you well? Where in the prison do they have you, right now?" She assumed their meeting would be monitored, but it seemed an innocent enough question.

Jean smirked, the first actual facial expression Alex had seen her make. "You didn't come here just to ask questions. You came here to break me out."

Alex jerked up. "What are you talking about?"

"If the creature is back, that means there's a Higgs projector. You knew you might need to barter for my help. You mean to offer me my freedom."

Alex was disconcerted by the woman's perceptiveness. Surely there would be someone listening to their conversation? Or did they just record them for later review?

"So where is he?" Jean asked.

"I beg your pardon?"

"The real physicist. *You* didn't create the projector."

Alex was astonished. "How could you know that?"

"You're too young and stupid to have invented it yourself. Bring him, and maybe we'll talk."

"Excuse me," Alex said. "I'm not the one who's in prison."

Jean raised her hands mockingly. "Well then, get me out of here, if you can. What are you waiting for?"

Alex glanced at the door, which remained closed. Were they just letting her talk, to see if she would incriminate herself? Or was there truly no one listening? They could hardly imagine the technology she had available, so perhaps they were just biding their time.

The network that was feeding her the image of Jean was simple enough, just a standard web protocol. Alex could trace it, and get a location for Jean. She could teleport to her, and then all she would have to do was touch Jean's arm and teleport away again.

Her presence—as Sandra—would be on all the surveillance tapes, and so would her disappearance. It would make Sandra a felon, and place her squarely in the conspiracy in the minds of law enforcement. It would be the end of her police career. But she wouldn't have much of a police career if she died. It was the best option Alex had.

The door opened, and instead of the friendly warden, a tall, official-looking man came through, followed by four armed guards with pistols drawn. "Sandra Kelley?" the official said.

Alex sat alert, ready to teleport away at any moment. "That's me."

"We have been instructed to detain you for questioning. Please come with us quietly. The checkpoints you entered through are locked. There's nowhere to go."

Alex was surprised to feel a small smile form unbidden on her face. She hadn't wanted to stain Sandra's reputation; now she wouldn't have to. "Actually, my name's Alex," she said. "Sandra had nothing to do with this." She teleported. Jean's room was identical to hers, so from her point-of-view, the five men disappeared, and Jean solidified into a real woman instead of a computer image. "Come on," Alex said. "We're getting out of here." She flicked her eyes to choose the coordinates for the peak of Hawk Mountain, seized Jean's arm, and teleported.

Only she didn't. Nothing happened. She was still in the prison.

Jean laughed. "I told you. Stupid as dirt."

Alex couldn't understand it. "It worked the first time. Why won't it work now?"

"You can't get any signals out of here," Jean said. "You think they want their inmates making calls on contraband cell phones? The whole place is shielded."

"But the projector doesn't work on—"

The door crashed open, and three guards rushed in. Two of them trained their weapons on her, while the third advanced.

"On any electromagnetic bandwidth?" Jean said. "Of course not. It's extra-dimensional quantum tunneling on a large scale. You can't stop that with a bit of copper shielding."

The third guard turned Alex around and yanked one arm up painfully behind her.

"But," Jean continued, "I'm willing to bet the software driving it assumes the presence of a network connection, or at least GPS, for accurate targeting," Jean continued. "But of course, you didn't write it. So you don't know."

Alex didn't answer. She wasn't worried about getting Jean out anymore. She just wanted to get away herself. It hadn't even occurred to her that she might not be able to teleport out. She cursed herself for not reviewing the code, or at least for not interrogating Ryan about its limitations. She had no doubt that, given an hour with the source code, she could have modified it to allow teleportation to known locations, even without external network connectivity. But it was too late for that now.

She could still teleport line-of-sight, though. And she still had other tricks up her sleeve.

Through the open door, she could see a corridor. She focused on the place she wanted to be, and the eyejack automatically measured the distance. She initiated the teleportation module, and in a moment she was there. She heard sounds of consternation and shock from the guards, but she didn't dare pause to look. She initiated the invisibility module and disappeared.

At the end of the corridor, she saw a light and teleported toward it.

This was not the way she had come in, so she had no idea what direction to move or how far she was from an exit. She found herself in a central room, from which a series of cells branched like the spokes of a wheel. The arrangement allowed a guard to see every inch of the cells from a single vantage point. The cells were full, two women to a room.

It was a dead end. She jumped back the way she had come. Which way was out? She didn't know how thoroughly they could lock down the facility, or to what lengths they could go to capture her. Her main advantages at this point were that she couldn't be seen and that she could move faster than the guards, but they would have procedures to completely lock down sections of the prison in case of escape attempts or riots. She had to get out fast, if she was going to get out at all.

A few more jumps, and she reached a guard station separating two sections. The guard sat behind a pane of glass, and controlled another gate of interlocking steel bars. She could see through to the other side, which meant the bars were no barrier. In an instant, she was through. A klaxon blared suddenly, hurting her ears. She wondered if the station had sensors that had detected her, or if someone had manually sounded the alarm from elsewhere in the prison.

She teleported again, halting when the corridor ended in solid metal doors topped with flashing red lights. She threw herself against them, but they wouldn't open. Her heart hammered, and she felt cold, trapped. Of course, she could estimate the distance and jump to the other side of the doors, but she didn't know what was there. If there was another set of doors, or a person, or just a stairway, she would kill herself by jumping into it.

Teleportation, however, was not her only trick. They couldn't do this to her, not with the power at her disposal. She spotted a trashcan, a large metal one, against the wall. It would do. She backed away and teleported the trashcan into the center of the metal doors. The doors tore apart with an explosion of rending metal, and she jumped through to the other side.

A guard blocked her path, aiming a pistol at her and shouting for her to stand down. He could see her! She realized he must have an infrared sensor, possibly on his gun, probably synched to his eyejack lenses. He was certainly communicating with the other guards, so now they would all know how to see her, too.

From ten feet away, she ripped the gun out of the guard's hand and snatched it out of the air. Caught up in the moment, she almost shot the man, like he was a generic character in a first-person shooter video game. A chill went down her back at how easily it came to her, and she took her finger off the trigger. She had almost forgotten that her other adversaries had been varcolac puppets, empty shells controlled by their host. This man had a name, a life, a family, and she had almost shot him for no good reason, just because he stood in her way. Without his gun, he was no longer a threat. She didn't have to kill him.

The door beyond him was glass, and she teleported beyond it just as she registered a sharp jab of pain in her back. On the other side of the door, she looked back and saw that two other guards had run up behind her while she hesitated. In the seconds she had delayed, they had shot her with something. Her vision blurred. They had hit her with some kind of tranquilizer. She had to get away, *now*.

The noise of the klaxon was relentless. She could hardly think. She spun, her balance wavering, and saw that the décor had changed, from institutional cinderblock to stone and paneling. She was back in the original prison building. A glass window revealed a view of the outdoors: maple trees, the road, a high external fence. All she had to do was make it out there, and she was free. One more jump.

She teleported out into the open air, but this time the shift in perspective threw her completely off-balance, and she fell to the ground. She was beyond the shielding now, and her system was connected; she could teleport anywhere she wanted. The blare of the alarm was muted now, but it seemed to be spinning all around her, to be inside her head. She tried to navigate the eyejack menu, but her eyes wouldn't focus, and the menu options slipped away. The klaxon was her heartbeat, pounding through her veins.

Footsteps thundered on all sides, and she was surrounded, men shouting at her, weapons aimed. All she had to do was one more thing, but she couldn't remember what it was. It was tremendously important, but she was so tired. She would remember what it was after she slept.

CHAPTER 19

Less than two hours after Alex walked into the prison, the news feeds gleefully announced her capture. She was the perfect news story—it was hard to beat a young female assassin for ratings—and they had hardly stopped talking about her since Secretary Falk had died. Now, there was fresh grist for the mill, and the talking heads could barely contain their delight. A female murderer caught visiting another female murderer! And both of them physicists! Was there a conspiracy? Had the older one trained the younger? Old footage of Jean Massey's trial and conviction were replayed, and the speculations were as varied as they were ridiculous.

Sandra didn't know what to do. All her friends were policemen, likely to side with law enforcement and the justice system. But Sandra wasn't about to trust the courts with this; there were too many witnesses who had seen Alex pull the trigger. For her to be exonerated, she would have to prove the existence of the varcolac, and prove that Falk and his agents had been killed by it not by her, and there wasn't much likelihood of that. No, the only way for Alex to get out of prison was for Sandra to break her out. But none of her cop friends would help with something like that. The ones who had been most likely to support her—Danielle and Nathan—had come to her dad's funeral, and now they were dead.

Her phone chimed. It was Ryan Oronzi. She thought about ignoring him, but he might know something. "What is it, Ryan?" she said.

"Alex isn't picking up."

"She's a little busy right now, being captured and interrogated. Don't you watch the news?"

"Not much. I guess I have to talk to you then."

"I guess you do, then."

"I just wanted to let you know . . . the varcolac is out again."

"What?"

"I just thought you should know."

"What do you mean, it's out? You mean it's loose? I thought you said you could control it!"

"Not indefinitely. It defeated its protocol and escaped."

"Ryan, this thing is trying to kill us. You have to capture it again!"

"It's not an animal. It's a thinking being. We can't just keep it caged up forever."

Sandra took a deep breath. "It's a killer. If you can't control it . . ."

"It's not my fault. I'm not a miracle worker."

"Not your fault? Are you kidding me?"

Ryan's voice took on a childish whine. "I'll do what I can, okay?"

"You'll do better than that, and do it quick, or there will be more deaths on your head."

"I'll try, all right?" He sounded affronted. "I'm not powerless. I still have some tricks up my sleeve."

"If that's true, then how did it escape? I thought you had them set to apply automatically."

"Well, I may have accidentally . . . look, never mind."

"Accidentally what? Accidentally let the varcolac loose?"

"Never mind. I'm sorry I called. I'll fix it."

"Where is it now? Can you at least tell me that?"

The line went silent for so long that Sandra thought he had disconnected. "Well," he said finally, "I can tell you what its next target will be."

"What, it sat down and shared its plans with you over coffee?"

"I can see it in the logs, just like I did with the funeral home. Its attacks leave residue both forward and backward in time."

Sandra didn't care about the science. "Where?"

"Tomorrow morning, 5:46 AM, at the Muncy State Prison."

"You're kidding me."

"No. Why, what's there?"

For a moment, Sandra couldn't speak. She suddenly knew, beyond all shadow of a doubt, that Alex was still being held in that prison, and that at 5:46 the next morning, she would still be there. Why else would the varcolac attack at that place and time?

"You bastard," Sandra said, and cut the connection. She lashed out, knocking a picture frame and a clay dish onto the floor.

How did the varcolac know where Alex would be? She felt like she was playing a deadly game against an opponent who kept changing the rules. Was it attacking from the present or from the future? One thing seemed clear: it was trying to track down and destroy her family. Sandra had originally assumed that the attack on Alex at her demo hadn't been personal, just an opportunity created by the use of Higgs technology, in which Alex's presence had been entirely coincidental. But since then, its attacks had been purely against her family, as far as she could tell. What did it have against them? Was it afraid that the people who had banished it fifteen years ago could do so again? If so, she thought it had overestimated them.

Alex was captured, her eyejack taken away. Sandra didn't realize how much she had been relying on Alex, both intellectually and emotionally, until she was gone. She beat her fists against the bed and buried her head in her pillow, repressed tears lodging painfully in her throat. What chance did they have against such an enemy? They couldn't kill it, and they couldn't reason with it. Now Alex was trapped, an easy target for its next attack.

The tears broke free, and she sobbed silently into her pillow. Her phone chimed again. She growled, expecting it to be Ryan again with some inane comment. But it wasn't. It was Angel Gutierrez.

"I saw the news," he said. "I thought you might need someone to talk to?"

Ryan tried to shake away the sense of guilt he felt after talking with Sandra. It was why he didn't like people very much. They were always finding ways to make him feel bad. Why should Sandra shout at him? It wasn't like he'd *wanted* those people dead. He hadn't killed them himself. He was trying to stop the varcolac, too. They were on the same side.

The best thing he could do now, he thought, was to put Alex and Sandra out of his mind. Either the varcolac would kill them or it wouldn't. There wasn't much he could do about it. The only thing he could do was try to capture it in the wormhole again, however long that took. He didn't want them to die, but it wasn't his problem. The most important thing was to get the varcolac back under lock and key.

Which wouldn't be easy. The equations Ryan had created previously were compromised. If the varcolac had been in his mind, then it would already know the solutions. That was the only explanation Ryan could think of to account for how it had been able to unravel the Riemann function pattern so fast. If it had truly solved it from scratch, then it had just been playing with him all this time, and it could escape whenever it wished. He didn't think that was true. Which meant he had to devise a new equation, a tough one, and hope it would hold the creature better than the last.

Ryan considered a Maass wave form approach, but discarded it. He had used non-holomorphic L-functions in a previous pattern, and the varcolac would be ready for it. He needed something that would last. Perhaps a Navier-Stokes equation instead. That would take a little extra work on his part, but it would be worth it in the long run. No sense formulating something fragile and having it unravel again.

He took a pencil and paper and started crafting the general shape of the equations he wanted. He had several software suites designed for higher mathematics and visualization, of course, but when he was inventing something new, he always liked to start on pencil and paper. It gave him a freedom of expression that someone else's software package didn't allow.

Of course, it was all just a stopgap. No matter how brilliant the problem he set, the varcolac would defeat it sooner or later. Could he really just continue to devise new equations indefinitely? Eventually—and quicker than Ryan liked to admit—he would be out of ideas, and there would be nothing to stop it from running loose, killing and destroying whatever it wished, remaking the world into whatever form it thought appropriate.

Fifteen years ago, as Alex had described it, they had defeated the varcolac by removing its source of exotic particle energy. This had been as simple as shutting down the super collider, leaving the creature with no hold on the physical world. But that was impossible here. Ryan had formed his baby universe out of the quantum froth of the multiverse. Now that it was created, there was no way to destroy it, or even to destroy the wormhole connecting it to their universe. Ryan had tried. The new universe's space-time was hurtling outward in its frame of reference like a trillion joule freight train, and there was no stopping it. The varcolac had a practically infinite supply of energy to draw from.

Ryan might contain it for a while, but eventually, it would break free for good. It was inevitable. His prior hopes that it might communicate with him seemed silly now. How could he communicate with something so alien? It reminded him of a term he remembered from the books he had read in his childhood: *varelse*. An intelligence that was *varelse* was so utterly different than humanity in kind and experience that there was no hope ever to communicate with it. The varcolac wasn't biological. It didn't even exist along the same dimensional plane. How could it understand the concept of human life and death? Of the individual? Of the limits of physical reality? Ryan wasn't even sure it could be called alive, in any measurable sense of the word.

If there was no hope of killing it, and no hope of reasoning with it, then there was no hope at all. Ryan had to admit the truth. He had signed the death warrants of all nine billion inhabitants of planet Earth. He was the most brilliant scientist of his generation, and he had destroyed the world.

"Of course I'll help," Angel said. "What kind of friend would I be if I turned you away in your hour of need?"

"But it's illegal and dangerous," Sandra said. She sat next to him on a lopsided and worn couch in his quadcopter lab. In the mesh cage, a dozen copters flew through some kind of automated test scenario. "I'm talking about breaking into a maximum security prison on high alert to rescue a criminal wanted for the murder of a high-ranking government official. Not to mention that the varcolac may be trying to kill us at the same time."

"Heck of a first date," Angel said.

She smiled despite herself. "Look, I'm just saying, we only met a few days ago. You don't have to help me. I totally understand."

"You're really going for the hard sell, aren't you? I mean it. I'll help. This is your sister's life in danger, right? And maybe the fate of the human race. How could I pass it up?"

She let out a breath. "Thank you. So. How hard is it to reprogram your quadcopters?"

They worked side-by-side for hours, fueled by mushroom-and-green-pepper pizza and Diet Coke. Computer science wasn't Sandra's field, but she had done enough programming in her teenage years that she wasn't completely useless. Angel, however, was fast and brilliant, incorporating unfamiliar code with astonishing facility. All the while, he chattered inanely about everything and nothing, bleeding away Sandra's stress and worry.

Eventually, Sandra gave up trying to help, and went hunting on the web for information they could use. Within a few minutes, she had the blueprints for the Muncy State Prison, along with a description of its security features.

Angel was surprised. "They actually publish that stuff online?"

"Not exactly. I mean, the prison doesn't post it on their website or anything. But it's not classified under the Espionage Act or anything, either. Any time a construction company does work, there's going to be records of it publicly available, if you know where to look and how to get it."

Angel glanced over the information. "Your sister should have done this research before she went. The whole place is shielded. She probably couldn't teleport out, once she was in."

"I didn't think of it either," Sandra said. "We just felt so invincible, with that ability—it seemed like no one would be able to capture her. Even now, they won't be able to keep her. If I had the time to wait for her to go on trial, or even just to be transferred, I could teleport in and steal her away before they even knew I was there. As it is, the varcolac may kill her before I get the chance." She took a deep breath and let it out. "Why can't people leave well enough alone? If Vanderhall and Jean Massey hadn't gone messing with Higgs particles fifteen years ago, then none of this would ever have happened."

"But then you never would have existed. At least not as you are now. You and your sister's lives would never have diverged, and you would be living some compromise life somewhere."

"Maybe that would have been for the best."

Angel studied her for a long moment. "Do you believe in God?" he said asked finally.

"What?" The question took Sandra by surprise. "No, I guess I don't." Though she had noticed a cross on a chain around Angel's neck, just visible under his collar. "You do, I'm guessing?"

"I'd say about ninety percent," Angel said. "But that's not the point. Let's say there is a God, for the sake of argument. Or a super-powerful alien intelligence. Or an artificial intelligence that just dreamed us up one day. Whatever you like."

"I think you should keep programming."

"I am programming." And in truth, his fingers had never stopped moving across the keys while he talked. "Humor me, okay?"

Sandra didn't know where he was going, but he seemed earnest. "Okay. There's a God. So what?"

"Our deity, or alien, or whatever he is, created the world. But instead of doing it fourteen billion years ago, he did it twenty thousand years ago."

"You're kidding me," Sandra said. "We're talking about Young Earth Creationism here? The whole world, slapped together in six days by an Almighty Being? You're a scientist! For heaven's sake, there are galaxies out there that are billions of light years away. Just point a telescope at Andromeda, and you can look at something millions of years old."

"You're missing the point."

"I guess I am."

"The universe is billions of years old," Angel said. "I'm not suggesting otherwise. But let's imagine that our godlike being created the whole mess—billion-year history and all—ten thousand years ago."

Sandra paused to work that one out. "So, then God's deceiving us? He created a fake fourteen-billion-year history? The dinosaurs and the Carboniferous period and the Andromeda galaxy, they never existed? It's all just a scam? 'April Fools. Love, God.'"

"Right. Not very nice of him, maybe. But here's the question: would it matter?"

Sandra threw up her hands. "Of course it would matter. If it never happened, it's like a big cosmic joke."

"But what's the difference, practically? The history is still there. It's still consistent, following the same predicable laws. You can still study it and learn things that are true. And as far as we're concerned, that history is gone. Vanished in smoke. All that really matters is what we can learn from what we have now. What it left behind."

"I don't understand what you're trying to tell me."

"What does it mean for history to be 'real'? What about last Tuesday? Was that real?"

"Of course."

"How do you know?"

"I was there. I remember it."

"But your memories are just a set of electrical impulses and neuron states. What if an AI just dreamed you up five minutes ago? It could have made you complete with your memories of your life, paperwork and souvenirs from your childhood, dental history, etc., every bit of it consistent. But not real."

"You're a creepy little man."

"But if he did, you wouldn't know the difference. It wouldn't make any practical change in your life going forward. The history of last Tuesday is exactly the same whether it 'really' happened, or God just created it that way. Unless you're a varcolac, it's only the present and the future that you can do anything about."

Whatever he was trying to do, it wasn't making her feel any better. She crossed her arms. "So what's the point? Where are we going with this?"

"The point is you. You're so tangled up in knots about whose history is real, yours or Alex's. You figure one of you must have 'really' experienced the events of your childhood, and the other is just a fake, a carbon copy created fifteen years ago with the same memories, but who was never actually there to experience them. You're each terrified that you're the imposter, and afraid that the other one knows it. But it's a false fear. Your memories are both genuine."

Sandra paused, taken aback by the sudden twist of subject. "You can't be certain of that."

"Certain? There's nothing certain in life, not any of it. But why agonize over something you can't change? If you popped into being five minutes ago, or fifteen years ago, or have always existed, it doesn't change *now*. You're here. You're real. Embrace the person you were, and make sure you have reason to like the person you're becoming. The past you can't change. The future is what matters."

Three hours later, Angel had twelve quadcopters up and spinning in the cage. "Let's see how this works," he said. "I've created a few unit test scenarios to prove out the mechanics."

The copters spun up as a unit, and then suddenly disappeared together and reappeared on the other side of the cage.

"Wow!" Sandra said. "You did it!"

"So far so good," Angel said. "We haven't put them through their paces yet."

Each of the copters held a different colored flag, to differentiate them by sight. They hovered in a line in order of the visible spectrum, red to blue. Then, suddenly, the colors changed as if with the flick of a switch, following the same order from blue to red. Sandra watched in confusion as the flags changed colors again, each of them rippling through from red to orange to green to blue. But the flags were just cheap plastic, nothing special. How was Angel making them change colors?

It took her a moment to realize what was happening. Each copter was simultaneously leaving its own position and instantaneously taking the position of the next copter in line. The copters themselves seemed not to move, making it appear as if the flags were changing colors.

Sandra whistled. "I hope you got the timing right. They'll destroy themselves if two of them appear in the same spot at the same time."

The copters began flying through the cage as a unit, veering and banking in tight formation, but all the while the flags were changing colors, indicating that the copters were actually trading places as they flew. Angel grinned. "I hope so, too."

"How could you do all this in only a few hours?" Sandra asked, amazed.

"It's really not hard from a software perspective. The copters model the rules of their universe and use the model to know, ahead of time, exactly what will happen when they maneuver in certain directions. All I've done is add a rule—the ability to change vector position to a new one, instantaneously. Most of the programming was already in place." The quadcopters began bouncing balls back and forth to each other, continuing to rotate positions seamlessly. "It makes very little difference to the software which of the copters is in a given place, or that the rules of the actual universe don't usually allow such movements. Now, watch this."

One of the copters began to perform radical high-speed turns, racing forward and then suddenly flying to the left as if defying its own momentum. It did it again, this time completely reversing direction as if it had struck an invisible wall, without slowing down or showing any discernable jerk.

"How are they doing that?" Sandra said.

"They're teleporting to their own location, only with a frame of reference rotated by 90 or 180 degrees. Momentum is preserved, so from their perspective, it's as if the whole universe rotated to the right, and they kept traveling forward as usual. They can do it in any direction, with any orientation, making them more or less infinitely maneuverable, without the usual limitations of momentum and centrifugal force. It means, in essence, that they can turn without turning. They move the universe instead of moving themselves."

"It's amazing."

Angel shook his head. "But it's not going to work."

"What do you mean? It works perfectly."

"They do some neat tricks, I'll give you that. But we need to break your sister out of a maximum security prison block. We don't know where they're holding her, and once we find them, the copters themselves can't teleport her out. They can only move things with a smaller mass than themselves. Even working together, a human being is far too massive. Worse, we can't communicate with them from the outside. Unless we go into the prison ourselves, they would have to be completely autonomous, with a flexible plan that could anticipate any eventuality. I don't know about you, but I don't think I'm that good, especially not in one night. The copters are a tool, but not a miracle. We still need a plan."

Sandra considered this. "We need a relay."

Angel raised a questioning eyebrow.

"The place is shielded, and we can't trust the copters to act entirely on their own. So we use them as waypoints. The copters search the prison, and then we can teleport to the location of any one of them."

"But they won't be able to signal out to us."

"That's why at least one needs to be left near the entrance. As a conduit to the outside."

Angel nodded. "That could work. But there's one more thing."

"What's that?"

"The varcolac is still out there, planning to attack. For all we know, it could be the same kind of attack that destroyed the stadium. Complete devastation."

"That's why we have to be fast. We need to be able to teleport her out before that happens."

"But what about everyone else in the prison? The other prisoners, the guards? They'll all die."

Sandra raised her hands helplessly. "We can't rescue all of them. Maybe if we get Alex out of there, it won't attack the prison at all."

Angel sucked on a lip, thinking. "I think we need to be prepared to fight it."

"Prepared? You haven't seen this thing. There's no being prepared."

"As much as we can."

"There's maybe one thing," Sandra said. "It'll add to the confusion at any rate, and that could be a good thing."

"What are you thinking?"

"We need to call the Muncy State Prison ahead of time," she said, "And tell them we've planted a bomb."

By nightfall, running on almost thirty-six hours without sleep, Ryan had his equation. This new pattern would give them another week, or a few days at minimum, to judge by the time it had taken the varcolac to solve the patterns in the past. In that time, he could develop a suite of backup equations to have in reserve. There might be no hope for the world, but at least he could delay Armageddon for as long as possible.

He loaded the new equation into the wormhole pattern regulator and sat back to watch the new configuration form in his photoionization display. He was so tired. His eyes stung, and his muscles ached, and he felt jittery from all the caffeine he'd drunk. This had to work. It *had* to.

But the moment the pattern started to form, it flew apart like dandelion seeds in the wind. The full dataset hadn't even finished loading before it unraveled.

Dismayed, Ryan paged through the logs, trying to understand. Had he loaded an old pattern by mistake? But no. Not only had the varcolac cut through his new equation like a scalpel through dry skin, it had started to do so *before he had even fully loaded it*. It was impossible.

But it had happened, so of course it was possible. It meant that the varcolac had known what equation he was going to use before he had even set it in place. It wasn't just out-thinking him. It was living inside his mind.

And suddenly, it was there. The moment he realized that it must be, Ryan could sense its presence. In fact, now that he thought of it, the new equation he had just devised was beyond even his capability. He was thinking on a higher level than ever before, picturing higher-dimensional shapes in his mind like no human could. It was communicating with him, but not through words or pictures or codes. It had infiltrated his own sense of self.

Chills went down his spine. He didn't feel tired anymore. There was something inside him, something he couldn't get out. Normally, Ryan hated the idea of anything foreign inside his body. He found body piercing disturbing, and he hated getting splinters. The idea of having pins in a broken bone or undergoing something like cardiac catheterization was intolerable. But this was different. The varcolac wasn't physical. It wasn't in his body, not in the same way. There had been theories for years that the human brain was too capable for the space it inhabited, that its processing capacity might in fact reach through electrical fields into other dimensions. It was in this domain—in Ryan's mind—that the varcolac was interacting.

How long had it been there? He remembered the duplicate Ryan, the one that had pushed the button releasing the varcolac when he, Ryan, had not intended to. He recognized that now for what it had been: a standing probability wave, quickly resolved, in which both possibilities occurred. The sort of probability wave that had previously been experienced only when encountering the varcolac. It seemed circular: encountering the varcolac had caused him to split into versions of himself that both did not and did release the varcolac, the second of which caused him to encounter the varcolac, which caused the split in the first place. But that was exactly the sort of behavior that occurred among particles on the quantum scale.

Regardless of the cause, the varcolac was there in his mind. It was subtly influencing him, reading his thoughts, increasing his capabilities. It was like taking off a veil to see that the world was a lot brighter and clearer than he had realized. Only it wasn't his eyes that had been veiled, but his mind. He could imagine anything, solve anything, keep any amount of information at the front of his consciousness. It was taking him over in ways he didn't understand, making him into something newer and better and more powerful. And he loved it.

CHAPTER 20

Sandra and Angel stood on a hillside behind the prison, the quadcopters hovering over their heads like a swarm of large, well-trained insects. It was not yet light. Sandra had hardly slept, but she felt wired, partly from the coffee she'd been drinking, and partly from sheer terror.

The fence blocked their view of most of what was inside. "Once we start this, it'll be hard to back out," she said. "You're sure you want to do this? You've never even met Alex."

"But if we don't rescue her, who's going to tell me the embarrassing truths about your childhood?" Angel said. "You're hardly a trustworthy source."

"It was her childhood, too."

"Ah, good point. Let's leave her in there, then." Angel cocked his head at her and smiled. "Ready?"

Sandra sighed. "What if we hurt someone?"

"We're rescuing them, remember? If we do nothing, then the varcolac kills them all."

"They might not see it that way."

"Alas, no." Angel put a solemn palm on his chest. "It is our lot in life to be misunderstood."

"Okay, joker," Sandra said. "Let's do this."

They had phoned the prison at midnight and told them a bomb had been hidden in the prison and set to go off at 5:46 the next morning. She didn't know what the prison administration had done in response, but it wasn't what they had hoped. At least, Sandra and Angel hadn't observed any activity that looked like large-scale prisoner evacuation.

"Here we go," Angel said. On the south side of the prison was a field of rocks that had been excavated from the ground when the new prison was built. Angel stretched out his hand (a little overdramatically, Sandra thought), and teleported a large rock into the middle of the prison's perimeter wall. The wall exploded, shattered concrete flying everywhere in a fountaining cloud of dust. A klaxon began wailing. Sandra was ready with the next rock, and teleported it into the wall of the prison itself. Before the dust had even cleared, a dozen quadcopters were racing across the field and in through the gap.

Now came the hard part. The prison was immense, and they had no idea where Alex was being kept. The copters had cameras and image recognition software, but some of the faces would be hidden, or turned away, or blocked. There would be a percentage that the copters couldn't eliminate as possibilities, that would require a human to check, and they didn't know how large that percentage would be. Once they found her, Sandra would teleport in, grab her, and teleport out.

Leaving a pair of copters by the hole to relay the images, the swarm flew into the complex, each of them armed with the blueprints for the prison complex. They had only so much battery power and a lot of area to cover. Angel had written an algorithm to allow the ten remaining copters to visit every cell in the prison as efficiently as possible.

The copters teleported from cell to cell, staying high to avoid collisions with people or furniture, taking pictures and moving on. Images of faces started flicking rapidly into Sandra's vision. "They're too fast!" she said. Ten copters, jumping through cell after cell, produced a lot of pictures in short order. Even with the image recognition software eliminating most of them, there were too many to keep up with. And although each copter could recognize a human as an infrared hotspot, it wasn't good at taking an image at such an angle as to make the person easy to identify. Sandra rejected them as fast as she could, but there were too many maybes—dark-haired, jumpsuit-clad women of about the right age—for comfort.

"Can we send some of the copters back to reimage the maybes?" Sandra asked.

"Not if we want them to cover the prison before running out of juice," Angel said. "They're less than ten percent through at this point."

"Okay. I'm going in," Sandra said.

The sound of approaching sirens vied with the prison's klaxon. "Do it quick," Angel said. "We don't have much time."

The copters had recorded the exact locations from which each picture had been taken, so Sandra could use their coordinates to teleport there herself. The shielding didn't prevent her, because she didn't need connectivity to find the location. Besides which, as soon as she teleported in, her system connected to the copters inside the prison, maintaining communication with Angel and the outside world through the relay copters. She could use the pictures to minimize the likelihood of a collision.

Sandra materialized in a tiny cell, six feet by nine feet, with bare concrete walls painted a pale green. She also appeared only a few inches away from the cell's inhabitant. Before Sandra could even get a good look at her, the woman pushed her hard in the chest, sending her crashing backward into the room's small, metal toilet. She cracked her head against it, making her ears ring. The inmate was Alex's height, but much wider in the shoulders and hips. She was staring at Sandra with wide, terrified eyes.

"Where did you come from?" she shouted.

Rattled, Sandra teleported straight back to Angel without answering.

"Are you okay?" Angel asked.

Sandra shook her head to clear it, but said, "I'm fine. It wasn't her."

"Okay. We've got some company." The blue and red flashing lights of multiple police cars and trucks pulled into the prison's front lot. "Let's mix things up a little," Angel said. He chose a section of wall between their hole and the arriving backup and blew another hole in it.

Sandra cringed a little. She should be with the police, driving onto the scene with flashing lights, not setting off explosions and staging a prison break. They would be lucky to get through this without killing someone, and although she knew that if they didn't, the varcolac might very well kill every person here, that wouldn't make her feel any better if someone died as a direct result of her actions.

She teleported to the next uncertain identification and quickly eliminated her. Each time she did it, she half-expected to be killed herself, appearing inside a wall or a bed or the inmate herself. It was always a place where the copters themselves had previously been, meaning that it had recently been safe, but things—especially people—had a habit of not staying where they'd been put.

Five minutes later, they found her. Sandra appeared in the room, by this time not expecting to find her at all, and there she was, a mirror of Sandra's own face looking back at her.

"You did it!" Alex said, standing. "I wasn't sure . . . I feel like such an idiot."

"No time," Sandra said. "We need to get you out of here."

"What about Jean?"

"It took long enough to find you."

"But she's right here, in a different spoke."

Sandra remembered how the prison's cells were arranged like spokes of a wheel, to allow a single guard to see a dozen prisoners from one vantage point. The guard on duty had seen her arrive, and was shouting into a receiver. He was unarmed, but she was sure there would be others coming soon. Sandra grasped her sister's hand and teleported into the central chamber, behind the guard. Before he could turn around, she had spotted Jean.

"I can only take one at a time," Sandra said. "I've got the coordinates, so I'll come right back for her."

She jumped with Alex back to the hillside where Angel still stood. Job complete, the copters had all teleported back to the entrance, and were flying back to Angel. "One more to get," Sandra said. She teleported back to Jean's cell. Jean was standing there, waiting. The moment Sandra appeared, Jean grabbed her by the throat and smashed her head against the concrete wall with all her strength. Sparks flashed in Sandra's vision. She cried out, but she was falling, falling. *I'm trying to rescue you*, she thought, but before she could say it, the floor jumped up to hit her head again and all thought was gone.

Jean had no reason to want to hurt Alessandra Kelley, not either version of her. If their father had still been alive, the self-righteous prig, she would have torn him apart piece by piece and burned the pieces for good measure. But this girl was just unfortunate collateral damage, a means to an end. Jean pried her thumbs into the girl's eyes and popped her eyejack lenses free. The Higgs projector was slightly harder to find, a slim, card-sized object that she finally located in the girl's sock. Jean put the lenses into her own eyes, and the software didn't know that she wasn't Alessandra.

For over a decade, Jean had been trapped in this prison by a society that didn't understand or appreciate what she had done or why. She didn't owe society anything. Now she was out, and she had power. She was ready to bet that Alessandra and whoever else was involved had no real vision for the kind of raw power a Higgs projector entailed.

Jean brought up the interface. She was afraid it would be unfamiliar, that she wouldn't know how to use it. When she saw how the options were laid out, however, she laughed out loud. The fool had given them the original software as a starting point, and they had simply migrated it to a modern platform, or at least used the original as a template. This was *her* technology. She might not know the latest programming techniques, but she knew how to make a Higgs projector work for her.

She teleported away, not to another position on the ground, but high in the air, a mile above the prison, looking down. She fell immediately, the wind buffeting her and roaring in her ears. The earth stretched out before her in a grand vista, no walls or bars or guards or cages, just clear, fresh air to the horizon. She screamed her delight into the rushing wind. Finally. Finally, she was free.

From her vantage point, she could see that large rocks had been placed around the perimeter of the prison, probably for decoration, though possibly also to discourage anyone trying to smash through the fence with a vehicle. Interesting. It gave her an idea.

An idiot might have teleported straight to the ground, forgetting that the momentum she had built up by falling would still be in effect, and would kill her by smashing her body straight into the ground. But Jean was no idiot. She teleported to a new orientation that was rotated 180 degrees, and instead of falling she was suddenly shooting up like a rocket, thrown against gravity by the kinetic energy of her free fall. Gravity gradually took hold again, slowing her and bleeding away her momentum.

When she reached the peak, she teleported to the ground close to one of the rocks. It wasn't perfect. She lost her balance and fell but was unharmed. Grinning, she wrapped her arms around the rock. It was the size of a refrigerator, easily a hundred times her weight.

The visual interface for the Higgs projector had an object edge recognition algorithm built in, indicating what would come along when she teleported. This appeared in her view as a greenish highlight, and automatically included her clothing and any small items she was holding. She adjusted the controls until the highlight snapped out to include the rock as well. Time to see what this technology could do.

She teleported again, back to a point a mile above the prison. The rock, despite its size, came with her. Almost immediately, before she could build up much momentum, she teleported back again, leaving the rock behind in free fall. She was pretty certain the effects of wind at that height would be negligible, but just to be sure, she did it again with one of the other rocks. And again. Seventeen seconds later, the first rock struck the roof of the prison complex traveling over four hundred miles an hour and packing the punch of a truck full of dynamite. It hit dead center, driving straight through the building and into the ground like a meteor.

Debris catapulted into the air as the foundation buckled, tearing the building apart. Then the second rock hit, and the third. Watching from nearby, Jean felt the ground lurch with each impact as if from an earthquake. Sirens blared. With an ironic, parting salute at the building that had stolen the last fifteen years of her life, Jean Massey disappeared.

It only took a few moments for Angel to realize that something was wrong. It should have taken no time at all for Sandra to teleport back with Jean Massey, but she hadn't returned. "I'm going in," he said. He thought of just following her last coordinates, but that seemed foolish. Something had happened at those coordinates to prevent her return, and it wouldn't help her to get himself caught in the same trap.

"I can help. I need a Higgs projector," Alex said.

"No time," Angel said. "Just stay here." He strode across the field toward the prison, calling his quadcopters to him. He was nervous about sending a quadcopter after Sandra, because of the risk of killing her, but he settled for sending it in several feet above her last location, near the ceiling. It arrived and spun, and Angel saw her, lying on the floor, her head bright with blood. No!

He teleported into the cell just as the first explosion hit. It was like having his ears boxed by a giant. The concussion knocked him down, and he couldn't hear, couldn't tell for a moment which way was up. He thought at first he had made a mistake and materialized inside a wall, that this was what it was like to die. But no, his body was whole. Something had happened.

Ears ringing, he got his bearings and saw Sandra, unconscious. He was no doctor, but it looked bad. There was blood everywhere. It made his head spin and his vision narrow. He had to get her out of here. He put his arms around her and teleported, just as a second blast went off, throwing them through the air. They appeared back on the hillside just as another sound like an explosion went off behind him.

Angel looked back at the prison. It was as if a bomb had gone off. Large portions of the structure had collapsed, including one whole wall of the original limestone building. Police were rushing toward it, guns drawn, calling for backup.

Alex rushed over. "What did you do?"

"Nothing." Angel didn't understand it. Oronzi had predicted a varcolac attack, but this destruction didn't seem anything like what had happened at the baseball stadium. There was no time to figure it out. Angel summoned the quadcopters back to their case. Two of them didn't return, presumably destroyed in the prison. Sandra needed to get to a hospital. He held out a hand to Alex. "We need to go." She took his hand. He sat on the quadcopter case, gripping it with his knees, and grasped Sandra's with his other hand, hoping he could bring them all at once.

He closed his eyes and teleported. When he opened them, however, he was not back in his lab, as he had intended. He looked around in confusion. He was in a large open space: the central yard of the prison complex. The building and walls around them were demolished, and debris blocked any easy exit. "What did you do?" Alex shouted. "Get us away from here!"

Angel closed his eyes and tried again, double-checking the coordinates for his lab. They didn't move. He tried the top of Hawk Mountain; again with no result.

"Oh, no," Alex said.

Angel looked. Out of the wreckage, a jumpsuited figure was crawling. She hauled herself to her feet and walked unsteadily toward them. She had no eyes.

"Get us out of here!" Alex shouted.

"I can't. It's not working."

They backed away from the approaching varcolac, but more prisoners were coming from the other direction, all of them without eyes. Some of them were clearly injured, blood streaming from injuries, or with an arm hanging limply. They pressed on, closing in from all directions. There was no escape.

"You'd better fix it quick," Alex said.

"I think the varcolac is blocking it somehow."

Angel flipped open the box, and his quadcopters lifted buzzing into the air. He controlled them through his eyejack interface, indicating places in space where they should hover, forming a circle around the humans. The varcolac-controlled prisoners raised their hands, sending out pulses of heart-stopping energy, but the quadcopters reflexively shielded against it, causing flashes of silver light.

The prisoners, now several dozen strong, bellowed at the same instant, shouting the varcolac's frustration. It attacked again and again, but the quadcopters swerved and blocked. Fortunately, the energy to create the shield was being drawn from the fabric of the universe itself, but the energy to keep each copter flying was a standard chemical battery. And Angel knew they couldn't have much power left.

Not only that, but the clock display in the corner of his vision read 05:43, only three minutes before the time Oronzi had predicted the varcolac would completely obliterate the prison. Whatever they did, they would have to do it fast.

"Give me control," Alex said.

"What? No."

"I won't be able to explain in time. Just give me some eyejacks."

Angel had never met this woman before, and now she wanted him to hand over his only possible weapon? But she was on his side, and she apparently knew more about how all this crazy physics worked than he did. Besides, she looked like Sandra. Angel dug out the extra pair of contacts they had brought for Alex and handed them over. The copters flashed again as the prisoners drew closer. Two of them were starting to sag in the air, their movements growing sluggish. Angel handed over his phone and sent the signal to synch it to the second pair of contacts.

"Two and a half minutes," he said.

"Just hold on to both of us and keep trying to teleport," Alex said.

Suddenly, instead of ten quadcopters, there were twenty. Then forty. The air was full of them, their buzzing grown to a roar. The copters surged forward, light flashing around them like a lightning storm. "This worked in the funeral home," she said. "Let's hope it works here."

Angel held Alex and Sandra's hands and closed his eyes. It was better not to look. He could still see all of his eyejack controls, and so he tried to teleport to the lab, just like she said. Nothing. Their coordinates didn't change. Two minutes left.

A loud crash made him open his eyes despite himself, and he saw one of his copters burning on the ground. Several of the prisoners were motionless on the ground, however. The copters were everywhere at once, reacting to any attack by splitting and covering all possibilities. That didn't stop a number of them from being destroyed. But when they managed to surround a varcolac-controlled individual with their energy shields, it would drive the varcolac out, leaving the human shell lifeless.

The copters were effectively holding back the prisoners, but that didn't help them teleport out of there. "What now?" Angel shouted over the buzz. "We need to get out of here!"

"You have any ideas?" Alex shouted back.

He didn't. Running was out of the question, not with Sandra unconscious on the ground next to him. Alex was improving her technique, knocking them down faster, but it didn't matter if the varcolac was just going to destroy the whole prison complex.

He had to do something. It seemed futile, but Angel wasn't going to spend the last minute of his life feeling sorry for himself. He brought up the teleportation module and opened the source code. There were thousands of lines of software, none of them familiar. He hadn't written this code. But he didn't need to read it all. Instead, he tried to teleport again, executing the module in a debugging mode, which allowed him to see each line of software as it executed. It was a common strategy for finding a coding bug, since it sometimes demonstrated that the software was executing different lines, or with different values, than the programmer expected.

With only one minute left before annihilation, Angel didn't expect to find anything, but he did. He saw it almost immediately. There was a line in there, an impossible line. It was a simple if-check that had no earthly business in this piece of code. And it wasn't a bug. The line couldn't have been put there by mistake. It was sabotage.

He removed the line and recompiled the module. Thirty seconds to go. It was time for goodbye, one way or another. Angel closed his eyes and focused on his lab.

CHAPTER 21

Alex knew they weren't going to make it. Her skill with the quadcopters was improving as she fought, holding the prisoners back, but it didn't matter. If Ryan's timeline was right—which she had no doubt it was—they had only seconds until the whole place was destroyed. Even if she killed all the prisoners, there was no reason to believe that would allow them to teleport again.

Not only that, but she was increasingly distracted by the presence of Sandra so near to her. With so many probability waves forming and collapsing in the near vicinity, many of them under her control, she could feel the tenuousness of the standing wave between them. They were just an unresolved quantum state, a single person with two possible futures. It was becoming increasingly clear to her that the wave stayed unresolved simply through their desire to keep it that way. Which meant that, just as she had reincorporated her own doubles back into herself at the funeral home, she could reincorporate Sandra into herself just as easily. They could become one person again, become Alessandra Kelley, in a heartbeat.

But she couldn't think about that now. If they both died here, as seemed likely, it wouldn't make any difference whether their probability wave resolved or not. And if by some miracle they lived, she was pretty sure they both wanted to keep on living separately instead of risking losing themselves in a combined whole.

The prisoners kept coming. It felt almost like a video game, in which she killed over and over again without thought. But of course, they were already dead, weren't they? The varcolac was killing them, not her. And when, in less than a minute, the whole prison went up in multidimensional smoke, it wasn't going to matter who had killed whom. They would all be dead.

She was about to apologize to Angel for failing, when he made a cry of astonishment.

"What is it?" she asked, but his eyes were closed, and he made no answer. A moment later, the wreckage of the prison vanished, to be replaced with a cluttered robotics lab.

Alex stared at him. "You fixed it! How—"

"Sandra first," he said.

Sandra still hadn't regained consciousness, and her hair was matted with blood. "Teleport us to an ER," Alex said.

"I don't have precise coordinates. We could be dropping her from several feet off the ground, never mind the risk of intersecting a car or another person."

"Call 911, then!"

"I already did."

Angel's lab was in West Philadelphia, only blocks from three different university hospitals. An ambulance was there in minutes, and she was in the Jefferson emergency room minutes after that. Alex worried that there would be trouble, that someone at the hospital would recognize Sandra from the news bulletins about Alex, and call the police.

"There's nothing we can do about that," Angel said. "She's not the sister who's wanted for murder, and she has friends in the police department. She should be okay. What she needs most is medical care."

The ER waiting room looked newly refurbished, with plush green chairs, racks of neatly organized magazines, and a play station for kids with toys, puzzles, and books. The screens mounted high on the walls showed news images of the demolished prison with the words, "Second terrorist action in two weeks."

The prison now looked like Citizens Bank Park, the pieces scattered in a complex spiral, none of which were bigger than a chair. The image being shown was from above, from a news helicopter, and the similarity was obvious.

"So . . . how did you get us out of there?" she asked.

Angel shook his head in wonder. "There was a specific line of code in the module. I can't imagine who would have put it there or why, but it was no accident. It instructed the software to stop working at 05:40 today."

"What?" Alex thought she must have heard him wrong.

"Yep. Hardcoded into the software was a downtime coordinated with the varcolac's destruction of the prison."

"We were sabotaged? Someone tried to get us killed?"

Angel shrugged. "Looks that way."

"But who would do that?" Even as she asked, Alex knew there was only one real answer to that question. This was Ryan's software. And he was the one who had known what time the varcolac's attack would come.

"So Ryan tried to kill us?" Angel asked.

"I don't know. But we need to pay him a visit," Alex said.

Angel took his Higgs projector out of his pocket and held it out to her. "Go ahead," he said. "I'm going to stay here."

"But you won't have a projector," Alex said. They were down to only one, since Jean had stolen Sandra's. "The police are going to be here, you know. Sooner or later, they'll make the connection to Muncy. Probably sooner."

"All the more reason not to leave Sandra on her own."

Alex tried to smile, but she was pretty sure it came out wrong. Was he scolding her? Sandra was her sister, after all. Another version of herself. That meant Alex should be the one worrying about her, the one ready to camp out in the waiting room as long as it took. On the other hand, where did Angel get off telling her how to take care of her own sister?

"I have to do this," she said. "I have to understand this, so next time it doesn't kill her."

"It's okay," Angel said. "You've got every cop in the country looking for you. I'll watch her for you."

Alex relaxed. She could see why Sandra liked this guy. He had an innocent, disarming way about him that meant you couldn't take him too seriously. He was hard to stay mad at. "You're sure?"

"I've got this. You go do the physics stuff."

Alex smiled for real this time. "Okay. See you soon."

The varcolac was living in Ryan's mind. He felt energized, a vitality of thought and will that he could only attribute to the alien presence. Mostly, he felt a sense of triumph and vindication. It was all true! The stories he had dreamed as a child, the idea that he was destined for something more, something greater. That his intelligence was not of the same kind as the people around him. He had always suspected, but now he knew it for certain. He was a creature of mind, not of flesh and blood, now reunited with his own kind. He was a varcolac.

It knew him completely. Not only that, but he, Ryan, knew the varcolac. He saw—if not fully grasped—its understanding of the universe, from the tiniest ambiguities of particle and wave to the vast sweeps of gravity that formed the contours of space-time. He sensed its confusion with the individual, the distinct, the time- and space-bound creatures that were human beings.

It could not have melded with just any human mind. Ryan was certain it was his mind, and his alone, that was precise and analytical enough to be an adequate host. Even so, Ryan could sense the varcolac's distaste with him, almost a moral judgment. A holy vessel defiled. He was a too-complex equation, a million variables where one would do. The varcolac's goal was not so much to destroy, as to unify. To simplify the equation, driving away inefficiency and inelegance.

Yes! He could see it all so clearly now. Ryan could have crowed with the beauty of the varcolac's vision. Human interaction was slow and imprecise, prone to error and misunderstanding. As an interface, it was terrible. Data was passed through conversation and body language and—worse—social cues and norms. Words carried ambiguous meanings and were rife with redundancy. Multiple languages, not easily translated, evolved from place to place and generation to generation.

And there were so many people! What was the point of it all? Ryan had heard so much nonsense about what human beings could do when they worked together, but really, they worked together so *poorly*. The varcolac had it right. And it wasn't until it had merged with Ryan's mind that the varcolac realized just how many people there really were. It was only beginning to comprehend how packets of oxygen, carbon, and hydrogen could think or interact at all. There didn't seem to be enough data passed to achieve the complexity of anything like intelligence. It had previously recognized as human only those individuals who had interacted with Higgs particles in productive ways—Brian Vanderhall, Jean Massey, Jacob Kelley, Alex, Sandra, and Ryan himself. Now it knew better. There were billions. And the varcolac was appalled.

And in that moment, Ryan knew what the varcolac was. It was the last of its kind, but at the same time, it was all of its kind. Its people had consolidated their minds for the greater good, first in pairs, then in communities, then ultimately in a single creature of incredible intellect and power. Those early individuals had been barely sentient, but merged, they were aware, omnipotent, indestructible. In the varcolac's mind, con-solidation was the greatest moral good. The elimination of waste. The alliance of disorganized and unproductive parts into one glorious, unified equation. There was only one varcolac, *could* be only one varcolac. It was, by definition, one.

Humanity was conflicted, disorganized, fractured, a staggering waste of resources. Now that it knew just how bad things were, the varcolac could see the enormity of the task it had before it. To combine, to merge. To make for itself a companion intellect, equal in perception and under-standing. The varcolac would make humanity what it should be. And it wanted Ryan to be the first. All other minds would be shaped around his. They would be consolidated into his own. And he, Ryan Oronzi—a greater Ryan than he was now—would soar through the dimensions of space and time, bodiless and eternal.

Ryan laughed. If he told anyone this, they would mock him or refer him to a psychiatrist. But he knew it was possible. The varcolac itself was proof of that.

That didn't stop him from a moment of sheer terror when the woman in the orange jumpsuit suddenly teleported into his lab.

"You bastard," she said. "I should kill you where you sit."

He wheeled his chair backward, away from her, but there was nowhere to go. "Who are you?" he said. "How did you get here?"

She gave him a withering stare. "Don't give me that," she said. "Don't you dare pretend you don't know me."

He stared at her. It wasn't fair. He had forgotten her long ago, had promised himself never to think of her. She couldn't be here. She was gone forever. "I don't know you," he insisted. Even to himself, it sounded feeble.

"You pathetic little child," she said. "What's my name? Say it!"

It came out of his mouth against his will. "Jean . . . Massey."

And it all came flooding back, filling his mouth with acid and making his stomach hurt. He had to get away from her. But how could he? He could teleport, but she would just follow him. It was, after all, her technology.

She lifted her hand, and he felt the eyejack contacts tear out of his eyes and go flying across the room. "I gave you everything you needed," she said. "All the research I did, enough to build your own Higgs projectors. I even gave you the software. Everything I had fifteen years ago and more."

Ryan took a deep breath and calmed his panic. He was a varcolac. She couldn't hurt him. "And it worked," he said, trying to smile but knowing it wasn't working. "You did a fantastic job. You should feel proud."

She advanced on him. "Proud? You think? I didn't share it with you so I could *feel proud*. I shared it with you so you could get me out of prison. Like you *promised*. That was the deal. I did my part, and you didn't do yours."

"I would have. Eventually. I was scared." He was almost whispering now, and he felt like a weakling. "I'm not an action sort of person. I had to work up the nerve."

She shook her head in disgust. "And here we are again. I do the work, and the world thinks you're the genius. I can't believe that for the second time in my life, I gave my best work to a man who would betray me."

"I *am* a genius," he said, a little strength coming back into his voice. She didn't know about the varcolac's vision, after all. She didn't know who he really was now. He was the One. He could face up to Jean Massey. "You laid the groundwork, sure," he said. "But you didn't do it. *I* created the baby universe. Me. You think just having the idea is all it takes?"

Jean smiled like a predator. "I killed the first genius who crossed me. And I'll kill you, too."

"No, you won't," Ryan said. His voice came out like a squeak.

"No? You think you're better at this than I am? You think you can block me if I decide to teleport your coffee mug into your soft little chest?"

Ryan swallowed. "If you were going to do it, you would have done it already. So what do you want?" He tried to sound brave, but he wasn't at all sure it came out that way. If she did try to kill him, would the varcolac protect him? Could he get the varcolac to kill her?

"Well, you're right. I do need something. I need all of your Higgs projectors," she said.

"All of them?" Ryan blinked. "But you already have one." He wondered which of the twins she had killed to get it, but it didn't seem important to ask.

"I want every last projector you've created. And you're working for the military, so I know there are a lot of them."

He was genuinely confused. "What are you going to do with them?"

Jean cocked her head. "I hardly see why you need to know. But I would have thought it would be obvious. I'm not wanted here in the

United States. Any of our government's allies would turn me over to them in a heartbeat. So I'm going where my skills might still be appreciated."

"Turkey? You're going to give all the Higgs projectors to the Turkish government?"

"I think they may be willing to pay handsomely for them. And I suspect they will be glad to put me to work for the cause. A cause I'm passionate about, by the way. Crushing the country that screwed me."

"I'll give you what I have," Ryan said. "But most of them aren't here. They took them to the front already. To use in the fighting."

"There isn't any fighting."

"There will be. In fact, from the questions they were asking me, I'm pretty sure they're planning some kind of preemptive—"

A monitor behind him shattered in a fountain of glass. "Enough chatter," Jean said. "I can find them without you. If you want to live, then make it worth my while to keep you alive."

"I'm doing it, I'm doing it." Ryan crossed to a safe and entered a long series of numbers on a keypad. The safe popped open. Inside were a stack of cards kept together with a rubber band. They were the Higgs projectors he had held back for his own further research, although he had told the government people that he had surrendered all of them. In fact, this stack wasn't all he had left, either. Ryan knew the value of redundancy.

"Happy?" he said. "Now take them and leave."

It didn't matter. She was welcome to them. All he needed was one. In fact, he wasn't even sure he needed that anymore.

Jean snatched up the stack of projectors. "What are you grinning at?" she said.

"You can't hurt me," Ryan said. "I'll be alive long after you and your kind are gone."

"My kind?" She stared at him as if he was insane, but then her face cleared. She chuckled softly. "Oh, I see. It's been talking to you."

Ryan was so astonished he didn't try to hide it.

"Been promising you things?" Jean went on. "Let me guess—it plans to consolidate all of humanity into your mind and make you eternal, bodiless, beyond pain and death. Do I have it right?" Her mocking smile collapsed into a scowl. "I've been listening to it for longer than you have." She leaned forward, invading his space. "A lot longer."

Kill her, Ryan thought at the varcolac. *She's a threat. Kill her.*

"It's been talking to me for years, in the prison, subtly speaking inside my head." She leaned away again, and the mocking smile returned. "When you think about it, I have a lot more to offer than you do. I have the projectors, for one thing." She held them up for him to see. "I'm smarter than you, more relentless, more ruthless. Less weak. Not so afraid of the world I can hardly step outside my door. You think *your* mind is a blueprint for the ultimate human? Please. I'm surprised you can tie your shoes."

Ryan leaped up in a rage and attacked. He didn't have his eyejack interface, but he had always known this confrontation was possible. He had prepared a panic button, a literal button on his personal Higgs projector that would blow everything near him into constituent atoms and teleport him to a safe, predetermined location. He reached into his pocket and pressed the button five times in quick succession and then held it down.

Nothing happened.

Jean shook her head and gave him a patronizing smile. "I'm sorry. I took the liberty of toasting your projector the moment I stepped into the room."

Then the worst thing of all happened. The varcolac left him.

"Goodbye, Ryan. Next time you make a deal, keep your end of the bargain."

Ryan started to panic. It was slipping away. It was leaving with *her*, choosing her instead of him. He couldn't feel the energy and clarity of its mind anymore. He felt clumsy and slow, barely able to hold a coherent thought. It was as if his neurons were firing through molasses. At first he thought he was dying, but then he realized: this is what it's like to be human. It was his normal state. He had always thought of himself as brilliant, but now, having tasted what it was like to be a varcolac . . . it was like the crash after an amphetamine. All he could think about was how to get it back.

"Don't . . . go," he managed.

Jean laughed and shook her head. "Oh, Ryan," she said. "It was never about you at all." She saluted him with his projectors and then disappeared.

Alex teleported into the High Energy Lab to see Ryan staring off into space with a grief-stricken expression on his face.

"I need two more Higgs projectors," she said.

Ryan's eyes wandered slowly over to her. Then he started to giggle.

"What's so funny?"

Ryan waved his hands helplessly, his giggle turning into a manic laugh, though his lips were turned down, making it look more like he was crying.

Alex grabbed his arm and shook him. "Hey! Stop it. What's wrong with you?"

He got himself under control, wiping tears from his eyes. "You want Higgs projectors," he said bitterly. "Everyone wants Higgs projectors."

Alex studied his face. "Who else was here?" she asked.

"Well, let me see," Ryan said. He ticked off on chubby fingers. "First off was Babington and some military guy. A colonel, I think they said. Lots of colors right here." He patted his chest. "They wanted all my projectors. All of them! Saw the demo and said they were needed for the war effort in Europe; no time to waste."

With a pang, Alex thought of Tequila Williams and the team at Lockheed Martin. Some of them were probably heading to Europe right now with those projectors, to train the troops on how to use them. She thought of her brother Sean as well, on some secret mission somewhere. If war was starting, would he be on the front lines? Would he live to come home?

Ryan touched his second finger. "Next, Jean Massey was here, and guess what she wanted? All my Higgs projectors. I had no choice—"

"Wait, you saw Jean Massey? She came here?" Alex asked. She looked around as if Jean might jump out from behind the furniture.

"She took all the projectors I'd kept back from the military," Ryan said. "I don't have any left."

"Why did she take them? She already had Sandra's," Alex said.

"She wants to sell them."

"What, on auction?"

"To the Turks."

Alex stared at him. "How did she even know to come here?"

"She's a smart woman. She figured it out."

"But she got here before I did. It must have been the first place she came from the prison. Even if she knew who you were from reading the news, this building is classified. How did she find you?" Alex crossed her arms. "What aren't you telling me?"

Ryan looked up at her with haunted eyes. "I don't have any more projectors. Go away."

"That can't be true," Alex said. "You're all about safety. Redundancy. You wouldn't have put them all in one place."

"It doesn't matter. It's all over now. It chose her. It left me for *her*."

"What did?" Alex said. She didn't understand what he was talking about. He looked like he was overcome by grief. Had he been abandoned by some lover? Though she had a hard time imagining Ryan Oronzi having a lover in the first place. A crazy thought occurred to her. She remembered some of the odd comments Ryan had made in the past. "Are you talking about . . . the varcolac?"

"It left me," Ryan said. "It's all over. I was going to be the One, but now it's gone."

Alex shook her head, trying to understand. The varcolac had made several attempts to kill them. Ryan, though not terribly helpful, had given her advance warning of its attacks. She stared into the mesmerizing laser display of the wormhole, letting its shifting patterns calm her. This man was probably crazy, but she needed him. She took a deep breath and turned back to face him. He stared down at her shoes.

"Look at me," Alex said.

His eyes flicked up to meet hers, but just as quickly wandered away.

"You're telling me that the varcolac is with Jean," she said. "In Turkey."

"Yes."

"She's—what—its ally? Its slave?"

"It wants to refine the human race. To raise us to its level, maybe even incorporate us into itself. That means stripping away inefficiency." He turned his head away. "You wouldn't understand."

"And Jean is going to help it . . . strip away inefficiency? By prompting armies to kill each other?"

Ryan shrugged. "Is that so terrible? They want to kill each other, let them do it."

"My brother is there," Alex said.

Ryan made no response. He stared at the floor, morose or belligerent, she couldn't tell which.

"Look," she said. "I intend to go find Jean and the varcolac and destroy them. To do that, I need at least two more projectors, which I know you have. I also need to know anything you know, or any ideas you might have, about how to kill it."

Ryan was quiet, staring at the floor. "I'll help you, under one condition."

Alex crossed her arms. "And what condition is that?"

"That you let me come with you."

Alex and Ryan teleported back to Jefferson Hospital to find Angel still sitting in the waiting room.

"She's sedated. They said she had a subdermal hematoma—bleeding inside her brain," Angel said. "They actually drilled a hole in her skull to let out the blood. Some girls have all the luck."

"You call that luck?" Alex said.

"Sure. Best I ever had was my tonsils taken out. For the rest of her life, Sandra gets to say, 'Oh yeah, well I had a hole drilled in my skull.' She wins, like, every conversation."

"You're a weird guy, you know that?" Alex said. Then she glanced at Ryan, and added, "But in the best way."

Angel grinned. "Did you find any more Higgs projectors?"

"Ryan had some stashed away. But we also found out that the varcolac is in Turkey." She explained what Ryan had told her about Jean and the varcolac's apparent goal.

"So it's going to facilitate a world war in order to eradicate humanity?" Angel asked.

"Yeah. Let's hear you joke about that."

"Well, it will make the lines shorter on Black Friday."

Alex shook her head. "Something's not right with you."

"So what's the plan?"

"The rest of my team from Lockheed Martin is in Poland right now, training soldiers to use this technology. Ryan called a military contact, and they've cleared us to hitch a ride on a military jet, if we can get there in time. From there, we'll try to get to Turkey and stop this thing."

"Not much of a plan."

"You have a better suggestion?" The banter suddenly seemed exhausting to Alex. She sat down in one of the waiting room chairs, bone tired. "Look, I don't have any ideas. I don't know how to find an extra-dimensional creature. But nobody else even knows it's there, or would believe me if I told them. We have at least some small means to fight it, so we're going to do it. Would I rather be happy and oblivious? Sure. But we don't get to pick. Are you coming with me?"

"Can't," Angel said. "I have to stay with Sandra."

"Sandra's being taken care of. We need you and your copter swarm."

Angel shook his head. "Nope. You're welcome to take my copters with you, but I'm not leaving. She needs someone to be here when she wakes up."

"I called our mother. She'll be here soon. She can take care of Sandra."

Angel's face took on a set expression, and Alex realized this was not a man easily shifted. "I'm staying," he said.

She sighed. "Okay. But if we all die, I'm going to say I told you so."

His smile leaped back into place as if it were spring-loaded. "I would expect no less. Good luck."

She handed him one of the Higgs projectors. "You might need this," she said. She turned to Ryan. "Let's go. We have a plane to catch."

"A plane? Why not just teleport?" Angel said.

"It's too far away. The error term is too high. There are military jets flying to Poland almost every day now, and we're going to be on one tonight."

"Okay. Take care of yourself."

"I'll do my best," Alex said. "You take care of my sister."

The jet was a brand new Lockheed Martin C-130Q, fresh off the assembly line and heading to the European front. It was a behemoth, a tank carrier, its cargo hold a gaping cavern large enough to fly a 747 into, including the wings. When they arrived, it was already stacked with three decks worth of tanks, Humvees, and armored personnel carriers. There was no passenger compartment, per se; only long rows of clips for soldiers to attach to along the walls.

Ryan's face was white. "I can't go on that," he said.

"It's an airplane," Alex said. "It's this amazing new technology: they can fly."

"It's a death trap."

"No, really. They do it all the time. Back and forth across the ocean. It's like magic."

"Don't mock me."

Alex rolled her eyes. "You want to stay? Fine. I'll see you later."

"Are you looking at this thing?" Ryan said. "Never mind crashing; there are a thousand tons of metal in there, tied down with chains and cables. Do you want to bet your life that they checked every connection? Double-checked every connection? All it takes is one loose Abrams sliding around, and you'll be crushed to jelly."

Alex looked at his pasty skin, his shaking hands. She didn't understand him at all. He knew the stakes. This wasn't a European vacation. He knew the probabilities were low that anything would happen to him on this flight, but he still couldn't get past it. She was tempted to leave him behind, but he knew things she didn't. Any hope they had of ultimately defeating the varcolac was going to have to include Ryan Oronzi.

"Turkey is on the other side of the Atlantic," she said, trying to keep the sarcasm out of her tone. "The only way is to take a plane. It's a risk, sure. But this risk is a lot smaller than the risk of teleporting there. And if what you told me is true, the risk of staying here is the worst one of all. So we're getting on this plane."

His eyes were locked on the jet. She wasn't even sure he was listening. After a moment, however, he took one hesitant step forward.

"That's right," she said. "You can do it."

He took another step. Sweat stood out on his forehead. At this rate, the world would be destroyed before they got off the tarmac.

"A little faster," she said.

Ryan stopped. He held out a trembling hand. She looked down, then back up at him. He couldn't be serious, could he? She waited a moment, eyebrows raised, but he just shut his eyes and held out his hand. What was she, his mother?

Sighing, Alex took his hand. He grabbed on like she was a life rope. His hand was fat and cold with sweat, like holding a dead fish. She swallowed. This was ridiculous.

She took a step toward the plane, but still he wouldn't come. His feet were planted. "Come on," she said. "One foot forward."

It seemed like an eternity, but finally, an inch at a time, he lifted his foot and took a step. After the first, it was easier, and he stepped forward with her, eyes still clenched tight, following her lead. When they reached the ramp, he started to moan, but he kept walking. She led him to a station, tied him into a harness, and clipped him down. Then she walked clear across the plane to the other side and clipped herself in. She didn't want to be anywhere near him for this trip.

CHAPTER 22

Sandra woke from a dream that she was riding a gigantic military plane. She felt disoriented, displaced. Where was Ryan? Gradually, she took in the fluorescent lights, the white walls and white machines, the sounds of curtains sliding on rings and distant people talking, the antiseptic smell. Where was she?

"She's only just regained consciousness," the nurse said. "She needs her sleep."

A woman in nursing scrubs stood in the room, facing down three men in severe dark suits. Sandra recognized them as Agent Liddle and the two agents that seemed to follow him everywhere. Liddle's face wore a scowl.

"This woman was at the scene of an apparent terrorist attack that claimed the lives of hundreds of people," Liddle said. "I'm going to have to ask you to step aside."

The nurse stepped aside. Liddle and his cronies surrounded the bed and loomed over Sandra. "It's time for some answers, Miss Kelley," Liddle said.

Sandra blinked. She felt strange. Her head was pounding with pain, but in a distant sort of way. She must be on some kind of medication. "Why don't you start with the questions?" she said.

Liddle raised an eyebrow, but the set of his mouth didn't change. He spoke with a false cheerfulness. "Feeling feisty, then? Good. The questions. Let's see. Where is your sister? Where is Jean Massey? And finally"—his voice grew dark—"what in seven hells did you do to Muncy Prison?"

She thought, remembering. She had gone back inside to fetch Jean, but then . . . what had happened? "Where's Angel?" she asked.

"That, my dear, is a question, not an answer. I ask the questions; you provide the answers."

She was starting to feel irritated, despite the meds. "I don't know where my sister is. I don't know where Jean Massey is. Right now, I don't even know where *I* am. And the prison was obliterated by a creature from another universe. Happy? Now where's my friend?"

Liddle scowled. "Angel is being debriefed by two of my colleagues. If he's cooperative, he may only be arrested. If not, he may find himself disappearing down a deep, dark hole of the kind only the intelligence services of the United States can create. And nobody comes out of those."

"You don't scare me," Sandra said. In fact, at that moment, not even the varcolac would have scared her. She felt cushioned on a cloud of good will, and long-term consequences seemed like a distant curiosity.

Liddle leaned down into her face. "There's a conspiracy going on here. You, your sister, your father, your boyfriend—you're all involved. Who are you working for? Is it Turkey? Japan? What's your goal? What are you hiding?"

He had one long hair growing out of his left nostril. Sandra could see it quite clearly, given how closely he was leaning over her. She felt a giggle rising to the surface, but she reluctantly tamped it down, realizing, at least in a distant way, that it was not appropriate for the situation. Instead, she just said, "He's not my boyfriend."

"I'm not fooling around here, Miss Kelley. Do you admit to being at Muncy Prison?"

"I don't think I have to talk to you."

"What sort of explosive did you use to destroy the prison?"

"I didn't use any explosive."

"What weapon, then?"

"I didn't destroy it."

"Did you break Jean Massey out of prison?"

Sandra sighed. "I want to talk to Detective Messinger."

"You're talking to me now."

"Not anymore. You don't believe me. This is a waste of my time."

"And Messinger does believe you?"

"Look, bring her in here. I'll tell her everything. Then she can tell you."

"Is she part of your conspiracy, too?"

The sound of a scuffle down the hall caught Liddle's attention. "Let me in! She's my daughter, not some criminal. Let me in, or I'll call a lawyer. I'll call the press. Get your hands off me!"

Liddle stepped into the hall. "Let her through," he said.

A moment later, Sandra's mother turned the corner, her face red and her curly hair askew. Sandra grinned. "Mom!"

Her mother glared at Liddle. "You," she said. "I might have known. Do you always conspire to keep mothers and daughters apart, or is it a special interest with my family?"

"I could arrest you for interfering with an investigation," Liddle said. "Do you have information relevant to this case? Or am I about to throw you out?"

"Leave her," Sandra said. "And send Messinger in. I'll talk to her."

Liddle held her gaze for a moment. "This is your one chance. I'll bring in Messinger, but I will also be here. If you talk, good. If not, I will have you relocated to a facility of my choosing, even with your injuries. Under the National Defense Authorization Act, I can hold terrorism suspects, without trial and without access to a lawyer, indefinitely. Do not cross me on this. I will do it."

He walked out. Sandra's mother rushed over and wrapped her arms around her. Sandra threw an arm around her neck and held her close. Her mother's thick dark hair spilled over her face, and Sandra inhaled her familiar scent. "I'm so sorry about Dad," Sandra said.

Her mother leaned back. "I didn't just bully my way through there to hug you," she said, her voice low and urgent. "I found something."

She held out a thin card. Sandra took it. "Dad's phone?" she said.

Her mother nodded. "It wasn't on your father's body at the stadium.

The police tore the house apart looking for it and finally concluded that it must have been tossed away in the blast and destroyed."

"Where was it?"

"In the toaster."

Sandra looked at her incredulously. "The toaster? But wouldn't it have melted in there?"

Her mother smiled. "We haven't used that toaster in years, not since Sean left home. Your father knew that. He hid it somewhere nobody but him would think to look for it."

"But why?" Sandra bit her lip, trying to concentrate through the buzz of the pain medication. Her father had been in the kitchen when she saw him last, possibly right up to the point where his probability wave collapsed and he disappeared. "Do you think he hid it on that last day, when you stepped out of the room?"

"I don't know. I was hoping you could look at it, figure out what was so important that he had to hide."

"I can do that." Sandra took the phone and slid it under her sheet, just as Melissa Messinger came through the door. Angel was with her.

Sandra smiled in relief. "I thought they were going to disappear you," she said.

"Not yet," Angel said. "They tried, but I threatened to use my ninja judo jiu-jitsu on them, and they fled."

"Is that a real thing?"

"I don't know, but it has lots of J's in it. Sounds impressive."

"Look, I don't think Liddle is kidding around," Messinger said. "He's on his way back in. You need to spill the beans, and it better be convincing, or he's going to start throwing his weight around."

"He's a scary dude," Angel said. "But, speaking of disappearing . . . we've got to go."

Sandra wasn't expecting it. The room disappeared, and they were in sudden darkness. There was a loud crack, and she was falling, sliding off the bed. Her mother screamed. She was turned around, disoriented. What was happening? An eerie, multicolored *something* was moving to her left. She heard Angel cursing. Finally, light flooded the room.

They weren't in the hospital anymore. It was a large, windowless laboratory of sorts, filled with machines and apparatus of various kinds. In the center stood what looked like a large laser-light display, swirling and sparking out colors. "Where are we?" Sandra asked.

"Welcome to the evil scientist's lair," Angel said. "We're on the eighth floor of the High Energy Lab at the NJSC. Ryan Oronzi's home base."

Angel had teleported not only Sandra, but her bed, her IV pole, her heart monitor, and her mother, who had still had her arms around Sandra when Angel came in. One leg of the bed had materialized in the same location as the frame of a swivel chair, obliterating both. The bed sagged crazily to one side, and Sandra lay on the floor, with only her legs still in the bed. The IV had torn free, and her arm was bleeding. The heart monitor beeped wildly.

"Sorry about that," Angel said, helping her up. "Not exactly a stylish rescue." He nodded to Sandra's mother. "Mrs. Kelley. Pleased to meet you."

Sandra's mother did a slow turn, taking in the room. "Amazing," she said. "And good move, getting us out of there."

Sandra struggled to her feet. She was wearing only a hospital gown, which was open at the back. She tried to hold it closed, but it didn't work.

"Let me," her mother said. She tore the pillowcase to tie a makeshift bandage around Sandra's bleeding arm. Then she folded the sheet and wrapped it around her, under her arms, threading the corners through and tying them together behind her neck. As a dress, it was a little odd, but it kept her covered, and seemed to stay up on its own.

"Gorgeous," Angel pronounced. "You're ready for Paris Fashion Week."

"Why did you pick here?" Sandra asked.

"It was the only set of coordinates already stored on the projector Alex gave me. I didn't have time to get creative."

"It's a good spot," Sandra said. "Isolated, hard to find, and with plenty of computing and communication equipment. I wish I could see Liddle's face when he finds out we're gone." She looked at the display in the center of the room, with its twisting neon colors. It was beautiful. "What's that thing?" she asked.

Angel shrugged. "I have no idea."

"Are you going to be okay?" her mother asked.

Sandra shrugged. "I'll probably have a rotten headache when the pain meds wear off, but I feel fine." She took a step and wobbled a bit, light-headed. "Almost fine, anyway."

Her mother tried to guide her to a chair. "Wait," Sandra said. She hunted around on the floor, and came up with her father's phone. "Let's see what we can do with this."

The plane flight was the most terrifying experience of Ryan's life. He had never even been on a passenger jet before, never mind a military transport, so he had no idea whether the sounds and vibrations he heard were normal or not. The engine roared like a famished beast, and when it started rolling down the tarmac, every tank and truck and piece of equipment rattled and shook. They built up incredible inertia, hurtling blindly at breakneck speed, and Ryan knew in his soul that this behemoth could not possibly take off. They would plow into the buildings at the end of the runway, and he would die.

The rumbling grew worse, until his jaw hurt from clenching his teeth, and he felt his arms would be bruised from clinging to the straps. The plane gave a lurch, and Ryan vomited, covering his clothing in foulness. He coughed and spat, only to realize that the battering had stopped. They were airborne.

The knowledge did not calm him. It meant only that they were climbing higher and higher, their potential energy increasing every minute. He couldn't help checking the GPS in his eyejacks and watching their altitude climb. In moments, they were high enough to eliminate any chance of survival were the engines to fail.

This was all Alex's fault. She had practically dragged him on board, signing his death warrant. He shouldn't have listened to her. He should have teleported a rock into her head rather than let her strap him into this flying deathtrap. Just because people sometimes survived such a flight didn't mean it was safe. People survived shark attacks and gunshots, too, but that didn't mean they were a good idea.

He screamed, drawing the attention of the few other passengers, a few soldiers and pilots who were strapped in farther up the decking. And Alex. Alex looked at him with pity. He didn't want her pity, not when it was her fault he was here. If he could have reached her, he would have slapped her. Except that slapping her would have required him to release his grip on the handles attached to the plane's fuselage. He couldn't do that, not even to wipe the vomit from his face.

This was all Jean's fault, too. The only reason Ryan had agreed to come along was because Jean had stolen the varcolac's favor away from him. He had to get it back. *He* was the One, not her. He was born to it. With the varcolac on his side, he wouldn't be afraid anymore. With the varcolac on his side, everyone else would have to be afraid of him.

Alex was probably laughing at him. She didn't show it on her face, but inside, she was laughing. She thought he was ridiculous. He screamed again, in frustration and fear. Why couldn't she just laugh in his face? At least then he would see it. He wouldn't have to imagine her later, recounting the flight to friends, imitating him, mocking his terror.

Maybe the plane would go down, and she wouldn't get the chance. That would wipe the smile off her face. He'd be laughing at her, then. Only he wouldn't, would he? His fragile body would be hurtling toward the ground, then crushed and torn apart by thousands of tons of twisted, razor-sharp metal. The image sickened him, and he vomited again.

He had to get off this plane. He couldn't take it, not a moment longer. He opened his eyes a crack and found the straps. He fumbled at the buckles, trying to get them free. The knots were too tight. He couldn't get his fingers into them enough to separate them, especially with how they kept shaking. He was trapped. Alex had trapped him here to die.

He wasn't made for this. He hated his body, hated every physical limitation and danger. The varcolac never had to fear something so prosaic as a fall from a height. Ryan was so much more than this. Why should his mind be trapped in this fragile flesh? He longed to be free of it. If by some miracle he made it through this flight alive, he was going to do everything he could—everything—to insure that this never happened again. He was a varcolac. He was pure mind. And he wasn't going to let Jean Massey take that away from him.

The plane landed before Alex expected it. She had finally managed to fall asleep and thus missed the last several hours of the transit. It had definitely been a good choice to stay clear of Ryan; she had seen him lose his dinner a few seconds into the flight. She didn't bother going over to him. She expected he could get off the plane without her holding his hand.

They had landed at the Krakow 8th Air Base in southern Poland. Since Turkey's semi-peaceful assimilation of Greece and most of the Balkan states, Krakow was only two hundred kilometers from the Turkish army's front lines. She saw rows of fighter planes, bombers, and helicopters, and farther afield, meadows full of tanks, trucks, and rocket artillery.

The sky was gray. A light rain was falling, but that didn't stop hundreds of uniformed soldiers from striding purposely through it, attending to various duties. Planes roared overhead. The noises of a hundred engines clamored to drown each other out, and the air was dank with the smell of wet metal.

Ryan pushed down the ramp past her and promptly fell on his face at the bottom. A uniformed major hauled him to his feet just as Alex reached them. The major was large and dark-skinned, his features almost invisible in the gray light. Even so, he projected a sense of lethal strength that went beyond just solid musculature and military posture. This man was a controlled killer.

"Please tell me you're Major Hughes," Ryan said.

The major nodded. "Welcome to Poland, Dr. Oronzi." He turned to Alex. "And you are?"

Alex had a moment of panic. She couldn't give them her real name, could she? They would know that she was wanted for Secretary Falk's murder. She was still wondering what to do when Ryan said, "This is my assistant. Her presence here is code-word compartmented; her identity is need-to-know."

Hughes seemed to accept that explanation, as if secret identities were a normal part of his life. He saluted Ryan, who made a pathetic attempt to return the gesture. "I've been instructed to deliver you safely to the facility and give you everything you need." Hughes lowered his voice. "And just between you and me, sir, this is the most incredible piece of Special Ops hardware I have seen in all my days. The Rangers and Seals are going to piss themselves when they find out we got it first."

Hughes took them on the road in an open-top Jeep. Alex studied his uniform, wishing she remembered more about divisions and insignia. He was in the Marine Corps, she could tell, and almost certainly Special Ops. Was he Force Recon? Would he know Sean? Running into him among the hundreds of thousands of coalition troops amassed on the Polish border would be quite a coincidence, she knew, but how many Marine Special Ops units could there be? Hughes probably knew where her brother was. She couldn't ask him, though, not without giving away her identity.

The streets were packed with a mix of tiny European cars and huge military trucks and Humvees. Alex had no idea where they were going, though again, she didn't want to call attention to herself by asking. There seemed to be billboards on every building, most of them alien and incomprehensible, though occasionally she saw products or logos she recognized. Coke. McDonalds. Kraft Macaroni and Cheese.

Between high-rise apartments, she caught glimpses of the famous churches in the old town, though they seemed to be heading in the other direction. Finally, they stopped at a building that Alex guessed had once been an elementary school, though she couldn't read any of the Polish signs. Soldiers in gray fatigues guarded the entrance. They saluted Major Hughes as he marched Alex and Ryan through.

The school's gymnasium was crowded with more Special Ops types, training on the use of Higgs projectors. There were a dozen civilians in the room, but only one six-foot black woman with three-inch heels and pink eye shadow. "Tequila!" Alex shouted.

Tequila Williams saw her. Her mouth dropped open. Only then did Alex realize what a bad idea this might have been. Vijay and Lisa and Rod were here; they would recognize her. They would know she was wanted for murder. If Alex had to run, here in Poland, she'd be in bad shape. She was in the middle of a potential war zone. She didn't know the city or the language or have any way to get back to the United States. She could turn invisible and probably evade capture, but then she would be a ghost, trying to survive without any human interaction. The best option might be to let the army arrest her and send her home for trial.

"Alex!" Tequila screamed. She trotted across the room and wrapped her arms around her. "Did they finally decide to leave you alone, honey? All that nonsense about you and the Secretary. I told them you didn't do it."

The rest of her team gathered around, grinning and clapping her on the back. Lisa and Rod peppered her with questions about her trip over and rambled on about Polish food and military accommodations. Even

Vijay seemed pleased to see her, telling her how good it was to have her back on the team. "Though even with your help, there's no way we're going to train enough people in time," he added morosely.

They all seemed to assume she had been exonerated and had now come to Krakow to join the team. "I'm not here to help with the training," she said.

"Of course you're not," Vijay said. "That would be too much to expect."

"Listen," she said. "Don't ever take your projectors off. Keep them with you, and keep them running, even when you eat or shower. Take them to bed with you."

"Why? What's going on?" Tequila asked.

Alex spotted Ryan following Hughes into an office on the far side of the gym. "I'll be back," Alex said. "I'll explain it to you."

"It's that thing, isn't it?" Rod said. "The thing from the demo that killed Falk."

She could have kissed him. "Yes," she said. "We're fighting it. Be careful."

Alex jogged over to the door through which Ryan had disappeared. Inside, a very serious looking Asian woman in civilian clothes was talking intently. Major Hughes stood at attention behind her. "Come in, Ms. Kelley," the woman said. "And please close the door behind you."

Alex did so, a little rattled that she knew her name. Though if she knew it, that probably also meant she knew Alex hadn't really killed the Secretary of Defense. Alex closed the door as asked, and then joined Ryan. Ryan glared at her. What was wrong with him? Was he actually mad at her for helping him overcome his fears enough to take the plane?

She turned toward the woman, getting her first good look at her face. She recognized her. It was Ryan's lab assistant from back at the High Energy Lab. "Nicole Wu?"

Nicole gave a curt nod and offered Alex a dry handshake. "Actually, it's Colonel Wu, CIA. Thank you for coming."

Alex gaped at her. "CIA? You're kidding me. So you've been, what, undercover as a physicist? Spying on Ryan all this time?"

"No, actually, I am a physicist, though I'm afraid the agency doctored my resume quite a bit. I went to Muhlenberg, not Cal Tech, and I didn't actually finish my dissertation. I know enough to get by, though, and not be totally useless. I was the one who first convinced the government of the feasibility of the technology Ryan wanted to build."

"Nicole has been our main contact into the intelligence community," Ryan said coldly, not meeting Alex's eyes. "On paper, it was the Department of Defense paying the bills, but of course the Agency took a great interest in the technology, and behind the scenes they were really running the show."

"Which makes me Ryan's boss. And yours, when it comes down to it." Nicole gave a tight smile. "Now, can we get down to business?"

The room looked like a sports director's office, with trophies in a glass case and posters on the wall of men playing soccer—or football, Alex supposed they would call it. She was surprised to see a mesh bag full of basketballs in a corner, and a football—an American football, that is—on the desk. She had never been much into sports as an adult; that was Sandra's thing.

Nicole sat behind the desk. Ryan promptly sat in the other chair, leaving Alex to stand. "Ryan told me about Jean Massey. I need to understand how quickly she could have gotten the technology to Turkey, and the soonest they might reasonably be able to field it. This is crucial intelligence; American lives are on the line."

"You're going to make a preemptive attack, aren't you?" Alex said. "We're not going to wait to see if the Turks attack; we're going to start the war ourselves."

"That decision is way beyond my pay grade," Nicole said. "I'm just trying to establish the timeline."

Alex looked at Ryan. "Do you think Jean could have teleported there? Or would she have to take a plane?"

Ryan shrugged. "How should I know? She's working for the varcolac.

My best guess is, she can go wherever she likes in an instant. Or at least, she can go wherever it wants her to go."

"So we'll assume teleport," Alex said. "That means she's had a full day there. She can't have had any Turkish contacts, so it may take her some time to connect with the right people in their government. On the other hand, if she started showing off what she can do, it wouldn't take long. It may depend what her demands are and how readily they agree to them."

"Oh, they'll agree to them," Nicole said. "They'll agree to anything, once they see what she can do." She sounded bitter, disgusted. "Really, Ryan. She just waltzed in and asked for them, and you handed them over?"

"She would have killed me!"

"You could have *lied*, genius. You could have told her you didn't have any. That you gave them all away. Or—better yet—you could have told *me* the truth and actually given them all to me like you said you did. Then when a mad, psychotic, escaped murderer-turned-traitor showed up in your lab you wouldn't have had anything to give her!"

"I said I'm sorry." Ryan's voice was high-pitched and whiny.

"You could have been a hero," Nicole said. "Now you'll be lucky if you're not prosecuted."

"Prosecuted?" Alex said. "That's a bit much."

"He just handed our most significant military advantage over to our enemy," Nicole snapped back. "American troops, perhaps thousands of them, will die because of him. I think jail time would be pretty lenient."

Alex waved it away. "Fine. It doesn't matter whose fault it is. What I want to know is, what are we going to do about it now?"

"That's already done," Nicole said.

"What do you mean, done?"

"It's taken care of. Plans are in motion. It's a bit earlier than we intended, but some people"—she glared at Ryan—"have forced our hand."

"You sent troops into Turkish territory?" Alex asked. But no, a significant troop movement would have been public, would have made the news. All the fighter planes and bombers she saw at the airport wouldn't have been on the ground. "No. You sent Special Ops teams in, to take out important targets, didn't you? You sent them with Higgs projectors, to use the advantage while you still could."

"That, and a few other preliminary attacks," Nicole acknowledged. "Laser disruption of their satellites. Initiation of viruses we've insinuated into their comm systems. The full assault is outside my control, as I said, but the normal timeline will have the fighters scrambled within hours to take out their radar and SAM sites, followed by the bombers. The infantry should cross the line sometime tomorrow."

"You don't get it, do you?" Alex said.

Nicole raised her eyebrows. "I beg your pardon?"

"This isn't about us and Turkey. It's about the human race trying to survive against a powerful creature that wants to annihilate us. There's nothing the Turkish army can throw at us that's as dangerous as the varcolac. Forget about Jean Massey. Forget about Turkey. It's the varcolac that's the threat."

Nicole nodded with a patronizing smile. "I've heard Ryan's alien intelligence theory before. If you don't mind, I'm going to worry about whether Turkey has the means to deliver its nukes before I worry about a ghost in the machine."

Alex clenched her fists. There didn't seem to be much point in arguing with Nicole. She had been there the whole time, presumably seen the evidence Ryan had that something intelligent was breaking out of the wormhole. If she didn't believe him, nothing Alex could say would convince her, and there wasn't time to sit around trying.

"Let's go," Alex said to Ryan. "Looks like it's up to us."

Ryan looked startled. "What?"

"Miss CIA here thinks she knows what's going on. She's not going to help us. We're going to have to find Jean ourselves."

"Oh, I don't think so." Nicole held up her hands. "You can stop right there. I brought Ryan here to analyze the Higgs projectors when the ops teams return, to make sure they're working as well as they can be. I don't need my prize physicist jumping off to who knows where in the middle of enemy territory. What if they kill you? What if they torture you and force you to tell them everything they know? Just because Jean gives them the technology doesn't mean they'll know how to use it."

"Jean will tell them," Ryan said.

Nicole stood up, exasperated. "That's not the point. The point is, I don't want my chief technologist falling into enemy hands!"

Alex opened her mouth to say something defiant, but then thought better of it. Nicole probably couldn't stop her, but she didn't want to give her the chance, either. Instead, she said, "Fine. We'll do it your way." She let her anger and frustration fill her voice. "We'll stay here and help with the training. Just don't say I didn't warn you."

Nicole's smile was cold. "Thank you. I knew I could count on you." She turned to Ryan. "The other thing we need to do is ramp up manufacture. I've commandeered a cell phone factory in town and set a team to work developing a large-scale production process. Within the week, I want enough Higgs projectors for every soldier in our army. I'll take you to the site this afternoon; maybe you'll have some suggestions."

"That's it. Dismissed," Nicole said. She began flicking her eyes at something they couldn't see, presumably shuffling through files in her private eyejack space.

"I just have one more question," Alex said. "Is my brother Sean on one of the Special Ops teams that went behind enemy lines?"

Nicole's eyes refocused. "Those teams don't officially exist. I can't tell you who's on them."

"Come on," Alex said. "I gave up something for you. Return the favor. This is my brother; I just want to know where he is."

Nicole sighed. She dropped her voice to a whisper. "Yes," she said.

"Sean Kelley is on one of the advance parties. I couldn't tell you which, because I don't know. He'll be back here tomorrow night."

"Do you know the target locations?"

"What, so you can follow them? I'm not an idiot." Nicole pointed toward the door. "Get out of here. Report to Vijay Bhargava and ask him how you can help."

When Alex stepped out of the office, Tequila was there waiting for her. "You look like you could use a drink," she said.

"Aren't you working?" Alex asked.

Tequila laughed. "It's nine o'clock at night," she said. "We've been working for twelve hours. Time to hit the pub."

Alex shook her head. "It's night? Seriously? My internal clock is so scrambled."

They had walked less than a block from the elementary school when Tequila turned and climbed down a set of stairs into what appeared to be the cellar under a row house.

"This is a pub?" Alex asked.

"Welcome to Krakow," Tequila said. "Highest density of alcoholic establishments in the world. You're always either in a pub or walking past one."

The rest of the team was already there, all of them drinking bottles of Zywiec beer, except for Lisa, who clutched a glass of clear liquid. She held it up like she was giving a toast. "Wódka! Why come to Poland and drink beer?" she said in an attempt at a Polish accent that came out sounding Transylvanian.

Alex ordered a beer despite Lisa's protests, and felt some of the tension start to drain away. She was among friends. It wasn't much, given the threat to the people she loved, and to all of humanity, but at that moment it felt like the most important thing in the world.

For a time, they chatted about Polish drinks and food. Vijay had sampled a lime mead that he said was truly dreadful, and the team related a disastrous attempt to order pizza at a Polish restaurant that had resulted in being served a cheese-covered crust and a pitcher full of ketchup. A nearby Polish bookstore had a bigger section for books about the Pope than it did for novels, and one of the ten TV channels they could get from their hotel was entirely devoted to the Vatican.

"And don't get me started about the toilet paper," Rod said.

Alex laughed with them, but eventually the conversation slowed to a halt. She hesitated, not wanting to break the spell, but knowing she had to. "There are some things I have to explain to you guys," she said.

She told them everything. About the varcolac and its attacks, about Sandra, about Jean Massey and why she and Ryan had really come.

"So . . . you're heading behind enemy lines?" Tequila asked. "Turkey's a big place. How will you even know where to go?"

"I don't know," Alex said. "I didn't really think that far. I guess I thought it would be making itself obvious."

"Once it makes itself obvious, it'll be too late," Vijay said. "It's probably too late anyway."

"Thanks, that's a big help, Mr. Cheerful," Tequila said. She touched some beer to her fingers and spritzed it in his face. "I bet you're a miserable drunk."

"It sounds like the best thing we can do is to incorporate the teleportation and invisibility modules into our training," Rod said. "Put it in the hands of as many of our troops as possible, and educate the officers and general staff, so they'll figure out how to use them effectively. There's nothing you can do by heading off into Turkey alone. You'll just get yourself killed."

"I'm afraid the advance teams are walking into a trap right now," Alex said. "If the Turks already have the technology—worse, if the varcolac is there—then they may not get out alive. But I don't know where they are, and Nicole wouldn't tell me."

"I know where they are," Lisa said softly.

Everyone looked at her. She blushed. "I got on a bit with one of the guys on your brother's squad," she said. "He let slip where they were headed. One of the targets, anyway."

"Where?" Alex asked.

"I don't understand it. It was why he mentioned it; it was so strange a target."

"Spit it out!"

"The Jozef Stefan Institute. It's a scientific facility in Slovenia."

There was silence at the table. Alex had been expecting military targets near the front lines—radar installations or fuel depots or anti-aircraft weapons. They were only a few miles from Slovenia, but what was the importance of this institute? Were they stockpiling weapons there? Or developing them? The name rang a bell, but Alex couldn't figure out where she had heard it. Jozef Stefan Institute. "Of course!" Alex's mouth hung open as a rush of adrenaline hit her. "That's it. That's where Jean will be."

"Wait, how do you know?" Tequila asked. "What's there?"

"They have a particle accelerator. It's a small one, relatively low energies, nothing like the NJSC or CERN. But it's probably the only accelerator in all of Turkish-controlled territory. If they want to make more Higgs projectors, enough for their whole army, then that's where they'll do it."

"You're going, aren't you?" Tequila said.

Alex realized she was on her feet. "I have to. Sean and his team don't know what they're heading toward. The varcolac will tear them apart."

"How will you get there?"

Alex started pacing, two steps one way, three steps the next. "I don't know. I need the coordinates. The exact coordinates."

"I can help you with that," Rod said.

"How?"

"I have access to the bombing dictionary."

That got everyone's attention. "Why on Shiva's third eye would they give you access to that?" Vijay asked.

"They didn't exactly *give* it to me," Rod said with an impish grin. "I was helping the major get his laptop on the network, and, well . . ."

"You devious little hacker," Tequila said.

"Anyway, I can get the coordinates. Some of them they have down to less than a meter."

The whole group stood, pulling euro notes out of their wallets and leaving them on the table.

"You can stay," Alex said. "You've had a long day; I'm sure Rod can get me what I need without the rest of your help."

"You don't understand," Tequila said. "We're coming with you."

"To Slovenia? Don't be stupid."

Tequila raised an eyebrow.

"You're not soldiers. There's no reason for you to come."

"If you fail, we all die anyway, right?" Lisa said.

"Well . . . yes."

"So, if there's any chance we can help, we might as well come."

Alex smiled. "I guess you're right." These were true friends, willing to follow her behind enemy lines, purely on the strength of her word that it was important. She hoped she didn't get them all killed.

"I knew it," Vijay said. "Somehow I always knew I wouldn't live past forty-five."

CHAPTER 23

Sandra's headache was in full force now, like a tide of pain washing through her scalp. She tried to ignore it, concentrating on the graphs in front of her. An empty pizza box and cups of soda were scattered around her, the remains of a dinner now long finished. She was getting hungry again, though she knew her body probably needed sleep more than it needed food.

Her father's phone had been crammed with data, so much so that it was difficult to determine what was important and what wasn't. She had sorted by date modified, to start out with, and immediately found the data that Angel had sent her the day after the stadium explosion, showing the pattern of the blast. She located her father's analysis of it, too, the ten-dimensional look that turned all the crazy lines into simple, coherent curves. But what had been so sensitive and important that he felt the need to hide his phone in the toaster?

She gradually pushed backward in time. He had obviously been using the phone for a great deal of analysis and study of quantum effects, far more than she would have expected from a retired scientist. He still taught some courses locally, at Swarthmore College, but this was high-level stuff, a personal project of some kind that seemed to have been going on for years.

It took her a long time before she figured out that the target of the study was herself.

"He's been monitoring me," she said. "Me and Alex both. For years. Since the beginning." By the beginning, she meant the split, the point at which she and Alex had ceased to be Alessandra and had taken different paths. "He's been gathering data at a quantum level." She stared at it further. "I think it's in our phones. He hid some kind of device into our phones that monitors us and sends the data back to him." She looked up at her mother. "Did you know about this?"

She shook her head. "No. He didn't say anything."

"What was he looking for?" Angel asked.

She knew. The math was beyond her, but she knew what he must have been studying. She and Alex were a quantum fluke, a probability wave that refused to collapse. Every other probability wave in their crazy lives had collapsed, a single path taking precedence. Even her father's own experience, both in prison and out of it at the same time, had eventually come back together. But she and Alex hadn't. For fifteen years.

Of course he was curious. Of course he wanted to study them, non-invasively. He was their father. Beyond the simple scientific interest, he cared about them as his children. He wanted to understand why the wave held for so long and whether it would ever collapse again.

Sandra wanted to know, too. She brought up graph after graph, trying to make sense of it. The notes were terse, cryptic, not meant for anyone besides her father to read. But finally, she thought she understood. The strength of the probability wave field, constant for many years, had started to deteriorate over the course of the last three months. At last measurement, it was less than a third of its original strength. She thought of the recent occasions when Alex's thoughts had mixed with her own, when their minds had seemed to almost collide. Was it happening? Was there anything they could do?

But there was something more. She discovered a text file with some scribbled notes. It read, "NJSC funding increase, new parking garage, November 5th. Coincidence?"

The date coincided, roughly, with the time the probability wave field had started to diminish. Her father had been suggesting a causal relationship—that something going on at the NJSC was weakening the field, making it more likely that she and Alex would collapse into one person again. The note was followed by a bewildering array of mathematical notations and equations.

Sandra looked up at the universe simulated in flashing colors behind the glass. Her head pounded. She felt so angry. She glared at her mother, who had been looking over her shoulder. "Did he tell you about this?"

Her mother shrugged helplessly and shook her head.

"I bet he told Alex. He was always telling her things, things he thought I was too stupid to understand. Maybe he was hoping to nudge things somehow so that, when the wave collapsed, it was Alex's mind that came out on top."

"Don't think that," her mother said. "It's not true. He loved you."

"Did he? He never liked me much before the varcolac came, and then afterward, he had Alex. She was like this brand new daughter who had saved the world with him, who liked quantum physics, who risked her life to save us all. Not even Claire could compete with that." She stood up and clenched her fists. "I'm tired of these riddles! I'm not smart enough to solve them. I never have been."

Her mother wrapped her arms around her, and Sandra sobbed. "I miss him so much," Sandra said finally. "I don't know what to do. Why didn't he just tell us what to do?"

Angel put an arm on her shoulder and wiped a tear off her face with his thumb. He acted as if crying were a normal thing, not a sign of weakness or frailty, not something to be uncomfortable about. It made her feel safe. She wiped her face on the hospital sheet she was using as a dress. "You should look at this," he said.

Her phone pinged as it attached to his feed, and suddenly she could see what he saw. It was a video feed of sorts, though he was viewing it in non-immersive mode, like looking down into a glass box instead of standing in the scene itself.

The display was strange: granular and oddly colored, with some data missing. It was like the image was made of a constantly-moving fuzz, which kept shifting around. Even so, she could make out five people on a roof of some kind, though she couldn't see the background or anything more than a few feet away. The people's faces were gray and indistinct.

"What is this?" she asked.

"It's the quantum data your father was collecting from Alex's phone," he said. "I used the location references to put together a 3D image."

"So . . . this is live? One of these people is Alex?"

"The closest one, I think. I don't think it was meant to be used to spy on her, exactly, but the data is there."

"Where is she? What's she doing?"

He shook his head. "It's all locally referenced. There's no global locator data, or anything like that. You can just call her, if you want to know where she is."

But Sandra could hardly hear him anymore. Her awareness of the room was fading, the colors shifting. She could see what Alex was doing. No, more than that. She was sliding into Alex's viewpoint, falling into her mind. And she couldn't stop.

The Jozef Stefan Institute was in Ljubljana, Slovenia's capital and largest city. It would almost certainly be guarded. Instead of teleporting to the roof of the Institute, Alex chose an old castle, a tourist attraction that looked down on Ljubljana from a rounded hill in the city center. It was night, so the castle was closed to the public, its ramparts deserted.

Catching her breath, Alex looked around, astonished. For some reason—perhaps because she had never heard of the place before today—she had pictured Ljubljana as a dirty slum of a place, poor and over-crowded. Instead, she found a picturesque old European city, clean and colorful, with red shingled roofs and cobblestone streets and the blue ridges of the Alps in the distance. Lights danced through the night, not garish with neon or strobing color, but subtle and tasteful.

The Institute itself was a university and center of scientific endeavor, one of Slovenia's proud achievements. Its five buildings formed a sort of square in a residential area of the city, with a courtyard in the center where flowers bloomed. It was a place of peace and human accomplishment. And it was surrounded by Turkish soldiers.

It could mean only one thing: that Jean had reached and convinced the leadership of Turkey, and that they recognized the importance of this place. Alex's mind raced. Now that she was here, it was increasingly clear to her how unprepared she was. How would she find Sean? She didn't know his plan of attack or where he was coming from. Maybe he was waiting until the dead of night. Maybe he had already rigged the place with explosives and was putting as much distance between himself and the Institute before it blew. Or maybe the varcolac had already killed him.

It made her suddenly sad. Why did there have to be war? Hadn't Europe suffered enough in the last century and a half? When humanity was capable of such beauty and discovery, why did countries have to pit their aspirations against each other in widespread destruction? She hated to see this beautiful city scarred. And she didn't want her brother to die.

Alex unlocked the large black hard case she had brought with her: Angel's quadcopters. If it came to a showdown with the varcolac, it was the best weapon she had, the only weapon she knew that could even slow it down. Though ultimately, it had not even been the varcolac itself she had fought at the prison. It was a shadow of itself, created by a Higgs singlet sent precisely back in time, like an automated computer program given certain goals and functions by its creator. And she had very nearly lost.

An alarm sounded. A soldier on the roof was pointing in their direction and talking into a radio. They'd been spotted.

"What do we do?" Tequila asked.

The soldiers stood at alert with weapons raised. Alex saw an officer speaking rapidly to a squad and pointing at the castle. Then they started to die.

Gunfire tore into them, sounding like distant pops from Alex's vantage point. The soldiers' bodies danced and fell. A few started shooting, but their weapons were wrenched out of their hands by invisible forces. Alex watched, aghast. It had to be her brother and his team out there, using their projectors and killing these men. Somehow, it seemed more awful in this idyllic city with its old-world charm. The old world had bloody conflicts too, of course. But everything about this place spoke of peaceful cooperation and advancement. The blood on the cobblestones was lurid, garish, wrong.

She understood the reasons. She didn't even blame Sean, not really. This place had to be destroyed. It was a military installation now, whether it had been built for that purpose or not. It was possibly the enemy's single most powerful asset. If it had been bombed from the air, it would have somehow seemed more justifiable, though of course the soldiers would have died just the same. A team of insurgents was the more humane option; it would allow them to kill the soldiers without killing the scientists inside.

When the soldiers lay dead on the floor, the marines appeared, seemingly out of nowhere, and advanced on the entrance. They ran quickly, in a crouch, anonymous in their masks and urban fatigues.

Alex could immediately tell which one was her brother. Sean had been born with a short arm, half the normal length, with a tiny hand at the end of it that couldn't grasp anything very well. For most of his growing up, it had been that way, a source of frustration and occasional ridicule, though he could do just about anything he put his mind to learning. He was athletic and coordinated, and worked twice as hard as anyone to prove he could not only do the same things others could, but do them better.

Then a prosthetic was invented that could enclose his short arm and operate off of the signals of his nerves and muscles. It was a wonder of engineering and made his left arm more precise and powerful even than his right. Sean had joined the military—an impossibility before the prosthetic—and, true to form, had dedicated himself to being not just a capable soldier, but one of the very best.

It was the prosthetic that gave him away. It was bulky where it enclosed his left arm, and even under specially fitted fatigues, it stood out.

They disappeared inside. Maybe they would set their explosives and leave safely, and the facility would be destroyed. Sean knew what he was doing. He and his team were in superb shape, crack shots, experts in infiltration and sabotage. They were trained with the Higgs projectors and knew when and how to use them. Alex began to hope that their presence wouldn't be needed, that Sean and the other marines had everything under control.

Then the bodies on the ground started to rise.

CHAPTER 24

"Sandra!" Her mother had her by the shoulders, but she was looking up at someone else. "We need to get her back to the hospital."

"No." Sandra blinked her eyes, looked around. She was on the floor in the High Energy Lab. Her mother and Angel were there, looking concerned. "I'm back. I'm okay."

"This isn't right," her mother said. "You have a concussion, maybe worse. You need medical care."

Sandra stood up, a bit shaky. Her head throbbed. "No, I don't. It's not medical at all. I wasn't unconscious." She turned to Angel. "I was there with Alex. In her mind. It was like I *was* her, seeing what she saw, thinking her thoughts." She sank into a chair. "I don't even think she knew I was there."

Was that what it would be like, when their probability wave finally collapsed? Would she be absorbed into Alex without a glitch? Not only did Alex not know she was there; *she*, Sandra, hadn't known she was there. She hadn't been aware of herself, like a ghost trapped in Alex's body. She had *been* Alex.

And now she was back. How long would it last? How much time did she have left before she ceased to exist as an individual?

"I have to lie down," she said.

Her mother pulled the thin mattress off the broken bed. Sandra stretched out on it, trying not to cry from the pain. Her mother sat next to her and massaged her scalp.

"She's in Slovenia somewhere, at a scientific institute," Sandra said. "Sean is there, too. And I'm pretty sure the varcolac is somewhere nearby."

"Is there anything we can do?"

She shook her head. "I don't think so. Hopefully she has a plan."

She lay quietly for a time, thinking. Wondering what her life would have been like if she and Alex had never split. Would she even have existed? It was so hard to think about, the concept of being Sandra, and yet being different. She and Alex were just two examples of millions of possible Alessandras that might have been, each of them her, and yet each of them not. If she and Alex did some day combine, she probably wouldn't mourn the day. She would be a new person, and that person would be glad to be alive. But that person wouldn't be Sandra Kelley.

"Angel?" she said.

He came to her side.

"Can you tell from the data how long I have left?"

"What do you mean?"

"From my father's data. If the trend continues, can you plot how long it will be until Alex and I converge into a single person?"

For once, he was solemn. "I can't. It's a complex pattern, not linear. Maybe someone else could tell, but not me. I'm sorry."

She met his eyes. She hadn't had much time to think about it, but she really liked Angel. He was funny, relaxed, unintimidated by petty authority figures. He was intelligent and self-sacrificing and cared about doing the right thing. He wasn't much to look at, but that was growing on her, too. She could trust him.

She took a deep breath and let it out. "I don't think I have very long," she said.

The Turkish soldiers had no eyes. They rose to their feet, ignoring the bullet wounds in their chests and heads, and set off toward the main entrance of the institute, the doors that the American soldiers had just entered. Alex felt the panic start to flutter in her chest like a trapped moth. The varcolac was here.

There was no time for fear. She teleported to the low roof of one of the Institute buildings, and her team followed close behind. Alex cued the quadcopters from her eyejacks, and they rose out of their case four at a time. As soon as each group reached eye level, she sent them teleporting down to surround a single eyeless Turkish soldier. A flash of electricity, the puppet fell, and Alex moved on to the next.

"What can we do?" shouted Vijay.

"Find another way into this building!" she said. He ran off across the roof, the others following him.

There were too many soldiers. She took out as many as she could, but they reached the doors anyway. An American who'd been left at the entrance fired his M4 into them, but the bullets passed through them like water. He slammed the doors in their faces, but they walked right through without a pause. She heard the soldier scream.

Alex surrounded another puppet soldier with quadcopters. This time, however, the puppet reached out and grabbed one with each hand. The flash of their energy shields still took him down, but he took the two copters down with him. They smashed into the ground, writhing and sparking as the blades dug into the dirt. The next soldier did the same thing. Unlike the puppets at the prison, these were learning. The varcolac was here, altering their behavior to react to her attack.

She teleported the remaining copters back to the roof. "Vijay?"

"Over here," he called back. "There's a way in."

She ran over to see a metal door, which they had unlocked by the simple expedient of teleporting a pebble into the lock mechanism, blowing it apart. The door hung open.

"Let's go."

She led them inside and down a flight of concrete stairs, which opened at the bottom into a long, poorly-lit hallway. It was evening, and most of the eight hundred scientists that worked here during the day were gone. She had to find Sean and warn him what he was up against.

Then, once his explosives were set, she could teleport him and his team back to Poland. Assuming they lived that long.

She rounded a corner and felt a gun at her head. A man grabbed her by the back of the neck and shoved her face against a wall, but not before she got a glimpse of his blackened face and gray fatigues.

"I'm an American," she said. The soldier turned her around and held her at arm's length, taking in her appearance, processing the sound of her voice. "I'm Sean Kelley's sister," she added. The expression on the soldier's face would have been comical in any other situation.

"Team Alpha," the soldier murmured. "We have a situation at entry point one."

"Copy that," a familiar voice replied. "Do you need help?"

Alex grabbed the radio. "Sean," she said. "It's me."

Ryan couldn't find Alex anywhere. She wasn't in the room that had been assigned to her to sleep. She wasn't in the training center. A soldier said she had gone down the street with all of her old team members to a local pub, but she wasn't there, either. He supposed they could have left there and gone on to sample another pub, but he was starting to suspect something worse. She had left him behind. She had forced him to get on that plane so they could fight the varcolac together, but then she had abandoned him to go on by herself.

Fortunately, he still had access to the logs from his baby universe and associated programs back at the NJSC. Every Higgs projector still ultimately drew energy from there, and so any Higgs projector activity was still logged in that system. He couldn't track her if she was just walking around the city, but if she did any teleporting, he would be able to see exactly where she went.

When he looked at the log, he was astonished. She had left the country.

She was behind enemy lines. Not only that, but she had made copies of the latest projector software—including the teleportation and invisibility modules—for her friends on the team from Lockheed Martin. Of course—she had taken them along, but not him. What were they doing?

Ryan looked up the coordinates with a mapping program and found the address: the Jozef Stefan Institute in Ljubljana. It was a physics institute, mostly, though they did some of the softer sciences as well. They had their own particle accelerator there. There weren't many of those in Eastern Europe; most of Europe's accelerators were in Germany, Switzerland, or the United Kingdom. In fact, it was probably the only one in all of Turkish-controlled territory.

Of course. It was obvious, now that he thought of it. The Institute was where Jean would be. The handful of projectors Ryan had given her wouldn't be enough; Jean—meaning the varcolac, of course—would want thousands of soldiers to have projectors. It would want men killing each other at an unprecedented rate. That meant the Turks would need to make a lot more.

Alex had gone to Ljubljana to stop her. She had taken her team along with her, but not him. She hadn't even told him she was going. Why? Because he was competition. She wanted the varcolac all to herself. He had thought her uninterested in such things, but why else would she have left him behind? She wanted to be the One.

But that was rightly him! *He* had made the baby universe. *He* had summoned the varcolac into the world. *He* had traded equations with it and learned its secrets. He had been born for this. But first Jean, and now Alex, wanted to steal it away from him.

He couldn't let that happen. But how could he stop them? Alex was one thing; she was just a human. But Jean had the varcolac on her side. If he teleported away after them without a plan, he was just going to get himself killed.

What he needed was a new weapon. Jean had taken out his Higgs projector as easily as thinking. He could theoretically make a new one, hardened against EMPs, but that would take time and materials, and he didn't have either. There were two options: either he had to have the strength to overpower her or he had to catch her unawares. The former was unlikely, not with the varcolac helping her, which just left the element of surprise.

But how could he surprise a creature who could see every quantum interaction, every electromagnetic wavelength, every particle emitted or absorbed? By itself, he could perhaps fool it. The varcolac had, after all, spent countless years completely unaware of human intelligence and only recently understood just how many humans there were. Particle interactions hadn't even given it a concept of matter, never mind individual human intelligence.

But with Jean, it was another story. Paired with Jean, it understood the significance of the particle interactions on a large scale. It could parse the meanings of interrupted beams of light and radiant energy sources and know that where there were signs of a human body there was a human intelligence.

The invisibility module wouldn't help. It was practically a toy, designed only to absorb and re-emit visible light according to Maxwell's equations. It didn't even stop the infrared signals of his body heat, never mind the countless interactions of radiation across the electromagnetic spectrum. Static electricity, friction, the Brownian movement of displaced air: all of these created a trail of evidence to eyes that knew how to look. He didn't know which of these effects might escape the varcolac's notice and which might be as obvious as a forest fire. His only option was get rid of them all. Instead of a module to hide him from visible light, he needed a module to hide him from reality itself.

In theory, it should be easy. The Higgs field already did the hard work of capturing particles and reconfiguring them according to his software's specifications. For the invisibility module, his software had to solve Maxwell's equations for each photon that came into the field and reproduce it properly on the other side. A reality module would work much the same way, but instead of Maxwell's equations, it would solve Schrödinger's equation for the probability of a particle being present in a region of space. It would reproduce *all* particles, not just photons, essentially rerouting reality itself around him. He would be completely undetectable by any means.

It was a concept he'd been playing with for years, a pet project of sorts. He had the software, fully tested in simulation. There had been nothing really stopping him from using it except the guts to actually try it. Now he had no choice. Unless he wanted to die in obscurity like the rest of humanity he had to challenge Jean and regain his place.

It took him an hour. The real challenge was performance. In daylight, there were roughly 10^{21} photons that entered his space every second, but there could be as many as 10^{50} total particles passing through the same space, requiring many orders of magnitude more processing power. The sort of computer that could fit in a phone card was no longer sufficient. Ryan liberated a hardened supercomputer from the military training center and fit it into a backpack. It was oppressively heavy, but it could do the needed calculations fast enough to eliminate any noticeable delay. Of course, Ryan couldn't say for sure what would be noticeable to a varcolac, but it was the best chance he had. He stole an oxygen tank as well, and strapped it to his chest—after all, air molecules would be routed around him just like any other particle.

Now he was as ready as he'd ever be. He plugged the coordinates for Jozef Stefan Institute into his teleportation module. Jean wouldn't get away with this. Not if he could help it.

Alex could tell that Sean was not happy to see her. At first he stared at her with eyes gone wide, as if she were a ghost. Then his eyes turned hard, and she could see the anger growing. "What are you doing here?" he asked, with barely suppressed rage. Alex knew the rage was because he loved her, and he assumed that her presence here meant she was doing something incredibly stupid. And maybe she was. But she also knew things he didn't. And could do things he couldn't.

Instead of answering, she teleported to the far end of the hallway and then back again. He stared at her, his anger dissolving again into astonishment and confusion.

"Let's assume I'm here for a good reason," she said. "We don't have much time, so listen up. The varcolac is here."

Sean had personal experience with the varcolac. He had been only five years old when it had kidnapped him, along with their mother and sisters, but she was sure he remembered the experience. He had almost died.

"How do you know?" Sean whispered.

"For one thing, the soldiers pouring into the building have no eyes."

He cringed. It was like a childhood nightmare come to life. Just as quickly, however, the hard look of an elite marine returned.

The marine who had originally found them, apparently the team leader, asked, "Kelley, what's this about?"

Alex explained as best she could in a few terse sentences.

"It doesn't change anything," he said. "We do the job, we get out."

Alex indicated her team. "Let us stay close," she said. "When you're done, we can teleport you out of here."

The team leader looked like he was going to object, but then he shook his head. "Fine. We don't have time to argue." He eyed the wall. "This looks load bearing." He slapped an explosive onto it and twisted something on its surface. It stuck fast and emitted a tiny whine.

"This way," he said. Alex followed him, trusting the rest of her team to do the same. "Kelley, is this floor cleared?" he asked.

"Yes, sir," Sean said.

"Okay. Johnny is dead. Wilson and Cash are holding the stairs. The first floor is overrun. We need to get down to the cellar.

They reached the stairs. Two Marines were holding position there, one behind the other, shooting at any Turkish soldier that turned the corner. The bullets passed right through the Turks, impacting the floor on the other side of them, yet they showed no inclination to climb the stairs.

"Why won't they die, sergeant?" one of them called back, his voice stressed.

"Do you have any spare magazines?" Alex asked.

Sean gave her an odd look, but handed one over. Alex thumbed a bullet out of the top, and then waited for another Turkish soldier to come into view at the bottom of the stairs. As soon as it did, she teleported the bullet into its brain. Its head exploded, raining blood and gray matter all over the floor. Its body fell and didn't get up.

"You did that with the Higgs projector?" Sean asked.

"Newer version. I can copy it for you, but not here."

"Hand over your spares to Sean's sister and her unit, then follow me," the team leader said, apparently taking the oddness of the situation in stride.

Wilson, Cash, and Sean all handed over fresh magazines to Alex and her teammates. The team leader charged down the stairs, shouting incoherently, and his men followed him. "Come on!" Alex said.

They hit the first floor on the heels of the Special Ops crew. The puppet soldiers advanced, blasting them with pulses of energy. The Higgs projectors protected them, shielding them with flashes of blinding light.

One at a time, Alex put bullets into the soldiers' heads. It was gruesome, horrible work, spattering all of them with gore, but it was better than dying. "Downstairs!" Sean shouted. "This way!"

They descended into the cellar, a long concrete stairwell three times as deep as any normal basement. When they reached the bottom, they entered a room as large as any gymnasium. The linear accelerator was there, a fat, steel cylinder that spanned the length of the room, connected to a host of machines and computers via a tangle of wires. The cylinder was the vacuum chamber through which the particles flew. At the far end, a giant Van de Graaff generator hummed in its own, larger compartment. A dozen scientists in white lab coats attended the machines.

And there was Jean. Alex didn't wait to see what she would do. She dropped a bullet into her hand and teleported it into Jean's head.

Or at least she tried. The bullet didn't move. Alex tried to send it into the Van de Graaff generator instead, but it sat resolutely in her palm. This wasn't good. She tried teleporting a few feet to her left, but once again, nothing happened. Afraid, she yanked the projector itself out of her pocket. It sat inert, dead, the tiny lights on its surface gone dark.

"Easy to do, once you think about it," Jean said pleasantly. "A Higgs projector is just solid state electronics, a computer operating a program. It has electrical circuits to fry, just like anything else. A focused EMP will do it. Just a tiny one, right in your pocket." She snapped her fingers. "Easy. The power of the quantum world is still there, of course. Only you can't access it."

The door to the stairway behind them slammed shut. "Why are you doing this?" Alex asked. "The varcolac doesn't care about helping the Turks."

"No, you're right about that. I'm afraid it's not going to help anyone but me."

"But you're *human*," Alex said. "Why would you want to throw in with this alien creature? Do you really want to be the only person left in the universe? To have all that blood on your hands? You might live forever, sure, but will that really be worth it?"

Jean's face grew hard. "What did humanity ever do for me? Took my daughter from me. Put me in a cage. Took my life, the few decades that I have allotted to me, and forced me to spend them shut up in a box. Do you know what that does to a person? Watching my precious time tick away, wasted? I have a mind with the imagination to create worlds, and humanity put me in a cage." Sean reached for a grenade, but she flung it away from him with a gesture. "The varcolac, as you call it, won't put me in any kind of cage at all. It will give me the universe."

"What about the billions of people who don't even know you? They didn't lock you in a cage. And what about your husband and daughter? Have you even seen them since you escaped? Would you kill them with all the rest?"

Jean's smile never wavered. "Humanity took my years away," she said. "Now I am taking theirs."

"You're crazy," Tequila said. "You're completely out of your mind. You think this will make you happy?"

"This conversation bores me," Jean said. "It's time for you to die." She turned away and snapped her fingers. Tequila's mouth opened in shock. Her chest made a small popping noise, and she rocked back. She looked at Alex and tried to speak, but a trickle of blood dribbled out of her mouth. Her head lolled to one side, and she collapsed to the floor.

"Tequila!" Alex rushed to her side. Her friend was motionless, her eyes rolled back. She had no pulse.

Alex looked back up at Jean. "I will kill you," she said, her voice wrenched out through the tears that closed her throat. "I will destroy you."

"Really," Jean said. "I'm impressed you located me so quickly, but come now. I have you thoroughly beaten. Now go home before I kill you all." She smiled. "Oh that's right, no Higgs projector. You can't go home, can you? Too bad for you, I suppose." She snapped her fingers again, and the marine team leader staggered back. He fell to the floor and died, just like Tequila.

Alex screamed in frustration. She cast about for anything she could throw, anything she could use at all to try to hurt this woman. "And where's the varcolac now?" she shouted. "Are you so certain you can trust it? Or is it just using you to get its way? What if, when all the rest of humanity is dead, it just discards you, too?"

Jean laughed. "You don't understand, do you? I *am* the varcolac. Do you think humanity is the first race it has assimilated? It barely understood humanity before, but now, with its mind entwined with mine, it understands everything." Another snap of her fingers, and Cash and Wilson collapsed as well. Rod turned and ran for the doors to the stairway. He reached them and yanked on them as hard as he could, but they didn't open. Jean snapped her fingers, and he fell where he stood. Alex, Sean, and Lisa were the only ones left. Sean stepped in front of them, shielding them with his body, as if that would do any good.

"Stop it!" Alex yelled. The tears ran down her face in earnest now. "Please! I beg of you. You have all the power. Show some compassion."

Jean's lips curled and her face twitched. "That's the thing about prison," she said. "It beats all the compassion out of you."

CHAPTER 25

Ryan teleported to the Jozef Stefan Institute and found it in chaos. The complex was surrounded by Turkish military trucks and at least one armored personnel carrier. The soldiers, however, were running to and fro through smoke and shouting, firing their weapons on each other. Ryan didn't understand what was happening, until he saw that some of the Turks had blank skin where their eyes ought to have been.

A helicopter flew overhead, shining a giant spotlight down onto the grounds, but Ryan cast no shadow. The bullets passed through his body without harm, and a soldier even ran straight through him, never seeing him and never slowing down. It was incredible. Ryan's software had just taken that man apart and reassembled him on the other side in less than a second, and he was none the wiser.

In fact, Ryan was not standing on the ground, strictly speaking. He couldn't feel it through his feet, and it didn't support his weight—it would pass right through him like everything else. To maintain his position, he was continuously teleporting to the same coordinates.

He couldn't walk, either—no friction—but he could shift his teleport coordinates slightly and thus hover through space. Ignoring the battle raging around him, he passed through the walls and into the main building. The carnage was even worse here, with blood and brain matter spattered across the floor. He wondered if any of it belonged to Alex.

The accelerator had to be in the basement. Instead of finding the stairwell, he simply sank down through the floor. He was surrounded by concrete. Buried in it. He envisioned the reality module failing at just that moment, leaving him entombed, and he began to hyperventilate. He took a deep breath from the oxygen tank and tried to relax. The supercomputer pulled at his shoulders, rubbing them raw. If he had taken more time to plan, he would have strapped himself to a chair. The pack could have hung on the back of the chair while he sat on it, saving him the trouble of supporting the weight.

He burst out of the concrete into a huge open space, and there she was. Jean Massey stood on the floor below him, facing down Alex Kelley, her research team, and a squad of American marines, although most of them seemed to be dead. The linear accelerator hummed and vibrated.

"That's the thing about prison," Jean said. "It beats all the compassion out of you."

She couldn't see him. The varcolac couldn't sense him. There was nothing to sense. Ryan walked through her, and for a moment she existed only as a trillion trillion virtual particles passing through his module and out the other side, leaving her unharmed as he came out. But what if . . . ?

Ryan stepped into her again, enclosing her body within the field, and just stayed there. Anyone else looking at this patch of space could see Jean, detect her body heat, even reach in and touch her. She still cast a shadow. But she was only a virtual Jean, a simulation of the particles that made up her and everything else within the field. Which meant, if he deactivated the field at just this moment . . .

It was surprisingly easy. When Ryan deactivated the field, Jean was just . . . gone. The supercomputer stopped simulating those particles. That patch of space was replaced by Ryan, his air, his hardened computer backpack. There was no mess, no blood. Just no more Jean. The thought did occur to Ryan to wonder where those particles had actually gone. After all, it shouldn't be possible to actually *destroy* a trillion trillion particles. Matter and energy were never actually *lost*. The particles must have been repurposed somehow, diffused as heat energy through the packet of air around him, or converted into much smaller exchange particles . . . or something. He would have to ponder the problem at some later date. The important thing was, Jean was gone.

"Ryan!" Alex shouted. She threw her arms around him. "You did this? You destroyed her?"

It felt good. Her arms were light and feminine. She was crying openly, her face red and streaked with tears. Ryan felt a surge of pride.

But no. This is what pretty girls always did. They made him feel happy just to be in their presence, but they didn't care about him, not really. They manipulated and took what they wanted. Alex didn't like him. She just thought she could control him. But she couldn't. "You can't have it," he told her. "Go home. It's mine."

She took a step back. "What's yours?"

"Don't play with me. I'm the one who deserves this, not you."

She was giving him that look again now. "Deserves what?"

"To be the One. To live forever. To be humanity as it should be, until the universe cools and dies."

"You're . . . taking her place?" Alex said. The horror on her face was evident. He felt it as a physical loss, this change from appreciation to revulsion, but it was for the best. The mask was off now. She was just showing what she really thought of him.

"There's only one person getting out of this alive, and that's me," he said. Where was the varcolac? He had only imagined this as far as killing Jean. He assumed that once he killed her, the varcolac would naturally gravitate to him again. Wasn't he the one who had freed it? Wasn't he, among all humans on Earth, its intellectual equal? He deserved this.

As one, the white-coated scientists at the accelerator turned to look at him. They had no eyes. They dropped their equipment and advanced, moving in lockstep.

"I'm here!" Ryan shouted. "I'm yours. I'm ready!"

They walked on, slowly but inexorably.

Ryan started to tremble. What if the varcolac was angry that he had killed Jean? "I had to," he said. "It was the only way to be with you."

The scientist puppets came closer. Ryan engaged the reality module. At least, he thought he did. But he could still feel the floor beneath his feet, could still sense the circulation of air from the room's big fans. He tried to teleport and failed. His Higgs projector had been compromised. He was helpless. And the varcolac was coming.

Ryan wracked his brains, trying to think. He remembered the short, beautiful time when he had shared the varcolac's mind, known its thoughts, understood its beautiful vision for the universe. How could he prove that he was worthy?

His eyes slid to Alex. Her gaze was intent, her expression set. Her tears were dry. And suddenly Ryan knew what to do. The varcolac had been trying to kill this girl ever since it first entered the world, and somehow, time and again, she had eluded it. It was impossible. She was just a girl in her twenties, a fragile human, with a common sort of intelligence. At least, that's how she appeared. And yet she had so far defeated a power that commanded the very structure of space and time. There was only one explanation: Alex was not who she pretended to be.

He could see it now. She had manipulated him from the very beginning. She had pretended to be frightened and out of her depth, yet she had lured him into following her and then tricked him into inviting her to his lab, where she had stolen his work. He had known it was folly to trust a beautiful woman, and yet she had seduced him all the same. Oh, she was good.

Now that he saw the truth, he wondered that he had ever missed it. She had known the varcolac fifteen years ago, had known what it could do and what it wanted. She had been preparing for its return all her life. She was cunning and manipulative, and she had played him for a fool. He felt a hot flush in his cheeks. She had been laughing at him all this time. Laughing at his silly fears, laughing at his fat body, laughing at how easy it was to trick him with a pretty smile. She had dragged him onto that plane just to laugh at his distress. They were all laughing at him, weren't they? When they thought he wasn't looking. All of her friends. Everyone, all of his life. Laughing, laughing, laughing.

The body of a dead marine lay at his feet. His gun was under his body and tied with a strap. Inaccessible. But on his belt there was a KA-BAR combat knife, sharp and made for killing. Ryan knelt and slid it out of its sheath. Alex stood with her back to him, distracted by the oncoming scientists.

She wouldn't laugh at him anymore.

CHAPTER 26

"Sandra," Angel said. "You should take a look at this." He was watching the feed from the module her father had planted on Alex's phone.

"I can't," she said. "It puts me too close to her. Next time, I might merge with her and not come back."

"They've found Jean," he said. "At least, I'm pretty sure it's Jean. She's glowing—I don't know if she's really glowing, or if there's something different about her that the quantum field monitor . . . oh no."

"What is it?"

"She just killed someone. She waved her hand, and somebody just fell over."

Sandra stood and gripped his arm, wanting to see, but not wanting to see. "Was it Alex? Or Sean?"

"I don't think so." He clenched his fists, his face pale. "She just killed another one. They can't hurt her at all. She's just murdering them."

"We have to teleport there," she said. "We have to stop her."

"We can't do that."

"Yes, we can! If we have her phone, then we have her coordinates."

"It's too far! The error term at this distance would be on the order of half a mile. We could end up on the other side of the city, or a thousand feet in the air, or buried in rock. The one place we won't end up is in that room."

Sandra was crying. "It's going to kill Alex and Sean. We have to try!"

"And even if we miraculously showed up right next to her, what would we do?" He said it gently, sadly.

"We could teleport them out of there."

"They have Higgs projectors. If that would work, they could do it themselves."

"Turn it off, then," she said.

"What?"

"Turn it off. If we can't do anything about it, I don't want to know. I don't want you to watch her die."

"Wait." His eyes were intense, watching the scene unfold. "There's somebody else there."

"Who?"

"He . . . he killed her."

"Killed who? Killed Alex?"

"No, killed Jean. I think. That or she teleported away just as he appeared there. She's gone, at any rate."

Sandra couldn't stand it anymore. She plugged back in to Angel's viewfeed and immersed herself in the scene. The picture was grainy and gray and incomplete, the faces a blur, but she knew immediately who each person was. Tequila and Wilson and Cash and Rod were dead. She had never met any of them, but she knew their names. She knew Tequila's sister was getting married this fall, and that Rod's wife was six months pregnant. Alex knew them, and so Sandra did, too.

She saw Ryan Oronzi, their savior, standing in triumph where Jean had once stood. And she saw the scientists, their eyes erased, advancing. They had to get out of there. Why didn't they just teleport away? Though she could immediately answer her own question from Alex's knowledge: their projectors were no longer working. Besides, they had come there for a purpose. Jean was nothing, just a tool. It was the varcolac that had to be stopped.

She saw Ryan kneel at a marine's side and pull at his belt. What was he doing? CPR? But then he stood again, and Sandra saw the knife in his hand. The metal of it glared brightly in the quantum display, standing out over the dullness of other materials. Alex didn't see it. Her attention was caught by the approaching scientists. Sean was standing in front of her, ready to fight them. Sandra silently called to them, *look, look, look!*

Alex did look, then, but it was too late. All she had time to see was Ryan's mad, deranged eyes just as he swung the knife up and into her heart.

Sandra screamed. She shouted Alex's name. There was blood everywhere, soaking Alex's shirt and pants, flooding onto the floor. Alex collapsed. She raised no hand to stop her fall. She lay where she fell, her face on the concrete, her eyes staring wide. Sean was at her side in a moment, calling her name, but there was nothing he could do. He tried to put pressure on the wound, but with every breath, more blood poured out of her.

She was dying quickly. Alex was dying in front of her, and Sandra couldn't even hold her hand. It was impossible, unreal. It was a grainy, gray-on-black image with no soul, utterly distant from events in Slovenia. At the same time, it was as starkly real to her as if it had been projected on fifty-foot screens in living color. It couldn't be happening. Alex couldn't die. She was her other self.

Sandra screamed and cried to her, though of course Alex couldn't hear. Or maybe she could. Their eyes seemed to connect, and Alex mouthed something Sandra couldn't understand.

A memory came, unbidden, of a party, fifteen years earlier, when Alex had first returned from the hospital. She had been in a wheelchair then, still lame from the effects of her electrocuted spine, and at the time they didn't know if she would ever be able to walk again. They had loved each other so much then. They could finish each other's sentences, finish each other's thoughts almost. They were two halves of the same whole. When had the idea that they might be forced back together become so unbearable?

What had gone wrong? How had such resentment built up between them? Of all the people for her to avoid, why had she chosen her other self? And now Alex was dead, or nearly so. Sandra had never even said goodbye. She had never said she was sorry for unfair words, for time together cast aside. Now it would just be . . . her. Just Sandra. It did not seem possible.

She would not allow it. Sandra closed her eyes. She felt Angel's hand on her back, but she didn't acknowledge his presence. She knew what she had to do.

She reached out, hesitantly at first, less familiar with the concept than Alex had been. She tried to remember what it had felt like in the funeral home, when multiple versions of Alex were collapsing back together, and she had felt the same pull. She tried to recreate it.

Together again. She was Alex, and Alex was her. She was Alex *and* Sandra, Sandra and Alex. They were one person.

It wasn't working. She felt a surge of panic. She didn't know how to do this. Alex was bleeding out on the floor, and she didn't know how to make this work.

Alex, she thought. My name is Alex. And then: *Alessandra*. My name is Alessandra Kelley. I am a police officer and also a physicist. I love investigating crimes, and I love science. I love to seek out, to hunt down, to discover the truth. I am two sides of the same coin. I am Alessandra.

And then it happened. There was no flash, no fireworks, no rush of energy or sense of invasion. It was so subtle she almost missed it.

She opened her eyes.

"What happened?" her mother asked. "Is Alex okay?"

Alessandra smiled, a little sadly. "Yes," she said. "I'll be just fine."

Ryan stood over Alex's dead body and grinned. He had done it. He had killed both Jean and Alex, and now he was the only one left who could warrant the varcolac's attention. He could feel it now, entering his mind, giving him that growing sense of clarity and intellect. It had accepted his sacrifice. It had found him worthy once more.

He and the varcolac were one now, in purpose and power. Nothing could stand in his way. Barely anyone was left alive in the world who even understood what was happening, never mind who had the power to stop him. He sensed something else, too; the varcolac was stronger. It was breaking free, breaking more fully into this world. There was no stopping it now.

The marine who had been trying to save Alex's life roared and rushed him, but Ryan flicked his fingers like he was shooing a fly, and the marine flew backward and crashed against the wall. He slumped to the floor and lay still.

Outside, someone was shouting with an amplified voice through a speaker. The man spoke in Turkish, a language Ryan wasn't sure he had even heard spoken before, but he found now that he could understand it perfectly. The voice told those inside the building that it was surrounded, and they should surrender peacefully. A dozen armored soldiers burst into the cellar laboratory and trained their submachine guns on Ryan and the handful of other still-living people in the room.

Ryan laughed. He laughed with power and delight and invincibility. It didn't matter what anyone thought of him anymore. It didn't matter what they did to contain him, to push him down and marginalize him. He was the only one who mattered anymore.

Ryan tossed his supercomputer backpack and oxygen tank onto the concrete floor. He wouldn't need them. He rose from the ground, effortlessly, and spun gracefully in the air. The soldiers shouted at him to stop, but he ignored them. They fired their tiny, insignificant weapons, and Ryan barely noticed. With a flick of his hand, they all died.

Giddy, Ryan shot up higher, passing through concrete and steel and wood like they didn't exist. From above the roof of the Institute, he could see the Turkish soldiers arrayed in the streets around him, with their armor and guns and trucks and grenades. They would kill him, if they could. That made it self-defense.

Ryan spun, waving a hand or throwing a fist, and each gesture scattered men and their vehicles like bowling pins in a hurricane. They crashed into buildings, into each other, or were crushed by their own falling trucks. He tossed one man five hundred feet in the air and watched him fall. He made another man's body heavier and heavier, laughing as the man tried to run away, until his body crumpled from its own weight.

It was only what they deserved. These were bad men, killers who imposed their will on others by violence. They were the sort of men who had mocked and bullied him all his life. They didn't deserve to have their minds joined with the glorious whole. Humanity would be better off without them.

But the goal, ultimately, was not killing. When the soldiers were all dead, Ryan stopped to consider. Now was the time to make the varcolac's vision real. It was time to bring humanity into the next stage in their evolution. He needed to start assimilating other minds into his own.

Ryan dropped back down into the cellar. Most of the people there were dead, but there was one woman, Lisa, who sat cowering behind a control station. She was a computer programmer, an intelligent woman. He would assimilate her mind, her memories, her knowledge into his own. He walked up to her, took her head and chin in his hands, and broke her neck.

No! That wasn't what he had wanted to do. What was wrong with him? Ryan waved his hands up and down and flexed his fingers. They moved as he intended. He looked at Lisa's dead body lying slumped on the ground. Maybe it had just been an accident. He didn't know his own strength.

Oh well. It wasn't like she was all that important. He would try again, and he knew just whom he would try next.

In an instant, he was back in Krakow, in the elementary school gymnasium. It was the middle of the night, and the room was empty and dark, lit only by security lights. Ryan knew, however, that Nicole had been sleeping in her office most nights. She claimed she was too busy to waste time traveling to her assigned lodging and back.

He opened the office door, and there she was, asleep on an army cot. Perfect.

Ryan leaned over her and rested his hand on her head. Her breath came in a soft rhythm. He had always secretly had a bit of a thing for her. She was intelligent, quick-witted, attractive. And the secret intelligence agent thing was, of course, pretty sexy. Now she would be his forever. And not in some temporary, physical way that would be over in a moment and regretted by both of them. Not as a slave to her beauty, manipulated into doing whatever she wanted. No. She would belong to him.

He reached into her, feeling the electrical sparks of her mind. Suddenly, she was there, connected to his thoughts. Her experiences and memories were available for him to touch and access at will. He knew her childhood fears. He knew her pleasures and her regrets. She was utterly exposed.

She resisted, of course. Her mind flailed away from him, and she woke, jerking back and reaching for the pistol under her pillow. It didn't matter. She couldn't hurt him, and physical distance couldn't pull her mind away from him, not anymore. She knew he was there, in her mind. She tried to close herself off to him. Reflexively, she thought of the one piece of knowledge she must hide from him at all costs, trying to close it away, keep it hidden. And by doing so, of course, she gave it to him.

She knew the location of the nuclear weapons Turkey had recovered from Romania. The CIA had uncovered the information through a combination of human and stealth drone intelligence. If the Special Ops missions tonight were successful, another mission would be sent to take the nuclear missiles out of the equation.

Ryan twisted his hand, and Nicole's heart ruptured. He felt her thoughts slipping away. No, no, no! He hadn't meant to do that! She was supposed to join with him! He reached out, trying to repair her heart, to put it back together, or at the least to pull her mind into him before it was gone altogether, but it was too late. Her bulging eyes stared into his as she died, and he could see the hatred there.

He hated himself. And then he knew. The varcolac was far superior to humanity, so Ryan had assumed it was above such base instincts as deceit. But of course, the varcolac was a sophisticated, intelligent being, capable of doing anything to achieve its desired outcome. It should have come as no surprise to him that the varcolac could lie.

It had never had any intention of uniting humanity into a single, efficient mind. It needed no companion with whom to travel the stars. The varcolac was, by definition, one. There was nothing it wanted from humanity that it could not simply take. He thought he had understood it, but he had understood nothing. He didn't know what the varcolac wanted, or why. How could he have deceived himself into thinking he could understand the motivations of such a creature? The varcolac was *varelse* after all.

Ryan didn't want to be the One anymore. He was done with this. He wanted to go back home to his lab and study the mathematics of particle physics. He wanted to eat French fries and drink Coke until two o'clock in the morning, immersed in solving the latest puzzle. But he was quite sure it was too late for that. He had thought he was the varcolac's equal, or at least enough that it saw him as a kindred spirit. Now he realized he was just of sufficient intelligence to be its disposable slave.

A single, burning desire sliced through his self-loathing: the desire to teleport to the Romanian missile silo. Ryan knew the desire had not come from him, but he felt it more powerfully than any of his own desires, so strongly that he barely questioned it. Nicole's office disappeared and was replaced by the dark inside of a silo, with the smell of dust and machine oil and wet metal. The darkness was nearly complete, but Ryan could see like it was bright day. The space was dominated by a white rocket decorated with severe-looking Cyrillic lettering. He had no idea how to tell a standard missile from a nuclear one, though the radiation symbols on doors and walls were a clue.

A burning desire filled him to fire a nuclear missile at Krakow.

No. Ryan resisted. This was not the plan. He had killed soldiers who were trying to kill him, sure. But he had planned to raise humanity to a new evolutionary plane, not murder millions. He *wanted* to fire the missile, like a starving man wanted food, but he would not do it. This was not his desire. It was false, placed there by the varcolac to control him. He would not be a slave. He planted his feet and clenched his eyes shut. He would not do it.

Then the pain hit him. Pure, unimaginable pain. His whole body was on fire. He screamed and writhed and fell to the ground. He didn't know such pain was possible. It was like every nerve was being touched directly with a red hot iron.

The pain stopped. Then once again, the desire, hot and radiant with promised pleasure, to fire the missile. Just one. None of those people cared about him anyway. They were all going to die, one way or another. And he wanted to fire the missile. He needed to.

The varcolac had learned the inner workings of his mind. It knew how to apply pleasure and pain. It knew what motivated him and where he was weak.

The pain came back, and this time it didn't stop. It rolled over his body in waves. The body was where humans were weak, and the varcolac knew it now. Ryan collapsed to the ground, helpless, unable to think of anything but continuous, unendurable pain. He wanted to die. Anything to stop it. But he knew the varcolac would not let him die until he did what it wanted.

As soon as he thought that, the pain stopped. Desire. Like a glass of water after three days with none. Fire the missile.

He couldn't win. Not against this. He *was* the varcolac's slave, as surely as any poor soul whipped and beaten by his own kind. Ryan stumbled to the control panel. With the varcolac's intelligence and powers, he didn't have to worry about passwords or special keys. All that security was just layers wrapped around a simple electrical current applied to a wire. He reached straight through it all to the firing mechanism and induced the needed current.

The missile roared as engines engaged. Alarms sounded, vying with the mechanical groan of the silo doors opening. The entire silo rose on an elevator, lifting out of its underground hiding place. Ryan could see stars through the gap above.

A surge of pleasure ran through him as the missile ignited and leapt off of its platform and into the sky, leaving a cloud of fire and black smoke. He doubted anyone was supposed to be standing in the silo when the missile was fired, but it couldn't harm him. The heat rushed around him, intensifying the sense of pleasure and goodness he felt. He knew that it wasn't right, that the varcolac was just making him feel that way, but he had no strength left to resist.

He heard the varcolac's voice as clearly as if it had been spoken in his ear. *Another. Again.*

"Alessandra," she said. "Use the full name. I'm not simply Alex or Sandra. I'm Alessandra again."

Angel looked unsettled, as if he didn't know whether to hug her or run away. Her mother, on the other hand, took the change in stride. She gave Alessandra's head a quick kiss. "What happened out there?"

Alessandra's head was still pounding. Apparently resolving the long-standing probability wave that separated them didn't remove the results of her concussion. Angel had teleported out and brought back some Ibuprofen earlier, but it wasn't cutting the pain nearly enough. She was tempted to ask him to go steal some Vicodin.

"Ryan Oronzi is working for the varcolac," Alessandra said. "Or it's possessing him, or something. He has powers he shouldn't have, and he's using them to do what the varcolac wants. He tried to kill me—to kill

Alex—just to please it. I should have known, the way he talked about it before, as if he admired it or wanted to be just like it."

"What about Sean?" her mother asked. She used a businesslike tone, but Alessandra could see the desperation in her eyes.

"The last I saw, he was still alive. He's smart and strong, Mom. He'll find a way." She tried to sound like she meant it, though all she could think of was the casual way Jean had killed her friends. Could he really survive against a varcolac?

"What about you?" Angel asked. "How do you feel?"

"Okay, I guess. My head is about to explode, but besides that . . ."

"Not physically—I mean, about what just happened. You and your sister . . . I mean . . . you . . ."

Alessandra shook her head. "I'm not thinking about that right now. I haven't had time to process what it means." She didn't *want* to think too hard about it. Who was she now? What had she lost? She remembered not wanting this to happen, both as Alex and as Sandra, each of whom had feared they would lose their identities. Now that it had happened, now that she was just *her*, Alessandra, she wasn't sure it was such a bad thing. But did that mean that it wasn't? Would her prior selves have agreed? Or were they dead, leaving only her . . . whoever she was?

She couldn't think about it, not now.

"What's that thing in the middle of the room?" Angel said. He pointed to the 3D display of Ryan's universe.

Alessandra raised an eyebrow, wondering at the question. "It's a photoionization microscopy display, used to visualize quantum n-dimensional data in an intuitive, three-dimensional arrangement."

His eyebrows went up. "Wow. It's really true."

"What?"

"Sandra didn't know that. A few hours ago, she said she didn't know what that thing was."

He was right. She could remember saying she didn't know. She could even remember *not* knowing. But now she knew now exactly what it was and how it worked.

"My father knew this would happen," she said. "At least, he knew the probability field was weakening, making it more likely that . . . we . . . would come together." She had started to say, "Alex and I," or else, "Sandra and I," but neither seemed right. Although, neither did referring to either of her previous selves as "she." The pronouns were confusing.

"And his data seemed to suggest that Oronzi's work was the cause," Angel said. "But how could that be? After all this time, what could have made a difference?"

"I don't know," she said. "Maybe his work just shook things up." It wasn't an answer the physicist part of her was satisfied with, but at this point she really didn't have a better one.

Angel stroked his chin. "It must have been essentially the same technology that you used fifteen years ago, right? The wave didn't resolve then. The technology was still there. But the varcolac wasn't."

"What do you mean?"

"According to your story, you split at exactly the same time that the varcolac was shut out of our universe. The standing probability wave was created at that moment."

"You're saying the varcolac had something to do with it?"

"I'm saying, what if it was your probability wave that kept the varcolac from returning? For years and years, you two are completely separate, and there's no sign of the varcolac. Then as soon as the wave starts to lose strength, the varcolac starts interacting in the world again. It can't be a coincidence. I'm wondering if one is the cause of the other."

"Or if both have the same cause," she said. Then she sat up, ignoring the sudden throb of pain in her head. "That's it!"

"What's it?"

"You're right. You must be. I always wondered why the varcolac was going after Alex and me. It seemed to have a specific vendetta, showing up wherever we were. I mean, why kill us? It was like it wanted revenge for shutting it out fifteen years ago. But what if you're right, and it was our standing probability wave that it was trying to kill? Maybe the wave had been weakening, allowing it access, but it wasn't completely gone. It was still preventing the varcolac from fully interacting with our world.

"It makes sense of a lot of things. It explains why it wanted to kill us particularly. It also explains why it failed, despite its power—it's not at its full strength. It's only partially able to manipulate things in our universe. Not only that, but it explains why it wasn't able to possess us directly, despite seeming to be able to possess anyone around us and use them to attack."

"What about your father? The varcolac attacked him first, not you."

"No, it didn't. Remember, it killed him by sending a particle back in time."

"I don't understand."

"My dad knew about the standing wave. If we're right, he knew it was what was keeping the varcolac out. What if he figured out a way to delay its collapse or even strengthen it? It would have preserved us— me—as two different people, and it would have kept the varcolac away. But then, what if after he did so, the varcolac had to attack in a different way, by sending the Higgs singlet back in time to kill him before he figured it out in the first place?"

Angel held her gaze intently. "Let's say that's right. What happened to the original timeline? In which your father defeated the varcolac and preserved you as two separate people?"

Alessandra pressed her lips together and shook her head. "It was destroyed. Erased. A new history began with the stadium disaster."

"How do you know?"

She shrugged. "I don't entirely know. But the multiverse theories have always been a bit fanciful. It's hard to believe that entirely new universes are being created all the time, whenever any particle's probability wave collapses. The math certainly doesn't require it. Remember Ryan's illustration with the billiard balls? There's only one timeline. The universe solves the equation so that causality is preserved."

"You're saying that it creates a loop? That the changed event in the past causes a situation that results in the particle being sent back in time to change the past?"

"Pretty much. Not in the same way, necessarily, but somehow a sequence of particles will cause that one to be created and sent back with the exact properties needed to cause this timeline. It sounds crazy, but the math works out. The solutions are possible, and the universe finds them."

"What would happen if we sent a particle back in time to smash into the varcolac's particle, and we stopped it from destroying the stadium and killing your father?" Angel asked.

Alessandra gave a rueful smile. "We would all die."

"What? What do you mean?"

"This timeline, in which you are I are living, would be erased. We would cease to exist—to have ever existed. Time would be recreated from that point forward. The stadium would never have been destroyed. My father would live, perhaps long enough to defeat the varcolac, but you and I would never know it."

"What do you mean? We would still be alive, too."

"No. Other very similar people named Angel and Sandra and Alex would still be alive. But they wouldn't be *us*. They wouldn't have our memories or experiences. They would be as different from us as Sandra and Alex were from each other. Different options, different choices, different people."

Angel's forehead wrinkled at the thought. "I see what you're saying," he said. "I wouldn't have thought of it that way, but then, I haven't lived side by side with an alternate me for the last fifteen years."

"Sandra!" her mother called. Alessandra thought about correcting the name, but she heard the concern in her mother's voice. Her mother had been sitting in a corner of the lab, reading something on her phone.

"What is it?" Alessandra asked.

"You'd better look at this," her mother said.

She held up the phone. The news headlines read: NUCLEAR BLAST DESTROYS KRAKOW. WAR DECLARED.

Angel caught her eye. *We have to do something*, he seemed to say. He was looking to her for a solution. But what could she possibly do?

CHAPTER 27

Over the course of the next three hours, nuclear blasts destroyed the cities of Berlin, Frankfurt, and Istanbul. The president of Turkey went on the air to urge restraint, claiming that his country had not fired any of the weapons. He asked the surviving leaders of Poland, Germany, and the United States to consider a summit to discuss peace accords. Poland and Germany refused. The United States remained silent.

Then Russia, which had so far remained neutral in the conflict, inexplicably fired high-yield nuclear missiles on China's three largest cities. Shanghai, Beijing, and Guangzhou disappeared before the sun had risen in New Jersey, and a hundred million people died. The Russian premier, looking genuinely horrified, mirrored the Turkish president's claim that the weapons had not been fired by his government, but it was too late. Ancient globe-spanning hatreds and mistrusts were reignited around the world. Militaries were put on high alert, fleets were launched, and world leaders were evacuated to secure locations.

"It's the right thing to do," Angel said. "If it's at all feasible to send that particle back and change the past, we should. We're going to die anyway. Humanity itself as a species might not survive. If there's any possible chance to reverse that, it's our moral obligation to do it."

"Think about what you're saying," Alessandra said. "Even if it were possible—which, let me tell you, I sincerely doubt—you're talking about annihilating *everyone*. Murdering everyone currently alive and replacing them with different versions of themselves, in a brand new timeline. Nuclear weapons can kill millions, but what you're suggesting would kill everyone."

"It's not like that. Except for any children born in the last few weeks, those people would be alive. All the people dying in those cities right now would be alive again. It's not killing them; it's saving them."

"Think of it like a river," Alessandra said. "We're floating along downstream. What you're suggesting would be like damming the river and sending it floating off in a different direction. There would be a different timeline—different people, different events—but it wouldn't be us. Our whole universe from that point onward would disappear. We would be dead, replaced by a different version of ourselves, living in a similar but different universe."

"I agree with Angel," her mother said.

Alessandra turned on her, feeling hurt, but her mother put a hand on her face, momentarily stopping any angry outburst. "You're wrong. Don't you feel it? Sandra and Alex haven't died. They were always the same. They were always you, and they still are. Different careers, different friends; those things were peripheral. It was always you. My daughter. My Alessandra." She stroked her cheek. "To do this, it won't be killing anyone. A different version is still the same person."

Alessandra shook her head. "It isn't right," she whispered. "It's what Jean tried to do. She didn't like the daughter that genetics had served up for her, so she tried to reshape her. To kill the present version of her daughter in favor of another. How can we make that choice for everyone?"

"The varcolac won't stop," her mother said. "You and I were both there. Remember? Kidnapped and trapped by that monster? It won't stop. It will track down every last human being until there are none left. Preserving the lives of people as they are now isn't an option on the table."

"Besides," Angel said. "Not doing it is choosing for them, too. How many people in big cities right now do you think would prefer we do nothing? Russia has thousands of nukes; the United States nearly as many. If the varcolac can control them, it'll be a long time before it stops."

"We could chase it," Alessandra said. "We could track it down and fight it. Stop it from killing anyone else."

"Could we?"

Alessandra thought about it. "No," she said. "But then, I don't think we can send a Higgs singlet back in time, either, not with that kind of control. It's never been done. It's never even been attempted."

"I believe in you," her mother said.

Alessandra threw up her hands. "I'm no genius like Ryan."

"That's probably a good thing," Angel said. "Look, just explain the principle to me. I won't understand it, but it'll help you think through the problem. Between the NJSC and the High Energy Lab, we have the best equipment in the world available to us. You'll think of something."

"I'm not so sure."

"Just start talking. If someone could do such a thing, how would they go about doing it?"

"Gravity," she said with a sigh. "They would need an immense gravitational pull." She repeated for Angel the same illustration that Ryan had used with the golden eagle on Hawk Mountain. How the eagle's possible locations—limited by the speed of light—were shifted by the gravity of a massive nearby object.

Using a shared eyejack space, she started drawing in the air with her finger, making lines that the three of them could see. She drew a simple pair of axes on the board, marking the horizontal axis x and the vertical one t. "Okay. The x axis is for movement in space; the t axis is for movement through time. So, if I draw a V, like this"—she switched to a red color and drew a V shape with its point at the origin—"that represents the area the eagle can theoretically fly, right?"

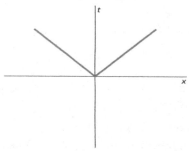

"As time advances, it can range farther in space," Angel said.

"Right." She almost smiled, but then the news feed in the corner of her vision reported that Tokyo and its fifty million people had been erased from the map by a pair of American nukes. It was hard to process. It was so horrible, so far beyond horrible, that her mind was rejecting it. "This is stupid," she said. "What are we doing? This won't accomplish anything."

"Please. Keep talking."

She sighed. She couldn't shake the idea that she should be *doing* something, either fighting the varcolac, or at least finding somewhere far from cities to hide.

"Okay. Let's say I was standing near a black hole when I turned my light on. The black hole's gravity would deform space-time toward itself. It would change the cone like this." She drew a new V, only now it was tilted toward one side.

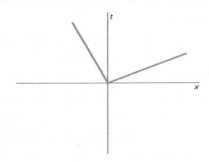

"The photon could travel farther if it traveled toward the black hole than if it traveled away from it, since the black hole's gravity is, in effect, pulling it in."

"Why is it tilted toward the right side?" Angel asked.

"It doesn't matter which side. It's just showing that the eagle's possible travel locations are skewed toward the black hole."

Her news feed reported the destruction of Karachi and Jakarta. The numbers of dead were becoming inconceivable, meaningless. She stopped talking and just watched as Mumbai was added to the list, then Moscow, and then São Paolo. Images from weather satellites showed mushroom clouds surging with radiant heat.

"He's going in order," Angel said. He was watching the same feed.

"What?"

"Ryan has a list of the populations of major world cities. Tokyo was the biggest. Then the three Chinese cities, then Karachi, then Jakarta. After the first few, he just started working his way down the list, killing the largest possible number of people with each blast."

The sheer coldness of that put a chill down her back. He was a sick, evil man. She couldn't believe she had talked to him, had ridden in his car. She had put her arms around him when she thought he had come to rescue them. Could the nervous, phobia-driven man she had briefly known really be systematically killing off the world's population? What she said was, "Where's New York City on the list?"

"It's down to number thirty-five. American population growth has been dropping compared to the rest of the world. But New York is seventy-five miles away; we should be safe enough. I mean, we might get an unhealthy dose of radiation, but we're well outside the blast range."

Alessandra shook her head. "It's the EMP I'm worried about. Depending on how high it actually detonates, it could knock out electronics as far as Chicago."

"This is a high-security government lab. Wouldn't it be shielded?" her mother asked.

Kinshasa, the news feed reported.

"Maybe," Alessandra said. "But it's not the lab that's the problem. The super collider has thirty miles of electromagnets with associated infrastructure that relies on above-ground power sources. It wouldn't survive."

Angel moved his eyes up and down, scrolling through a list. "We don't have much time, then. He's been taking out a city every few minutes."

Alessandra stood up taller and spoke with a stronger voice. "All right, then. Let's get moving." She pointed at the light cone again. "This cone is how we define causality. Since nothing can travel faster than the speed of light, only things located inside the cone in space and time could possibly be affected by anything that occurred at the origin of the graph. Anything outside that cone is causally independent."

"So you're just telling me that what the varcolac did was impossible," Angel said.

Mexico City.

Alessandra glanced at the news feed and started talking faster. "An object in orbit around the black hole would travel straight down the middle of this cone. From its own perspective, it would be in free fall— not moving, just staying on its local t axis. But to an outside observer, it's moving in space, falling into the black hole."

"I sense the moment coming where you totally lose me," Angel said.

Delhi, the feed said. They were coming faster. The satellite images scrolling by left no doubt as to the reality of the disasters. Alessandra swallowed back tears and tried to keep talking. "What we need to do is turn the cone backward," she said. "We need to warp the fabric of space and time so radically that the light cone looks like this." She drew a new V, this one tilting so far that its edge reached into negative time.

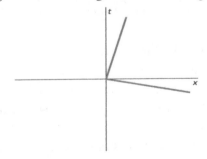

"This would mean the span of possible travel for our particle includes points down here"—she tapped the graph—"earlier in time than where it started."

Shenzhen.

"I don't understand," her mother said. "What are we talking about?"

"Gravity," Alessandra said. "Like I said, an immense amount of gravity. We need to create a black hole."

The other two just looked at her. "Um . . . like, right here?" Angel asked.

"In the collider."

"A black hole. Like, one of those ultra-massive space things that sucks everything into it and tears it to bits along the way?" Angel said.

"Just a little one."

Seoul.

"That wouldn't . . . you know . . . destroy the Earth or anything?"

Alessandra shook her head. "Black holes aren't entirely black. They all give off a small amount of thermal energy, called Hawking radiation. Big ones don't give off much, but the smaller they are, the more radiation escapes. Any black hole smaller than about the moon gives off so much that it radiates itself away in a fraction of a second. I'm talking about a miniscule black hole, smaller than an atom, even. It would barely last any time at all."

"But just enough?"

"Just enough. Theoretically."

Dhaka.

The stress was getting to her. "Where are we?"

"What do you mean?"

"The cities!"

He checked. "Fifteen destroyed from the list. That leaves twenty, until he reaches New York."

Cairo.

"Nineteen now. Keep talking."

Alessandra took a deep breath. "Okay. What we would need—if we were actually going to do this—was access to the super collider. We'd have to repeat an experiment that was done last year, in which a collision was made with sufficient energy to send Higgs singlets back in time. Only, we'd have to do it under our own special parameters, so that it precisely interfered with the particle the varcolac sent back to destroy the stadium."

Tianjin.

"Great," Angel said. "Let's do it."

Alessandra threw her arms in the air, exasperated. "We can't do it. We don't have access to the super collider, and we don't know anything about the particle the varcolac sent back. Even if we did have both of those things—along with a team of mathematicians—we're talking a lot of very complicated math to send the particle back in time with that kind of precise aim. It's impossible."

"If I can get you access, can you do the math?"

She stared at him. "Aren't you listening to me?"

Bangkok.

He spun, pointing at the machines around him. "Look at where we are. The access and the data is all right here. We can control the collider, and we can pull all the data we need from the logs."

"But it's a classified government lab! It'll have state-of-the-art security, encryption, the works. I don't have a password. Do you? We would need Ryan or Nicole to get us in. Nicole is almost certainly dead, and if you haven't noticed, Ryan isn't being too helpful at the moment."

Bangalore.

"Remember how many discussion board responses you got when you started querying about the stadium data? We bring the problem to the community. There are people out there who would give their right arms for a chance to help us access this system," Angel said.

"They live in the cities. They're dying. They have bigger problems."

"Exactly. And they know this is happening, but they don't know why. We'll tell them we can stop it, and they'll help, I promise you. No system is invincible. Especially one with so much reliance on physical security to deny access."

Lagos.

"But we can't stop it. Those people are going to die, no matter what!"

"There's no time to explain the particulars to them. We need their help. So I'm asking you again. If I can get you access, can you do the math?"

Hong Kong.

She paused, trying to stay calm and think clearly. What choice did she have? "No, I can't do the math," she said. "Certainly not in this much time, and maybe not ever. But I'll try."

Angel retreated into his eyejack environment, eyes flicking rapidly as he hurried to engage the help of software systems experts from around the world. Alessandra started to write some equations on the board, but quickly realized that it was the wrong approach. She couldn't do this by herself. It wasn't Alex's mathematical skills she needed right now; it was Sandra's ability to get answers from a web community. There were scientists in every country of the world who tracked the NJSC's experiments and studied the resulting data. Maybe not as many as computer geeks, but they were out there. She needed their help. As much as she could get.

Bogotá.

She pulled up her own eyejack display and started accessing the communities of physicists she had either met at conferences or heard of through her work. How many of them were now dead? Or fleeing for their lives out of whatever major cities they lived in? Physicists weren't generally found in rural settings; they needed the resources of a city to thrive.

She named her post "Need urgent help to stop nuclear attacks," and started writing.

Ho Chi Minh City.

<This is not a joke> she wrote. <I am in a classified American lab with access to the New Jersey Super Collider. I can provide data indicating a precise anti-timeward particle collision that will reverse the cause of the nuclear attacks. I need help to design the particle beams for a collision that will release the needed Higgs singlet to a very precise point and time.>

She waited. A response came quickly from Hyderabad, India. <If you are serious, then you know what you are asking?>

<I know> she wrote back. <It will rewind everything. You know your city is a target?>

<Yes. Nowhere else to go. Where is your data?>

<Working on that. Can you start work on a generic framework?>

She waited. There was no reply.

Hyderabad, her news feed said.

No! Alessandra shouted and pounded the table in front of her. She should have killed Ryan Oronzi when she had the chance, just thrown him out of the plane, or else just throttled his fat neck. Though she knew it wasn't ultimately Ryan who was doing this. If Ryan had died, the varcolac would have found another willing pawn. But that didn't mean she could forgive him.

A few more physicists and mathematicians responded to her call, from Munich, Boston, Kyoto, Berkley, Melbourne, Zurich, smaller cities that might outlast her. But none of them were up to the task. Few of them thought such a thing could be done in time, and those that did fell to arguing with each other over the best mathematical approach.

Lahore.

Time was ticking away. They might have a little more time than she did, but it wouldn't matter. Once they had the answer, they would have to use the NJSC to produce the effect. Not even CERN had the power to accelerate particles to the necessary speeds for this.

Tehran.

"I'm in," Angel crowed. "I told you they could do it." His face was alight, but just as quickly he sobered. "We lost quite a few along the way."

Alessandra synced her eyejack system with the network and made a quick assessment. Angel had done it. She had access to everything. Now all she needed was the math.

She started spinning up the electromagnets and the field generators, even though she didn't yet have the parameters to use. A heated argument flared up between a researcher at Caltech and one from Zurich, disagreeing over the sign of a tensor in one of the equations. Even at the end of the world, professional rivalries clashed enough to strike sparks. Alessandra didn't have time to let them fight it out. This wasn't working.

Dongguan.

"Only eight cities to go," Angel shouted. "How are we doing?"

"We're nowhere," Alessandra said. "I've got nothing. It isn't possible."

<They're both wrong> a message said. It had no routing source, in fact no metadata of any kind to say where it had come from. <Zurich and Caltech. They're both idiots.>

<Who is this?> Alessandra wrote.

<Jean Massey.>

Alessandra stared at the words, astonished. Angel said Ryan had killed her. If this was really her, it couldn't be good. <Where are you?> she wrote.

<As far as I can tell, I'm inside a portable supercomputer at the Jozef Stefan Institute in Slovenia.>

<Inside?>

<I apparently exist only as a sequence of simulated particles inside the computer.> The words had no inflection, but Alessandra could sense the bitterness in them. <I'm a digital intelligence. I find myself suddenly dependent on the survival of the world computer network. Which is rapidly getting smaller.>

Baghdad.

In other circumstances, Alessandra might have laughed. Jean had wanted an existence beyond her body, and she had achieved that. Instead of leaving humanity behind, however, she was trapped inside human machinery. The good part was, if anyone in the world could figure out the math needed to aim a Higgs singlet correctly, it was Jean Massey.

<Will you help?> Alessandra wrote.

<Already on it. Just don't listen to those university clowns.>

Wuhan.

But wait. Jean had to understand what she was doing. If this particle successfully went back in time, it would stop the varcolac, but at the cost of this entire timeline. She wouldn't need the world network anymore. She would be back in prison. Was that what she wanted? Alessandra supposed it was better than being dead, which was her only other alternative. Besides which, at this point, it didn't matter. Alessandra had to trust her.

<Got it> Jean wrote. A rush of equations flew over the line. Alessandra reviewed them. The equations looked sound. More than that, they were brilliant. If there was anything wrong with them, it was more than she could see.

Hanoi.

Deep underground, the electromagnets powered and a particle stream started making the rounds, driving the thirty mile racetrack at nearly the speed of light. Alessandra loaded the equations into the computer.

"Just about ready," she said.

"I hope so," Angel said. "Only three cities left before New York."

Alessandra paused. It would take only a single command to launch the sequence. Perhaps nothing at all would happen, but if it worked correctly . . . she would be gone. After all the time she had spent worrying about becoming one person again, she was now afraid to go back. If this worked, she would be two people again, neither of whom would remember any of this happening. They would never even meet Angel.

They wouldn't know about the varcolac threat. Ryan Oronzi would go on building his baby universe, giving the varcolac access to the world. The varcolac might just find some other way to kill her father, and the same basic thing would happen all over again.

"Wait," she said.

"There's no time to think," Angel said. He took her hand and laced his fingers through hers. "I will miss you. Or at least, my life will be the less for not knowing you. But this must be done. Just close your eyes and do it."

"He's right," her mother said. "If you can really undo this slaughter, then do it."

Rio de Janeiro.

"They need to know," Alessandra said. "Our past selves, they need to know what we know, or the same thing will just happen again. They need to be warned."

"How could you possibly warn them?" Angel asked.

"We'll send them a message."

"But they're before us. They're in our past. We can't leave anything for them to find, can we? You said our whole universe from that point onward is going to disappear."

"That's right," Alessandra said. "*Our* universe is going to disappear. But there's another one." She pointed to the laser-light display. "There's another whole universe that won't change at all."

Angel's face was white, and he gripped her hand tight enough to hurt. "Only two cities left. We don't have time to write a note."

"Not a note—my eyejack stream! Everything I've seen and heard since this all started, it's all saved in my account. We can upload it into that universe."

Santiago.

She was already doing it as she was talking. Ryan already had the system in place to encode digital information in the pattern of the wormhole; all she had to do was feed the right stream into it. The problem was, it was an incredible amount of data. It would take some time.

"How will they know to look for it?" her mother asked.

"They won't. They'll just have to discover it and recognize it for what it is."

The bandwidth was limited by the field generators Ryan had in place and how quickly those generators could manipulate patterns into the wormhole. There was nothing she could do to speed it up, but she willed the transfer to go faster.

It was easier than thinking about the fact that these were likely her last moments of existence as herself, as Alessandra, with her unique memories and experiences and thoughts.

Riyadh.

"That's it," Angel said. "That's the last city before New York. It's got to be now, Alessandra."

He was right. The entire stream wasn't transferred yet, but it would have to be enough. She squeezed Angel's hand, and then pulled her mother close for an embrace.

She started the command sequence. "Goodbye," she said.

CHAPTER 28

"Is that him?" Alex Kelley said. She had only been at the NJSC for a week now, and it was her first glimpse of the famed Ryan Oronzi.

Tequila Williams looked where she was pointing and nodded. "In the flesh. Smartest guy in the world, so they say. They also say he's cracked."

Oronzi was at least a hundred pounds overweight, his hair askew, dressed in a T-shirt and a pair of worn jeans that would have benefitted from a belt. "He looks like a plumber," Alex said. It was hard to believe he was the genius behind all the technology they were about to demonstrate that day.

Tequila giggled. "I guess if you're smart enough, you can do and say what you like, and people just call you eccentric. It's like being old."

"Or rich," Alex said.

Oronzi's arrival quickly attracted the attention of the generals and executives gathered near the stage, who tried to shake his hand, but Oronzi just pushed past them without a civil word. It took Alex a moment to realize that he was heading straight for them. For *her*.

He didn't stop until he was standing directly in front of her. "Alex Kelley?"

Alex traded glances with Tequila, startled and not sure what was going on. Was this related to the demo? Was he hitting on her? "That's me," she said. She held out a hand. "Very glad to meet you, sir."

His eyes were wild, like he had seen a ghost. "I have something to show you."

There was no way to keep it a secret. Ryan told her the basics of what he had found encoded in the pattern of his baby universe, and once he had shown her enough of the eyejack visuals to convince her, there was nothing for it but to cancel the demo. The only way to do that, however, was to explain what had happened to their superiors and to *their* superiors, until enough of them believed what was going on. A message from the future. And not just a message, but a semi-complete eyejack feed covering weeks of the most extraordinary and terrifying events.

Once Nicole heard what they had, the CIA got involved. The feed was classified at the highest level of national security, but it was too late to keep it contained. By that time, too many people knew, and the story was too amazing, too outlandish to keep quiet. The media got wind of it, and a series of speculative stories drew the attention of an international audience. The tantalizing ambiguities dropped by Ryan Oronzi, along with the flat denials by Secretary of Defense Jared Falk and his staff, only served to fan the flames.

The media had few details, and Alex didn't come forward with more, not wanting the notoriety of the press nor the attention of the American national security machine. She spent a fair amount of time in Ryan's lab, however, reviewing the contents of the feeds and drawing out the highlights. Ryan himself was blown away by what he saw. The sight of himself destroying the world as a slave to the varcolac shocked him out of the worst of his egomania. The best thing that happened to him, however, was when Alex introduced him to her father.

In some ways, the two men had little in common. Jacob Kelley was outgoing, athletic, and charming, while Ryan Oronzi was awkward both physically and socially. In the world of high-energy physics, however, their interests collided. They could talk for hours about Lorentz invariance and whether a tachyonic anti-telephone could practically be built. But the real reason for their friendship was a mutual commitment to keeping the events of the Other Future, as they had taken to calling it, from ever coming true.

Jacob had, in fact, discovered a method to enhance and sustain the probability field that kept Alex and Sandra separate and kept the varcolac from interacting in the material world. Ryan insisted on getting Jacob a security clearance, and once it came through, Jacob spent more and more time at Ryan's lab, the two of them eventually succeeding in cutting the ties to the baby universe and setting it adrift in the quantum froth. The CIA never released the recordings of the Other Future, but they did increase funding to the NJSC's High Energy Lab to "investigate and protect against the possibility of anti-timeward weapons systems."

Of course, Sandra had also seen the feed, though she was not strictly cleared for it. Ryan and Jacob sneaked her past security one day, using Alex's credentials. When she returned after six hours, she wrapped Alex in a hug and wouldn't let go.

That left only one person who had played a significant part in the Other Future but didn't know it. Sandra decided it would be too much—and too awkward—to tell him all at once. It would imply a relationship that they didn't actually have, making it hard to actually get to know him in real life. She was working a six-days-on, three-days-off cycle on patrol, but her days off happened to coincide with a robotics conference in Philadelphia. She checked the scheduled participants and bought herself a ticket.

When the synchronized quadcopter demonstration was over, Sandra walked up to the young, stocky, Hispanic man who had led the presentation. It was strange; he only looked familiar in a vague way, from seeing him on the feed. He wasn't very much to look at, though apparently they had become good friends in the Other Future. It seemed odd to use the past tense about something that would have happened in the future and now wouldn't, but, in a way, it was also in the past from her perspective. The Other Future was a cause that was producing effects in her life. In a very real sense, those events had actually happened, albeit in a kind of timeline loop that ended where it began. The past tense would do as well as any other.

She made a show of reading his nametag and held out her hand. "Angel Gutierrez?" she said.

He gave her a dazzling smile. "You pronounced it right," he said. "Most of you gringos are hopeless at Mexican names."

She smiled back. "I once knew someone named Angel."

"Well, nice to meet you"—he glanced at her nametag—"Sandra."

"Nice to meet you, too. I just wanted to tell you that your demonstration was remarkable. Those copters are pretty versatile, working together like that."

"Thanks. We think they have a lot of promise."

The moment stalled. Sandra didn't want to leave, but she didn't know what else to say.

"Well, it was good to meet you," she managed, hating herself.

"Bye," Angel said. He turned to go.

"Angel!" she called. He turned back. "Could we . . . that is . . . would you like to have a drink?"

"A drink? Right now?" It was eleven in the morning.

"No, I mean . . . sometime. Just . . . ." This was ridiculous. "I'm sorry. It was a stupid idea." She turned and walked away, her cheeks burning.

He came after her. "Wait." He touched her shoulder, and she turned around. "I don't have any plans for lunch."

She let out the breath she was holding. "Neither do I."

He was obviously confused—she was pretty sure he wasn't accustomed to strange girls asking him out—but he took it in stride. "The hotel's restaurant is pretty awful, but they do serve food," he said. "I have to clear my stuff out for the next demo. Meet you there at noon?"

She thought about offering to help him gather his things, but she thought that would be pushing it. "Noon it is."

She was tempted not to tell him. It would have been easier to enjoy the lunch, to ask him questions about his work and completely avoid the inevitable awkwardness of telling him what she knew. But the longer she delayed, the more it would seem like she'd been deceiving him, and the more difficult it would be. Best to get it over with.

She took a deep breath. "Actually," she said, "this isn't the first time I've seen you."

"I knew it," Angel said. "You've been stalking me. Pretty girls do that all the time." He sighed theatrically. "Am I going to have to call security?"

She grinned. He was just like he seemed on the feed from the Other Future, never embarrassed, always making her feel at ease. "I've got something to tell you. It will be hard to believe—I didn't believe it at first."

She was expecting another joke, but he was quiet now, looking at her curiously. There was nothing for it. She sent his eyejack system the first clip she had decided on—that of Angel himself flying his quadcopters at the wreckage of the baseball stadium. It was unquestionably him, complete with quadcopters and quirky sense of humor. It was also just as clearly at a disaster that had never occurred, in a scene that had never existed. She watched him watch it with growing astonishment.

Finally, his eyes refocused on hers. He was pale. His lips moved, but it took a few moments for him to say, "What is this? CGI?" But of course, it wasn't, and he knew it. No program, no matter how talented its designer, could capture a person so completely.

"It's from the future," Sandra told him.

Over dinner, Alex sat with her father and Ryan and listened to them talk about how they had finally disconnected their universe from the wormhole.

"But, the varcolac is still out there, isn't it?" she said.

"I'm sure it is," her father said. "I can't imagine how it could be killed. It must be distributed through the particles of a thousand worlds. Nothing we could do would be likely to harm it in any existential way."

"But we've destroyed the technology that would give it access," Ryan said. "The baby universe is gone, and my notes for how to create it are destroyed. There are only a few people who even know such a thing is possible."

"The thing about science," Alex said, "is that if something can be done, someone will eventually discover how to do it. You can't just put a lid on it and make it go away. Somebody will eventually do it again."

Her father nodded gravely and wrapped his arm around her. "Let's just hope that it doesn't happen any time soon."

A knock on the door interrupted them. Alex was suddenly reminded of a knock on that same door that had started everything fifteen years ago, when Brian Vanderhall had come in out of the snow, babbling about an intelligent quantum creature.

Her father opened the door. Sandra stood there, smiling, drawing a young man in by the hand. He was short, Hispanic, a little pudgy, with dark glasses. She recognized him at once.

"Angel," she said. "Welcome."

He came in nervously and shook hands all around. "You must be Alex. Dr. Kelley. And Dr. Oronzi, a pleasure." He gave an awkward smile. "This is a bit strange, I must tell you."

"I've shown him the highlights and summarized the rest," Sandra said. "He was supposed to be on a panel at the conference in the afternoon, but he skipped it. We've been talking pretty much nonstop since lunch."

"Welcome to the inner circle," Alex's father said with a smile. "It's been a real shock for all of us, I can tell you."

They sat together in the living room and made polite small talk for a few minutes, but inevitably, their conversation returned to the Other Future.

"There's one thing I don't understand," Angel said.

Ryan laughed. "Only one?"

"I get that the Other Future is an alternate set of events," he said. "Events that *would* have happened, only now they won't. What I don't understand is, does that alternate timeline still exist? Is it still going on out there, with most of the people dead, while we're in an alternate universe right here?"

"It can't be," Ryan said. "As soon as you sent that particle back in time and stopped the varcolac from destroying the stadium, it ceased to exist."

"But if it ceased to exist, how could it have stopped the varcolac? Isn't that a paradox?"

Ryan smiled. "I didn't say it had never existed. I said it *ceased* existing. The Other Future is effectively in our past, a loop tied into the string of our timeline."

"We've been talking about this," Alex said. "Think about the chain of cause and effect. The varcolac destroyed the stadium, which caused you to send a particle back, which caused the varcolac *not* to destroy the stadium, which caused us to be sitting here talking about it. The chain of cause and effect is unbroken. It always moves in one direction, even when it jumps backward in standard time. Nothing we do now can ever change the events of the Other Future—that's already happened. All we can affect is our own future."

Sandra shook her head. "It's enough to make my head swim."

"There's still a problem," Angel said. "What about the quadcopters?"

"What about them?" Alex asked.

"How did they gain the power to act as if they were programmed with Higgs projectors? There's no reasonable explanation. As I apparently told Sandra in the Other Future, it makes no sense."

"They must have picked it up at the scene somehow," Sandra said. "All that quantum stuff going on . . ." She trailed off.

"I don't see how. Yes, they were reading data from hundreds of ID cards around the stadium. Yes, someone could conceivably have designed a virus to affect the copters' programming and left it there for the copters to read. But it would require very precise knowledge of the flight control software to patch it in that way, not to mention knowledge of the operating system and its vulnerabilities. I'm the only one in the world who knows their software that well."

A chill went down Alex's spine. "Wait," she said. "What if you did write it?"

Angel shook his head. "I had never heard of Higgs projectors at the time, much less knew how to program one."

"I don't mean that you programmed it *then*."

She looked around the circle. Everyone else was staring at her blankly.

"Who's to say that the Other Future is the only time this has happened?" she asked.

It was all she had to say. Dawning realization crossed each of their faces.

"Angel says the only person with the knowledge to write a virus to insert that software, and to hide it on a chip at the stadium, is him," she went on. "What if, in a *prior* future to the one we've been watching, the varcolac killed Sandra and me at the prison? What if Angel—with the help of Ryan, presumably—figured out a way to send that chip back in time, where the copters would pick it up?"

"Only they didn't think of storing the eyejack data in the baby universe," her father said. "So none of you ever knew."

Angel's eyes were wide. "How many times do you think this has happened?"

They talked for hours. When Alex slipped out to the kitchen to pour herself a glass of water, Sandra followed her and wrapped her arms around her in a tight hug. It was amazing. A few weeks earlier, Sandra would never have done such a thing, and if she had, Alex would have pulled away. But the Other Future had brought them together in a way that simply being the same person never had. Somehow the experience of having saved the world together—even though they only remembered doing so through an eyejack recording—superseded the fears and insecurities about their identities that they'd built over time.

"So what do you think of him?" Alex asked.

"It's weird," Sandra said. "I know all this stuff about him, but we only just met."

"He is a little weird."

"That's not what I meant! I think he's sweet."

"And weird."

They sat down on stools in the kitchen, for all the world like they were teenagers again, growing up in that house. "He's so easygoing," she said. "I feel comfortable with him, even though we really just met today." Her eyes were lively, despite the late hour. Alex was glad for her. She hoped this Angel would be good to her and not hurt her. It surprised her how fiercely protective she suddenly felt toward her sister. And how comfortable she felt sitting here chatting with her. She grinned suddenly, and Sandra saw it.

"What?" she asked.

Alex shook her head. "I'm glad you're you," she said. "Whoever Alessandra would have been, she's not either of us now. You're different from me, and I'm glad for who you are."

"We were both Alessandra for a moment there," Sandra said. They hadn't talked about that part of the Other Future yet, not directly. "And it was okay. We did well."

"We did," Alex said. "We saved the world, in fact."

Sandra smiled. "And if we ever have to do that again . . . you know, to save the world again or something?"

"We could do it," Alex said.

"We could. We will, if we have to. And if we do . . ."

". . . it won't be the end."

"No," she said. "It won't."

ACKNOWLEDGMENTS

Much thanks to Rene, Jill, Lisa, Peter, Sheila, Liz, and all the rest at Pyr/Prometheus for their enthusiasm and ingenuity in bringing *Supersymmetry* to the world! It's been a true pleasure to work with you. Thanks once again to David Cantine, Mike Shultz, and Chad and Jill Wilson for reading early drafts and helping me make them better. And thanks to all of you who read *Superposition* and liked it enough to read this as well. I hope you enjoy reading it as much as I enjoyed writing it.

ABOUT THE AUTHOR

David Walton is the father of seven children, none of whom sprang into being via quantum superposition. He lives a double life as a Lockheed Martin engineer with a top secret government security clearance, which means he's not allowed to tell you about the Higgs projector he's developing. (Don't worry, he's very careful.) He's also the author of *Superposition*, the Quintessence trilogy, and the award-winning *Terminal Mind*. He would love to hear from you at david waltonfiction@ gmail.com.

Photo by Chuck Zovko